CROSSOVER

CROSSOVER

Michael Jan Friedman

POCKET BOOKS
New York   London   Toronto   Sydney   Tokyo   Singapore

POCKET BOOKS, a division of Simon & Schuster Inc.
1230 Avenue of the Americas, New York, NY 10020

ISBN: 0-671-89677-6

First Pocket Books hardcover printing December 1995

10 9 8 7 6 5 4 3 2 1

For the Mick

Acknowledgments

A lot of times, when I hear an author paying tribute to an editor on a page like this one, the cynical side of me wonders if the author's polishing the old apple. I mean, it never hurts to be nice to the guy who signs your paycheck.

In this case, however, I have no choice but to pay said tribute. The editor of this opus, Kevin Ryan, deserves all the praise I can heap on his tousled head.

First off, the idea of bringing together Spock, McCoy, and Scotty came out of Kevin's addled and slightly antic brain. After all, he is one of this planet's most loyal Trek Classic fans. But his contributions didn't end there. Perhaps because he really wanted to write this baby himself, he put as much of himself into it as I did.

From a writer's standpoint, that translates into the kind of agony you don't want to know about. From a reader's standpoint, it means you're getting a better book than if he'd minded his own business and left me alone.

Mind you, I'd say lots of other good things about

ACKNOWLEDGMENTS

Kevin—making particular reference to his work with Jonas Salk, his efforts to stamp out organized crime, and his walk on the moon—but thanks to his exacting edits, I'm out of time.

Besides, enough is enough.

Michael Jan Friedman
Long Island, New York
August 1995

HISTORIAN'S NOTE

This story takes place in the eighth year of Jean-Luc Picard's command of the *Enterprise*-D—after the events chronicled in *All Good Things* . . . and prior to those described in *Star Trek Generations*.

CROSSOVER

PROLOGUE

The Vulcan heard the footsteps outside his door several seconds before the Romulan arrived. The warning gave him the time he needed to bring his meditation to a close.

A moment later, he was waiting by the entrance, alert. Continuing to track the sound of footsteps, the Vulcan calculated the precise moment when the Romulan would enter his quarters.

The Vulcan's superior hearing gave him the necessary advantage. Though Romulan hearing was comparable to the Vulcan variety, the Vulcan himself was of mixed blood.

As was often the case in nature, the hybrid exhibited characteristics superior to those of either parent species. It was a simple and logical part of the evolutionary process.

In this case, the Vulcan had chosen to keep his superior hearing a secret from his Romulan hosts—a decision he now realized was wise indeed.

Just as the Vulcan knew they would, the footsteps stopped in front and the door opened almost instantly. The Vulcan waited a heartbeat for the Romulan to take a step inside his quarters. Then he struck, aiming the first blow at the Romulan's head.

Reacting quickly, the Romulan dodged to one side and partially deflected the Vulcan's hand. Nevertheless, the blow struck the Romulan on the shoulder, knocking him to the ground.

There was a brief moment, as the Romulan lay on the deck, during which he looked up at the Vulcan with uncomprehending eyes. Instead of pressing his advantage, the Vulcan waited to see what his adversary would do.

The Romulan lifted himself from the deck. Then the Vulcan saw the rage come.

On his feet again, the Romulan launched an attack of his own, striking viciously with a flurry of blows from either hand. With a precision and economy of movement characteristic of his people's defense techniques, the Vulcan met the blows, deflecting their force and lessening their impact.

Nevertheless, the fierceness of the counterattack surprised the Vulcan. What's more, if this went on much longer, he might find himself in an untenable position.

The Romulan was significantly younger than he was. And being younger, he could maintain the ferocity of his attack until after the Vulcan's strength had fled.

No matter, the Vulcan told himself. He had already accomplished his purpose. And it was in his power, he believed, to end the fight right now.

Waiting until the Romulan threw a blow and was thus off balance, the Vulcan grabbed the striking hand. Then he used a simple twist of his own body to toss the Romulan to the floor.

Landing solidly on his back, the Romulan was stunned for a moment—but only for a moment. When that was over, he gathered his legs beneath him and prepared to strike again.

"Enough," the Vulcan said evenly.

Standing, the Romulan drew back his fist, his eyes still full of anger.

"Cease your attack," the Vulcan said in a stronger tone.

The Romulan hesitated, trembling with the effort it required to restrain himself.

"This lesson is ended," the Vulcan said.

Finally, his words had the desired impact. The Romulan stopped moving entirely and regarded his mentor.

The anger on his face was gradually replaced with shame. As he regained control over his passions, his features went blank—except for the merest hint of curiosity.

"Teacher," the Romulan asked, "why did you strike me?"

The Vulcan eyed his charge impassively for a moment before responding. "Why do you think I struck you?"

Even though Sel'den's mask of control was securely in place, the Vulcan could see his student's discomfort.

"You were testing me?" Sel'den asked.

The Vulcan nodded.

Sel'den frowned. "And I lost control. I returned your attack. Instead of studying the situation and measuring my response, I responded emotionally. I did not even use the Vulcan fighting techniques you have taught me."

The younger man considered these facts for a moment, and then came to his conclusion: "I have failed your test."

Though Sel'den's control was impeccable, his humiliation was revealed by the green that tinged his complexion.

The Vulcan shook his head. "It was not my intention to judge you. This was merely an exploration of your development. There is no failure and no shame. We have both been enlightened. We now have much to discuss, and you have much to consider."

"Yet," said the Romulan, "when provoked, I abandoned my training. Clearly, I have not advanced as I should have by now. I have proved my mastery of discipline and logic to be inadequate. I have failed."

The Vulcan perceived the certainty in his student's face. He knew it was very much a Romulan tendency, the need for the absolute. He could see he still had much work to do.

"Consider this exercise in tonight's meditations," the Vulcan advised. "We will discuss it again tomorrow."

With the weight of shame and guilt temporarily lifted from him, Sel'den turned to the business that had brought him to his teacher's quarters. "We will enter orbit in exactly ten minutes," he said. "They are prepared to receive you on the bridge."

CHAPTER 1

The Vulcan led the way through the narrow, cramped corridors of the merchant vessel, from the crew and passenger quarters in the rear through the cargo area that was located in the center of the ship and made up most of the freighter's internal volume.

They were headed for the vessel's bridge. As always, Sel'den followed the Teacher dutifully.

On the way, he resisted the temptation to berate himself for his behavior in the Vulcan's quarters. Such self-recrimination was unproductive and illogical—as his teacher had taught him.

For the moment, he would only resolve to not fail again. Later, he would meditate as the Vulcan had suggested.

At the end of the long passage through the cargo area, a door hissed open as they approached it. Stepping through, teacher and pupil appeared on the small, efficient bridge. The other five students were already waiting for them, eager to see the first signs of their destination.

Immediately, the five Romulans raised their hands in the traditional Vulcan salute. Returning the gesture, the Teacher said, "Peace and long life."

As a planet loomed on the bridge's main viewscreen, Sel'den took his place at the communications console. He had programmed the ship some time ago with codes that would allow them to land on Constanthus. Nevertheless, he oversaw the clearance process personally, watching the planet's defense computer begin to access the ship's data banks.

The computer explored the ship's passenger and crew lists, scrutinized its manifest, and confirmed its authorization. From his station, Sel'den continued to provide the preprogrammed information and receive the proper authorizations.

Always careful when taking the Vulcan into a new environment, Sel'den was particularly concerned about this venture. After all, in the past, the Teacher and his followers had restricted their activities to Romulus—where Sel'den felt comfortable, having lived there all his life.

He had received his security training there. He knew the ins and outs of the place, to the extent that he could detect a problem from a long way off.

Constanthus, however, was another matter entirely. One of the Empire's outer worlds but one that was rising in importance, it was ruled with an iron fist by its governor. A dangerous place indeed for a unificationist.

Sel'den knew there would be subtle differences in security measures and internal politics here. Differences that he could not accurately forecast. Risks he could not fully assess.

But despite Sel'den's objections, the Teacher had insisted on the trip. The expansion of the movement to Constanthus was very important to the Vulcan. And though he had not chosen to share his reasons with his student, Sel'den had his suspicions.

As their small merchant ship glided through Constanthus's atmosphere, Sel'den glanced at his mentor—a tall, stately individual with pronounced cheekbones and dark, patient eyes. The student had never met anyone like his teacher before. He would be surprised if there were others of his stature even on Vulcan.

After a while, Sel'den felt the ship touch the planet's surface. Only then did he look up from his computer terminal.

He took a breath. The difficult part was over. Now all they had to do was disembark.

Leaving his station, Sel'den fell into line behind the Teacher and, along with the other students, followed him down a flight of stairs to the ship's personnel airlock. Opening it, they breathed in the air of Constanthus. Though it had a peculiarly acrid odor, perhaps due to the effects of some local plant life, it was largely the same air they breathed on Romulus.

The Vulcan was the first of their group to set foot on Constantharine soil. In the past, Sel'den had argued that the Teacher should always let others lead, to minimize the danger to himself and thus to the movement. But the Vulcan preferred to be the first to assume new risks, and Sel'den knew better than to question his teacher's logic in the matter.

When they were all assembled on the landing area, they were met by an older, burly Romulan whose jowls showed a lifetime of good eating. Sel'den recognized the man as

Belan, leader of the fledgling unificationist movement on Constanthus.

Belan approached the Teacher and nodded curtly, a gesture the Teacher returned. Sel'den knew they did not dare exchange the traditional Vulcan salute in the open landing zone, in full view of the technicians who were already tending to the ship.

Looking at the larger group for a moment, Belan simply said, "Welcome," and turned toward the exit from the large, squared-off landing pit. Without another word, at least for the moment, he led the group out of the pit via a set of broad stone stairs, and from there out into the streets.

The city—called Auranthus—was crude and graceless by homeworld standards. A series of gray boxes under a blue-green sky, devoid of the majestic arches and lofty spires that characterized the capitol on Romulus.

But then, that was often the case on the outer worlds, where beauty was sacrificed for the sake of practicality. Even the imported red-orange maqrana trees that lined each byway seemed strangely listless, as if uninspired by their surroundings.

Before long, they came to the city's manufacturing district, and a small factory building. Sel'den recognized the squat, square structure from the communications he had had with Belan.

After all, this was Belan's plant, where a portion of this world's building materials were made. It also represented the official reason for their trip to Constanthus, their ship having been loaded with minerals and other raw materials that Belan required.

They entered the building through the front door and walked through a small anteroom. A moment later, they found themselves at the entrance to a large, open space that was filled with, Sel'den estimated, approximately forty Romulans. Obviously a storage area, Sel'den saw that it had been cleared for use as a meeting place.

The faces of the Constantharines were unfamiliar to Sel'den. Nonetheless, they were Romulans and fellow believers in the great unificationist movement. As far as he was concerned, that made them his brothers.

As one, every Romulan in the echoing chamber lifted his or her hand in the Vulcan greeting. The Teacher returned the gesture and said, "Live long and prosper, followers of Surak."

"Peace and long life to you," Belan responded. "We are in a safe place and may speak freely here."

The Teacher nodded, clearly taking the statement for truth. Sel'den was not quite so confident.

He scanned the room. It had no windows and only two entrances—the one they had used and one opposite it on the other side of the room.

Gesturing, he assigned two of his fellow students to watch the entrance now directly behind them. Then he took another student with him as he made his way across the room to the other entrance.

Meanwhile, the Teacher was approaching a makeshift podium to address the Romulans before him. As interested as he was in what the Vulcan might say, Sel'den focused his attention on the door. Only when he was satisfied that it was secure did he turn around, watching as the Teacher spoke to the assembled group.

"Followers of Surak," the Vulcan began. He displayed precise control and betrayed no emotion.

As he had done many times before, Sel'den resolved to master the techniques of the Teacher. One day, he vowed silently, he would know such wisdom, such control. He would attain the enlightenment and dignity of the Vulcan way.

"You honor me with your presence," the Teacher continued, scanning the assemblage. "You show great courage in attempting to bridge the gap between two peoples, who are one in blood. In the weeks and months to come, I shall endcavor to share with you what I have learned about the teachings of Surak and the principles of logic."

As Sel'den heard the crowd become completely silent, he remembered the first time he had heard the Vulcan speak. And he felt himself once again moved by his teacher's words.

"We know," the Vulcan said, "that above all else, Surak was a Teacher. However, though he labored for much of his life to share his wisdom with others, he also remained a student. In fact, Surak once said the best pupil is the one who takes the most care in his teacher's education.

"This reminds us that since the ancient times, when we were one people, the relationship between student and teacher has been a sacred one. The basis of this relationship is the dialogue that brings both student and teacher closer to enlightenment."

The Vulcan paused for a moment, to give the assembled Romulans time to consider the weight of his words. But the moment was interrupted by the entrance of a Romulan at the far door.

Sel'den recognized him as Ganos—one of Belan's people, whom he had seen more than once in the course of their communications. Agitated, Ganos made no effort to control his emotions as he approached Belan.

"Someone here is using a transmitter," the Romulan reported.

To his credit, Belan retained his control as he faced the assembled Romulans. "We have been betrayed," he said simply.

No was all Sel'den could think. Then the first Romulan soldiers—disruptors in hand—pushed their way into the room through the door where Ganos had just entered.

For a brief moment the students posted at the door struggled with the incoming soldiers—but the struggle was short and deadly. It ended with Sel'den's comrades falling in agony to the crackling blue beams of the soldiers' disruptors.

Without hesitation, Sel'den produced his own concealed hand weapon and made his way across the room, motioning the student next to him to follow. Weaving through the confused crowd, his disruptor pressed against his thigh, Sel'den could only think: *The Teacher must be saved, his mission must continue.*

If Sel'den could hold off the soldiers, perhaps the Teacher could escape through the back entrance. He spared a moment to dispatch his comrade in the Vulcan's direction.

Then he continued toward the door, though he could see more soldiers pouring into the room every second. No matter, Sel'den thought. He would do what had to be done to save the Teacher. He started to lift his hand weapon.

"Sel'den—no!" The Teacher's voice rang out over the soldiers' commands and the murmurs of confusion.

No other instructions were required. Biting his lip, the student had no choice but to comply.

He dropped his weapon before anyone could see that he had it, and turned to look at his mentor. Beyond the Vulcan, other soldiers were now entering from the back door—the door Sel'den had been guarding.

Watching the chaos that reigned as the soldiers pushed and shoved their way though the assembled Romulans, he knew there would be no escape for the Teacher. Even if Sel'den managed to kill every soldier guarding one of the entrances, the others would overwhelm him and take his master.

The youth's body and spirit cried out for action. It took every ounce of control he had learned to keep from throwing himself at the soldiers.

At least a fight would give him an honorable death, which was more than he deserved now that he had failed his teacher so completely. And yet, obeying his mentor's order, he stood his ground.

Sel'den watched the soldiers subdue the few that struggled against them with short, deadly blasts from their pistols. Students fell, writhing in the hideous grasp of the roiling blue disruptor energies. The smell of their burning flesh made Sel'den retch.

Finally, however, a kind of order was established. A stillness settled on the crowd. A despair.

A few moments earlier, Sel'den had seen hope in the faces of the Constantharine unificationists. After all, they were greeting a great Teacher who would take them down Surak's path. But now those same faces were full of horror and disappointment.

Even those who had come from Romulus looked shocked. Sel'den felt shame for them.

Looking to the Teacher, he tried to draw strength from the Vulcan's apparent calm. He tried to emulate the precise and passionless thoughts that were the source of the Teacher's strength and dignity.

As if aware of Sel'den's scrutiny, the Vulcan turned to him. His gaze was steady and serene, acknowledging his student's struggle.

In the Vulcan's eyes, Sel'den saw no disappointment, judgment, or reproach. Only acceptance of what was—and what would be.

Meanwhile, the soldiers were securing each door exactly as Sel'den himself would have done, to make sure no one escaped. The ranking officer, a chief of security, surveyed the room with a practiced eye.

But there was more to his actions than mere efficiency, Sel'den thought. The officer was sizing up the unificationists. But for what purpose?

Suddenly, he knew. The realization struck him like a physical blow. It took every ounce of his discipline to retain his control—to keep the pounding of his heart from overpowering him—and to determine a logical course of action.

Even as the plan was forming in his mind, he was on the move, taking slow, careful steps toward the Teacher's makeshift podium. There was enough shuffling among the assembled Romulans that his intent was not immediately detectable to the soldiers.

But that wouldn't last long. Just a few steps later, Sel'den was by his teacher's side.

The Vulcan gave him a quizzical look, but Sel'den could not spare any response. The security chief and two soldiers had just reached the podium as well.

Unfortunately, the Teacher's position as speaker marked him as one in charge of the unificationists. That made him the target of a common ploy among Romulan soldiers.

To firmly establish their control over a group of prisoners—at least until a trial could take place—it was customary to identify a leader and deal with him or her ruthlessly.

Sel'den could not accept this. As long as his mentor

lived, the movement had life as well. It was logical, then, to preserve the Teacher's life at all costs.

Stepping forward, he intercepted the security chief and spoke in a level, even confident tone. "I lead these people," he said. "By what right are you here? By whose authority?"

The pose did not trouble Sel'den. In this case, the mistruth clearly served a greater good.

Sel'den couldn't see his teacher's face, but he could imagine his expression. Right about now, the Vulcan was coming to understand what danger he was in and what Sel'den was attempting to do about it.

At first, the Teacher would no doubt be disappointed in him. On the face of it, at least, Sel'den's act was an emotional one—an act of overweaning courage.

But this time, Sel'den knew that his logic was flawless. Surely the Vulcan would see that in time.

"You are their leader?" the officer replied. He turned to one of his men.

The Teacher reached out, protesting. "No, you do not—"

But it was too late.

Sel'den allowed himself a small regret: that he would not live to argue the necessity of his actions with his master. Then he heard the crack of the security chief's voice and saw a soldier drawing his disruptor.

Giving a final mental thanks to Spock, who had honored him with his teaching, Sel'den winced at the bright flash before him.

And felt the agonizing grasp of the disruptor's rampant energies.

And carried his gratitude to the grave.

CHAPTER **2**

This was just the sort of meeting that usually put Leonard McCoy to sleep.

In fact, he'd nearly dozed off on two occasions in the past hour alone. Fortunately—or not so fortunately, McCoy groused silently—he'd been able to gut it out each time and remain alert enough to follow the conversation.

At the moment, he was listening to the Starfleet cultural anthropologist who sat across the table from him in the *Zapata*'s conference room. Gibbs, the man's name was.

"In many ways," said the anthropologist, stroking his brown brush of a chin beard, "the Stugg are a people of contradictions. They showed openness when they originally invited Starfleet to visit their world seventy-five years ago, leading to Admiral McCoy's encounter with them. On the other hand, they have since asked all Federation personnel to leave their world temporarily on four occasions—with no explanation.

Drake, the tall, red-haired captain of the *Zapata,* nodded sagely. "Of course, none of the other periods of isolation lasted more than a standard month. Until now."

Admiral McCoy hadn't grown particularly fond of Drake. While the other four attending the conference— besides Drake and McCoy himself—were a collection of diplomats and Federation cultural contact "experts," the captain was at least reputedly a man of action. Yet he'd allowed the meeting on his ship to drone on in no particular direction.

"That's true," agreed Carmen, a painfully thin, dark-haired woman who'd made a career out of conflict mediation. "There is no precedent for an isolationist period of this duration in our experience with the Stugg."

Megipanthos, the director of the Federation's scientific exchange program, took a deep, noisy breath. Obviously, thought McCoy, the man had trouble with his sinuses. That, and he could stand to lose some weight.

"However," Megipanthos began—giving the impression that he was going to contribute something really important—"as we discussed, we have seen other unexplainable behavior in our dealings with the Stugg."

McCoy sighed, not bothering to hide it. In his day, he had watched starship captains size up a problem in an instant and spend whatever time they had—which usually was precious little—executing a brilliant and effective course of action.

And then there was *this.*

"How does the Prime Directive apply here?" Gibbs asked.

"Actually," replied Gildenstern, the woman from Federation legal affairs, "it doesn't. It's just not an issue. We have had contact with the Stugg for many years." She

16

frowned suddenly. "Of course, they could *invoke* the Prime Directive. . . ."

"Perhaps, in a sense," said Gibbs, "they *have* invoked the Prime Directive." He seemed downright excited by the idea. "Perhaps their silence is their way of invoking it."

The admiral silently groaned.

Carmen considered Gibbs's comment for a moment— a long moment, McCoy noted—before responding. "Well," she replied, "Federation law broadly defines how a culture may invoke Prime Directive protection. So it is possible."

"But not certain," Captain Drake added, with a certain ominousness.

That was the last straw. McCoy would not let this charade go on for another minute. He had wanted to— hell, he'd *insisted* on participating in this mission to get away from the drudgery of Starfleet command. And here he'd run smack-dab into the same old mind-set dozens of light-years away.

"I know," he said. "Why don't we just go to the Stugg capitol, beam down, and damned well ask them?"

An embarrassed silence descended over the room. When Drake broke it, he spoke to McCoy in the same tone he might have used in reasoning with a recalcitrant child.

"An interesting idea, Admiral." Drake leaned back in his chair. "Has your direct experience with the Stugg provided any insight into why that might be successful?"

The admiral made no effort to match the captain's soft, polite tone. "My direct experience as a Starfleet officer for over one hundred years has been that one should never overlook the obvious."

Drake turned to the anthropologist. "What do you think, Mr. Gibbs?"

The man shrugged. "Well," he replied, stroking his beard again, "with respect to Stugg interpersonal relationships, in certain social situations it is imperative for an individual to initiate contact even when anticipating resistance. In these situations, to fail to do so is considered worse than rude."

McCoy harrumphed in satisfaction.

"Of course," Gibbs continued, "in other situations, initiating interpersonal contact breaks a strong taboo and has serious social repercussions."

McCoy cursed under his breath, realizing where the conversation would soon be going. Megipanthos was the first to speak.

"We could develop a computer program," the director suggested. "Then try to extrapolate from our existing data base of Stugg interpersonal social conventions."

"Allowing us to project possible outcomes of initiating contact," Carmen added.

"Exactly," Megipanthos told her. "Of course, the findings would not be conclusive, but they would give us a clearly defined set of options—something to talk about, at least."

Just what we need, thought McCoy. Something to *talk* about.

This time he groaned out loud. How much more of this could he take? How much, in fact, could anyone take?

The next twenty minutes of the meeting focused on how to formulate the computer program, with a digression into the issue of whether the creation of the Stugg cultural data base would constitute a breach of the Stugg's privacy—considering that they may or may not have invoked the Prime Directive. Everyone at the meeting finally agreed that privacy was probably not an issue, but the legal affairs and cultural anthropology people agreed to assign staff to research the issue anyway.

McCoy couldn't be sure where the conversation went from there, because when sleep threatened to take him a third time, he didn't fight it. He embraced it with open arms.

A light tap was all that was required to rouse the admiral from his nap. When he opened his eyes, he saw Captain Drake's slightly embarrassed face hovering over him.

McCoy was used to the look, but didn't feel any embarrassment himself. If he needed or wanted to sleep, he'd damned well do it. At his age, he had learned to listen carefully to his body's whims.

"Admiral," said Drake, "there's a Priority One message for you from Starfleet Command."

McCoy felt a chill. Someone's died, he thought.

"You can take it in my ready room," Drake offered.

"Thanks," McCoy grunted automatically.

As he got up, he noticed for the first time how painfully silent the room had become. No one was talking—they were too busy looking at him.

"As you were," he told them. "Don't stop on my account."

Exiting the conference room, the admiral couldn't shake his sense of dread. One of the few regrets he had on reaching 145 was that he'd lived to see so many friends kick the bucket.

Through the years, he'd received "the call" more times than he wanted to remember. He had developed a peculiar sixth sense about it—an ability to recognize it with uncanny accuracy.

Now, as he crossed the bridge escorted by Captain Drake, he didn't permit himself to think about who it might be. Still, the feeling of horror was stronger than it had been in the past.

Whatever the message was about, he didn't want to hear it. Yet, at the same time, he couldn't turn away.

Entering the captain's ready room, he allowed himself to be guided around Drake's desk.

"Please sit down, Admiral," the captain said softly.

"No," McCoy said simply. "Thanks," he added as an afterthought. "If it's all the same to you, I'll stand."

Drake nodded. "If you need me, I'll be on the bridge," he said. Then he left the room.

McCoy paused only for a moment to put his hands down on the desk in front of him. He could feel the familiar tremor in his arms as they helped to support his weight.

"Computer," he said, "please relay message for McCoy, Leonard H., Admiral, to this station."

Without delay, the small screen in front of him produced an image of Admiral Keaton. Keaton was highly placed in Starfleet security and posted to Command headquarters on Earth. The fact that she was relaying the information personally told McCoy that whatever the message was, it was important.

"Admiral McCoy," she said curtly.

McCoy responded with a nod. "Admiral Keaton."

Her expression changed. "I have some bad news," she told him. "It relates to Federation security, but it's of direct interest to you personally." A pause. "It appears your former colleague and friend, Ambassador Spock—"

"Has been killed," McCoy finished for her, realizing he'd been right all along. Ice water trickled down his spine. "How?" he asked.

The admiral shot him a quizzical look before she spoke again. "No, Admiral McCoy. You misunderstand. To the best of our knowledge, Ambassador Spock is still alive. That is why we have a security problem."

Keaton gave him a second, even more quizzical look. "Why did you think he was dead?" she asked.

McCoy could feel the tightness in his chest release a notch. He took a breath, let it out.

"Doctor's intuition," he replied. "So . . . what's Spock done to make himself a security problem?"

She frowned. "What I'm about to tell you is highly classified, Admiral. Only people with Priority One clearance are privy to this information, and even then it's released strictly on a need-to-know basis."

"I understand," McCoy replied.

But he was thinking: *I was wrong about "the call."* That had never happened before.

It figured that Spock would give him a scare like that over nothing. Despite his annoyance with his old comrade, he couldn't help but feel a tide of relief wash over him.

Apparently, that pig-headed Vulcan had gotten himself into some kind of hot water. That was all right. McCoy had seen Spock overcome the odds before.

Too stubborn to die, the admiral thought. Like *me*.

"Ambassador Spock," Keaton explained, "has been involved in a private, covert operation on the planet Romulus for the last few years. He's working with a small group of Romulan insurgents called unificationists, who—"

"—are seeking a reconciliation and reunification with the planet Vulcan," McCoy remarked. "I've heard of them. But I'm surprised that Spock would get himself mixed up with a bunch of pie-in-the-sky idealists."

McCoy made a note to put that question to Spock when next he saw the Vulcan.

"I will assume he had a logical reason," Keaton responded. "In any case, Spock was among a group of unificationists who were recently taken prisoner on one of the Romulan Empire's outer worlds. A place called Constanthus."

McCoy leaned forward. "Taken prisoner?"

Damn that Spock. His feeling of relief died aborning.

"Do the Romulans know who they've got?" he asked.

Keaton shook her head. "No. The communications we've been able to intercept show they're so far unaware of it. However, if and when they *do* find out, we're facing a security breach that could be a most serious threat to the Federation."

The implications of Spock's capture were very clear to McCoy. As an admiral, he had learned more about Federation security than he had wanted to know.

He knew that if the wrong person fell into hostile hands it could be disastrous. Unfortunately, Spock was very *much* the wrong person. His Vulcan mind was like a steel trap, full of secrets the Federation couldn't afford to see exposed.

"What's the plan to get him out?" McCoy asked.

Though he would later decide that he must have been mistaken, for a moment McCoy was sure that Keaton had squirmed at the question. And he had never seen her squirm before.

"We're dispatching a Galaxy-class vessel to the Romulan neutral zone," she told him. "We would like you to join them, as an expert on Ambassador Spock. No one alive knows him better than you do."

McCoy was surprised. But the more he thought about

it, the more sense it made. After all, he *did* know Spock better than anyone.

"Of course," he responded. "I'll be glad to help however I can."

She nodded. "Good. The coordinates have already been forwarded to Captain Drake. You will rendezvous with the Galaxy-class ship I spoke of. Only you and the senior officers on board will know that Spock is in the custody of the Romulan Empire. This briefing and the one being given to those officers are being sent with the most sophisticated coding available to Starfleet today. I expect everyone involved to take all possible precautions."

Admiral Keaton eyed McCoy intensely.

"Let me remind you once again that secrecy is our greatest weapon here, Admiral. It must be maintained at all costs."

McCoy bristled at that. He hadn't reached his rank and age without a clear understanding of security.

"Thank you," he told her. "I know what a Priority One classification means. After all, I had that rating when you were still a plebe at the Academy."

McCoy made no effort to soften his tone, letting his displeasure show. Technically speaking, he didn't outrank Keaton, but he had certainly lived a damned sight longer than she had.

His words and tone had their desired effect. Keaton looked contrite. Or anyway, as contrite as McCoy expected she had ever looked.

"Of course," she said. "I didn't mean to suggest—"

"Fine, fine," McCoy cut her off. "Now, what's the name of the ship that I'm meeting?"

Keaton paused for a moment, as if she were delivering important news.

"It's the *U.S.S. Enterprise.*"

* * *

Montgomery Scott was sleeping when the call came, and he was still groggy when he reached the computer console. He had spent a long night reconfiguring the warp engines of his shuttlecraft.

The net result of his work was only a minimal increase in engine efficiency. Still, he had taken pleasure in getting any increase at all, after the computer had told him the system could not be improved even marginally—and definitely not, the computer pointed out, using the configuration Scotty had planned for it.

He activated the computer screen with a tap of his controls—and straightened when he saw why the computer had flagged him. It was a Priority One communication, heavily encrypted. Holding his breath, the engineer waited to see if the computer would be able to decode it.

It had been a simple matter to program his computer to scan subspace messages and news services for information that interested him. Among the subjects it was programmed to flag were a select group of names.

Doctor—nay, Admiral—McCoy was on that list. So was Captain Spock—or Ambassador Spock, as he was known these days. Of course, most of the information Scotty's computer scanned was on open public and Starfleet channels.

Coded messages were more difficult—he was no Uhura when it came to deciphering such things. However, Scotty knew that a number of the codes Starfleet used were based on engineering protocols.

As a result, he'd designed and added circuits to the communications system that looked for codes based on these same principles and then interpreted them based on Scotty's personal data base. The Priority One code that contained this particular message was based on the shifting harmonics of warp field physics.

After a long moment, the message finally came through, allowing him to eavesdrop on it. He smiled at the sight of Doctor McCoy, though he didn't know the woman on the other end.

Then Scotty heard the news Keaton was bringing, and his smile faded. He leaned back heavily into his padded chair.

Spock was in danger. Grave danger.

Even if the Romulans never found out the Vulcan's true identity, Romulan justice was swift and sure. And in the Romulan Empire, there was only one punishment for treason.

Scotty knew that the Federation was in a difficult position. It couldn't launch a full-scale attack to retrieve one man.

And even if such a thing were possible, it wouldn't work. Spock would be tried, convicted, and punished long before forces could be mobilized.

A smaller-scale rescue would have a little better chance, but a Starfleet vessel would never get very far into the Romulan Empire. This time, it seemed to Scotty, Spock would not escape death or have anyone there to help him cheat it.

The thought left him cold. Scotty felt he was listening to the death knell of someone he'd once believed was indestructible.

That, of course, was at a time when he was young— when they all were young. When they firmly believed their adventures would go on forever.

In those days, Scotty had been known as a miracle worker—though in truth, the engineer and his friends had accomplished their miracles together. Still, he'd believed that anything was possible.

Maybe in those days something could have been done for Spock. But Montgomery Scott had lived too long and seen too much to believe that anymore. In any case, he was alone now, and there was certainly nothing he could do by himself.

Scotty shook his head sadly. This time, there was no hope. None at all.

Unless . . .

No.

It would never work. . . .

Absolutely not.

. . . even if there was time.

And then Scotty felt that rush of ideas that never seemed to come on call, but always managed to appear when absolutely necessary.

Checking the navigational computer, he saw that he could cover the distance in a reasonable time—possibly even quickly enough to save Spock.

But there were too many variables. Too many things the engineer didn't know and couldn't plan for.

Scotty quit that line of thinking, deeming it unproductive. He wouldn't bother to calculate the odds; he could guess that they would be very high. And, in any case, the decision was already made.

He reset the shuttle's course. Starbase 178 and what he needed were twelve hours away, and he had a lot of work to do before he arrived.

Captain Jean-Luc Picard sat down behind the sleek, dark desk in his ready room and tapped the padd on his control panel.

The monitor in front of him displayed the long,

weather-worn face of a Starfleet commodore. Picard didn't normally hear from such a person unless the circumstances were grim.

"There's no easy way to say this, Captain." Commodore Edrich frowned, emphasizing the deep lines already in his face. "It's Ambassador Spock. He's been captured with a group of unificationists on one of the Romulan Empire's outer worlds. A place called Constanthus— literally, *Crossover*, for its position halfway between Romulus and the Neutral Zone."

Picard's mouth went dry. Spock . . .

"Do they know who he is?" he asked.

Edrich shook his head. "Not yet—so time is of the essence. That's why we're dispatching a consultant to help you. Someone who knows Spock like the back of his hand."

Picard shifted uneasily in his chair. "A consultant," he echoed.

The commodore nodded. "His name is McCoy. Admiral Leonard McCoy. He and Spock—"

"I know who he is," Picard interrupted. "And I know his relationship to Spock." Better than anyone could possibly guess, Picard mused.

"Then our business is finished. I am forwarding the rendezvous coordinates and formal orders to your ship," Edrich said. "Good luck, Captain."

Picard nodded. "Thank you," he replied.

With that, Edrich disappeared from the monitor.

The captain turned away from the blank screen to consider the stars outside his ready-room windows.

Time is a path from the past to the future and back again. The present is the crossroads of both. He wondered at the simplicity and wisdom of Surak's words.

In the past, he had traveled into the Romulan Empire

to find Spock and to determine the ambassador's reason for being there. Then, as now, Federation security had been at stake. Picard's orders had been to determine whether Ambassador Spock had turned to the Romulan side.

Undercover on Romulus, Picard had found Spock and discovered the Vulcan's work in the reunification movement. In the course of events, Picard had been able to help Spock—though truthfully, they had helped each other.

But that was in the past, when the Vulcan was living freely, if secretly, on the Romulan homeworlds. Now the ambassador was a prisoner of the Empire—a different matter entirely.

Picard felt his past and future with Spock merging into the same moment—the crossroads that Surak had identified as the present. In his mind, Picard despaired for the future of Ambassador Spock, the man who had helped shape the Federation's destiny and who had touched Picard's mind as well as his life.

Knowing that his options and the time to act would be severely limited, Picard could only resolve to honor the man and—whatever happened—to do his duty.

CHAPTER 3

The computer voice was cool, yet cordial.

"Starfleet shuttle *Romaine,* you are cleared for mooring. Welcome to Starbase one-seven-eight, Captain Scott."

A moment later, Scotty guided the shuttle to the coordinates transmitted. It glided into the appropriate bay, one of many on the large station.

As soon as the shuttle came to a halt, the computer notified him that the bay had been pressurized. For perhaps the tenth time that day, Scotty marveled at the pace of modern life.

Then he opened the shuttle door and descended to the deck outside. Abruptly, he came face-to-face with a smiling Starfleet officer. A quick look at the uniform pips told the engineer that the man was a commander—probably the one in charge of the station.

The officer had a large smile on his round, cherubic face. He put out his hand.

"I'm Commander Yuri Nelson, Captain Scott. It's a real honor to have you on my station."

Scott took the commander's hand. "It's a pleasure to be here, Commander."

"I wish we'd had more notice," remarked Nelson. "I would have liked to arrange something," he said as the two men walked across the shuttlebay.

Though Nelson was clearly enthusiastic about having a legend on his base, Scotty wondered if anyone else on the staff had heard of him. When the engineer last saw active duty seventy-five years ago, the grandparents of most of the station crew would have been young children.

"Will you be with us for very long?" the commander asked, stopping in front of a turbolift door. "We have quite a collection of alien artifacts here. No doubt, some pieces that would be of interest to you."

Scott shook his head. "I'm afraid nae, Commander. Nae on this trip."

Looking at Nelson's open, friendly features, Scott regretted what he was about to do. At some point in the future, he might have liked to come back to Starbase 178 and spend some time. But if all went well, the commander wouldn't be nearly so glad to see him the next time.

"I'll be back, though, as soon as I can," Scott promised. It was true enough.

By the look on his face, the commander was about to ask another question. Scott cut him off with a gesture.

"The tour?" the engineer asked. "The one I inquired about?"

"Yes, of course," Nelson replied. "The last one of the day leaves in a few minutes. This turbolift will take you directly to the shuttle. If you had time, we could arrange something more private. These public tours can be a bit basic for someone like you."

"It'll be fine," Scott assured him. "I'm glad ye could fit me in."

Nelson extended his hand and Scotty shook it again. "Believe me," said the commander, "that was the least I could do. It was good to meet you, sir."

Scott entered the turbolift. "The same here. Thank ye, Commander. I'll be speaking with ye."

A moment later, Scotty was in the turbolift, speeding toward the shuttle in what would no doubt be the shortest and easiest leg of his journey.

The turbolift came to a stop. The door opened onto a shuttledeck almost exactly like the one he had landed in.

Sitting on the deck was a large, short-range passenger shuttle. The deck was clear of people except for a single attendant waiting by the shuttle door.

As Scott approached, he could see that the attendant was a young woman wearing an ensign's uniform. She flashed him a smile, but her eyes looked thoughtful—even worried.

Probably nervous about having to give the red carpet treatment to an ancient Starfleet officer she'd probably never heard of—at least, until her commander briefed her on him. Scotty grunted.

"I'm Ensign Hammond," the woman told him. "Welcome aboard, Captain Scott. It's an honor to have you with us, sir."

"Montgomery Scott, lass. *Captain* Montgomery Scott, if ye want to get formal about it—which I do nae. In fact," he said, leaning a bit closer to her, "I'd like to keep a low profile on this tour, if ye know what I mean. No special treatment, please."

Ensign Hammond nodded, clearly relieved. "Yes, sir," she replied. "No special treatment. I've got it."

As Scott boarded the shuttlecraft and looked around

for a place to sit, he saw that the shuttle had four rows of five seats with an aisle down the middle. Nineteen of those seats were occupied—perhaps a third of them by children.

Nineteen faces looked up to watch him walk down the aisle. Apparently, he'd kept them waiting a wee bit. Giving the group a tight smile, he took his seat.

Without ceremony, the ensign sat down behind the controls and ran through the preflight protocols. Ahead of her, the shuttlebay doors opened to the blackness of space.

When he felt the craft lurch slightly, Scott forced himself to look away from Ensign Hammond. He recognized the irony of it. After all his years in space, he was uncomfortable traveling in a ship he wasn't piloting.

Of course, there were a few others he trusted at the helm of a vessel. But none of them were available, the engineer thought wryly.

Scott tried to distract himself by silently running through his plan, but that didn't help much. To call what he had in mind a plan was being kind in the extreme. The fact was, he had only the vaguest idea of how he would accomplish his objective.

Well, he mused, he'd simply do what he always did when facing a difficult problem under a tough deadline. He'd just take it one step at a time.

A flash of light from the starboard observation port caught his eye. As he turned, he couldn't help but grin at the sight. Hanging there in space, the *Yorktown* was even more beautiful than he remembered.

They were approaching the dry dock from out front, the dock's lights reflecting off the ship's command hull. It would have been more efficient to approach the ship from the rear and enter the shuttlebay directly, but this was a tour intended to show off the ship. And despite the lost time, Scotty couldn't find it in his heart to regret the view.

First, they skimmed along the smooth top of the main saucer section of the ship. All eyes in the shuttle, including Scotty's, were glued to the vessel—which dominated not only the observation ports, but also the viewscreen up above the pilot's seat. They came close enough to see the letters that spelled out her name.

U.S.S. YORKTOWN, it said. The call letters were NCC-1717.

No bloody letter, Scotty thought, in the old Starfleet typography. What's more, he liked it better that way.

They dipped down at the end of the saucer to a point just above the engineering hull. This gave them a good view of both the cigar-shaped engineering section of the ship below them and the engine nacelles above them.

Scotty had never taken to the newer starship designs, including those of the new Galaxy-class ship. The damned engine pods just seemed too short.

On the old Constitution-class vessels, the nacelles were long and graceful. Long enough, in fact, that they should have looked unwieldy. But they didn't. Instead, they conveyed a sense of power that the newer ships seemed to lack.

Of course, he knew that was just an illusion. Modern engine designs were so powerful, the warp speed chart had to be rewritten to account for their performances.

Still, though Scotty knew all of that intellectually, the illusion persisted. As they came around to the rear of the ship, it looked to the engineer as if at any moment she would shake off the dry dock like an old coat and blast out of the system in a blur of light.

Positioning itself directly behind the shuttlebay, their small craft began its approach. As it glided into the bay and took its place on the deck, Scotty could feel the vibrations from the shuttle doors closing.

Then he could hear the hiss of the air reentering the cargo bay area. And when there was enough air in the shuttlebay to transmit the sound, he could actually hear the air pumps at work.

Scotty noted that the pumps rattled a bit. It was a design flaw that he and every other chief engineer of this type of vessel had corrected. The fact that the *Yorktown* still had the flaw meant that the museum engineers had returned the ship to its original specs.

Normally, such thinking would have irritated Scotty. After all, the modifications and improvements made over the years by a ship's engineering staff were part of that vessel. Denying those efforts seemed . . . disrespectful, somehow.

But now, Scotty had to admit, he was of two minds about it. After all, the practice would make his job easier.

Ensign Hammond stood to face the captive audience in the shuttle as the door beside her opened to the shuttlebay.

"Welcome," she said, "to the Constitution-class starship *U.S.S. Yorktown* registry NCC-One-Seven-One-Seven. This ship was built almost one hundred and twenty years ago, in the year Twenty-two Forty-seven, at the San Francisco shipyard facility above Earth. The San Francisco facility is still operational today, producing components for state-of-the-art vessels like the Galaxy-class starships. These serve as the new flagships of Starfleet."

The ensign was clearly reciting a memorized speech for which she had no doubt lost enthusiasm long ago. The people around Scotty didn't seem to mind, however. And he was too busy thinking to be truly offended.

"In its day," Hammond went on, "the *Yorktown* and the other eleven Constitution-class ships were the most advanced Federation vessels in space. As exploratory vessels, they were out of communication range with Starfleet command for long periods of time. Much as they do today, ship's captains enjoyed broad discretionary powers in dealing with first contact issues, as well as matters of Federation security.

"Today, we're going on a walking tour of the *Yorktown.* We'll work our way from the shuttlebay to all of the major areas of the ship, and finally come up on the bridge. This is a modified version of the 'walking the ship' inspection ritual that is still performed by Starfleet captains. In the days of the *Yorktown,* an officer could walk every corridor and deck of the ship in a single duty shift. Today, it can take more than a week to walk every corridor of a Galaxy-class starship."

Hammond pointed out the shuttle door. "Out in the shuttlebay, we'll have a few minutes to explore the bay's museum, which includes artifacts collected from the voyages of the twelve Constitution-class starships. If you have any questions about individual exhibits, you can ask the ship's computer. And feel free to try any controls that you wish. You can't hurt the ship."

She looked around. "Any questions before we begin?"

A hand went up immediately. The ensign nodded at its owner, a young boy of about ten, Scotty guessed.

"Did the *Yorktown* ever get into a battle with the Romulans?" the boy asked.

"Well," said Hammond, "though the *Yorktown* was involved in a few battles, her chief accomplishments were in the area of galactic exploration."

The same hand went up again.

"Yes?" the ensign asked.

"Does it still work?" the boy wanted to know.

"I'm afraid I don't know what you mean," Hammond replied.

Scotty did. He spoke up.

"I think the lad is asking if the *Yorktown*'s still operational."

Ensign Hammond gave Scotty her professional smile. "Yes, she is. All systems are fully operational. Right down to the ship's synthesizers, which are capable of producing the uniforms, food, and other essentials that would have been necessary on a five-year mission."

"Are there any live photon torpedoes? Do the phasers work?" the boy asked insistently.

"No," the ensign replied—a bit tautly, Scotty thought. "Both the phaser and photon torpedo systems have been deactivated. There is little call for those types of weapons in the Starfleet museum."

The boy's hand went up one more time. This time he didn't wait for the tour guide to acknowledge him. "I thought you said that the ship was fully—"

"Now, if there are no further questions," the ensign said, turning for the door and heading out, "please join me on the deck—so we can begin our starship adventure."

Scotty was among the last to exit the shuttle. Reaching the deck, he scanned the bay at a glance. Given more time, he would have been happy to gawk at the museum's treasures with the others on the tour. But he knew he couldn't spare a moment.

Making his way across the deck, he noticed that the boy had cornered Ensign Hammond. Scotty wondered where the lad's parents were. No doubt, the ensign was wondering the same thing.

A moment later, he'd made his way to a display case—one that contained the device he had been looking for. Though it was listed in the museum's brochure, he had made up his mind not to count on it until he saw the wee bairn with his own eyes.

About a meter in height, the unit consisted of two circular sections, a larger one on the bottom and a smaller one on top. No power was being fed to the unit at the moment, but Scotty knew that when it was working the lower cylinder would glow with energy.

Scotty tapped the nearby intercom pad and said, "Computer, is this the original Romulan cloaking device retrieved by the *U.S.S. Enterprise* on stardate five-oh-two-seven-point-three?"

"Yes," the computer responded. "Thank you for your interest and enjoy your starship adventure on the *U.S.S. Yorktown.*"

The electronic voice was the same one that Scotty remembered from the *Enterprise,* but the personality was different. More friendly, less mechanical—a lot like the voice that had welcomed him to the starbase.

The change annoyed him. After all, the computer was a machine.

"Is the unit operational?" he asked. "Has it been modified in any way?"

"The Romulan cloaking device is fully functional and has been restored to its original specifications. Thank you for your inquiry and enjoy your starship adventure on the *U.S.S. Yorktown.*"

Well, that's it then, Scotty thought.

Suddenly, he realized he wasn't alone in front of the

exhibit. Turning, he saw the now familiar face of the youngster with all the questions.

"A ship like this stole that cloak from the Romulans," the lad informed him.

"Really," Scott said noncommittally.

"Yeah. It was a hundred years ago," the boy added enthusiastically.

"Is that so?" Scotty replied.

"Yeah. The starship got chased by three Romulan battle cruisers when they tried to get away with the cloaking device. Man, that must have been something," the youngster remarked with a flourish.

"It was," Scotty replied, too low for the lad to hear.

A moment later, Ensign Hammond called the group to the shuttlebay exit and led them out into the corridor. Their first stops were the cargo and recreational areas on the lower decks.

Scotty tried to remain as inconspicuous as possible and maintain a polite distance from the boy, who was now lecturing a young couple on the Earth-Romulan war.

Walking the corridors, Scotty could feel a vibration through the deck. The warp engines were on-line, though operating at minimal power.

That was good. It would make the execution of his scheme much easier. That is, the scheme that was still developing in his head—becoming firmer and firmer by the minute.

Scotty's breath caught in his throat as he followed the group onto the engineering deck. Again, he felt the desire to lose himself in the wonder of his surroundings, but he kept his mind on his task.

While the others were marveling at the engine core, Scotty discreetly headed for auxiliary control. On the way, he passed Ensign Hammond trying to coax the same lad down from a Jeffries tube.

"But you said we couldn't hurt the ship," the boy protested in a high-pitched voice.

In auxiliary control, Scotty seated himself behind the console and tested all of the engineering lockouts, using the shipyard presets he remembered from the *Enterprise.* The curators had completed their restoration down to the use of the factory codes—so they all worked, giving him access to most of the ship's engineering functions.

His first task was to change the codes, giving him sole access. Then he used that access to begin a minor overload to the warp engine systems.

Scotty had time for a few more adjustments, after which he was ready to try the prefix code. The curators— bless them—had restored that one as well.

He summoned the numbers from memory. Just another moment and he'd—

"Even if the entire bridge was destroyed," a recognizable boy's voice said behind him, "they could control the whole ship from here, even fire the weapons."

Scotty sighed with his whole body.

"What are you doing?" the lad asked.

"Just trying out the antiques," Scotty told him, keeping his voice even with great effort.

Ensign Hammond appeared in the doorway. "We're moving on, sir," she called to Scotty, purposely ignoring the boy.

"Of course," the engineer replied, getting up. "The lad was just asking me about the secondary functions of auxiliary control. Perhaps ye could explain them to him."

Joining the rest of the group, Scotty endured the remainder of the tour. But it was a blur to him, really. His mind raced ahead as he planned his next moves.

So engaged, the engineer barely noted the brief visit to the starboard engine pod, or the tour of the science labs, sickbay, the observation deck, and the crew quarters. An hour later, he made a point of being the first one on the turbolift going to the bridge.

He couldn't afford to have his time cut short up there. He knew he would get only one shot at what he had to do.

When the turbolift door opened, Scotty emerged, intent on his objectives. So intent, in fact, that he was unprepared for the sight that greeted him.

It was like stepping into a dream. He stared open-mouthed at the bridge, unable to shake the feeling he was home—that he was on the *Enterprise.*

Vaguely aware that he was holding up the people behind him, Scotty moved aside to let them out. Then he stood there for a moment, shaking his head.

Why did he have this feeling? This was the *Yorktown,* not the *Enterprise.* And though to the untrained eye the bridges of Constitution-class ships were quite similar, an experienced officer could always tell the difference.

After all, there were changes in the shipyard specs from ship to ship. There were design improvements, alterations in monitor sizes and shapes, fine-tuning of station ergonomics.

And yet, this bridge was absolutely identical to the one where Scotty had served.

Puzzled, he turned his head to read the dedication plaque next to him.

My God, he thought. It's nae possible.

But it was. The plaque clearly read:

CROSSOVER

A voice next to him said, "I thought you knew, sir."

Scotty turned to see Ensign Hammond standing next to him.

"This bridge module was removed from the original *Enterprise* during the refit in Twenty-two Seventy. When the *Yorktown* was decommissioned the bridge was damaged, so the museum used the *Enterprise*'s module."

Unable to speak, Scotty simply nodded. Once the ensign had turned away, however, he headed for his station and took a seat behind the engineering console.

He could feel his throat constricting as he worked. Calling up the prefix code, he changed it to ensure that no one on board the starbase would be able to access the ship's primary systems.

Then he increased the rate of the warp engine overload he had begun from auxiliary control. It would only be a few moments now.

Turning his attention to the rest of the group, Scotty saw Ensign Hammond explaining modular bridge design to the others, while the young boy lectured another child on the *Enterprise*'s encounters with the Romulans.

Both conversations were interrupted when warning lights went off on most of the bridge stations. Almost simultaneously, the ensign's communicator beeped.

"Hammond here," she said.

The voice on the communicator, which Scotty thought he recognized as the base commander's, instructed her to go to the communications station. Once there, she picked up an earpiece and listened to a private message. When the ensign returned to the group, she was all business.

"I'm afraid we'll have to be getting back to the starbase now," Hammond informed everyone there.

"Is there a problem?" asked one of the adults in the group.

"Are we under attack?" asked the boy—hopefully, Scotty would have sworn.

Hammond managed a semblance of her usual smile. "Nothing like that, I'm afraid. But there is a minor malfunction in the life support system. It's nothing to worry about, really, but I've been asked to escort you back to the base so maintenance crews can make repairs."

She gestured toward the turbolift. "So, if you will please enter the turbolift five at a time, it will take you directly to the shuttlebay and we can be on our way."

As the first group entered the turbolift, Scotty took the ensign aside. "Is there anything I can do?" he asked.

Hammond shook her head. "It's really just a minor malfunction."

Scotty pointed to the engineering control panel. "Nae according to those warning lights, it's nae."

The ensign dropped her professional smile. "There's a fluctuation in the warp engine, and the base is having trouble accessing the *Yorktown*'s systems. But it's probably nothing."

Scott shrugged. "Perhaps I could take a look at the engines for ye while ye get these people out. I'm still on active duty, and I do know the ship."

Hammond's smile returned. "No thank you, sir. I'm afraid that wouldn't be possible. Only base personnel are allowed to perform repairs. But I would appreciate some help keeping everyone together and getting them on the shuttle as quickly as possible."

"Aye," Scott said in a resigned sort of way, as he and the ensign joined the last group to get onto a turbolift.

During the ride, Scotty wondered how he would separate himself from Hammond.

He considered a number of options. One was to pull rank on her and send her on her way. Another was to overpower her and set the shuttle on automatic. Of course, he could simply hide in the *Yorktown* somewhere, until she had no choice but to leave him.

None of those choices seemed palatable to him. And worse, none of them was certain to work. Scotty recognized that his fragile plan was in imminent danger of falling apart. And failure at this point meant more than just embarrassment for him.

As they walked out onto the shuttledeck, the ship's computer began announcing yellow alert through the intercom system. Scotty knew it was an automatic response to the overload.

Ensign Hammond didn't wait for the question this time. "It's nothing to worry about," she said, "just a precaution. However, we should all board the shuttlecraft now."

She ushered the nervous line of people on board. When the young boy came up to the shuttle entrance, he asked in a loud voice, "Are we under attack? Is it the Romulans?" His eyes were alight.

Before Hammond could respond, the boy broke away from her and headed for the shuttlebay doors.

"I want to see," he announced.

The ensign looked up at Scotty, stricken.

"I'll get him," Scotty reassured her, racing after the boy. "Get the shuttle ready," he called behind him as he went.

Damn, the engineer thought. The boy could get himself killed—and it would be his own fault for initiating the engine overload. Seeing the lad turn right at the end of a corridor, Scotty dashed after him.

He took one turn and then another, homing in on the sound of retreating footsteps, glad that the lad didn't have the presence of mind to slip into a turbolift. But it didn't take long for Scotty to realize that he was losing ground.

In a footrace against a ten year old, he was hopelessly outclassed. So he bowed to the inevitable and came to a halt when he saw the boy dart around another corner.

"STOP!" he shouted in a booming voice. "You're endangering the mission!" he called out.

He heard the boy's footfalls recede for a few more seconds—and then silence.

"What mission?" the lad's voice called out.

"Dinnae question orders, just get over here," Scott bellowed.

The boy peeked around a corner. Scotty scowled at him, his face a deep red—an effect that was easy to achieve after his run. The boy took one look at Scotty and skulked over, hands in pockets.

"I just didn't want to miss anything," he said.

"Enough foolishness," Scotty told him. "Come back with me to the shuttlebay. *Now.*"

He'd saved the lad, he thought. Too bad he couldn't have saved Spock as well. However, he'd run out of chances to get the solitary time he needed on the *Yorktown.*

By the time he got the boy back to the shuttlebay, the maintenance team would likely be there. And that would be it.

Then it struck him. He and the boy wouldn't be going back to the shuttlebay. Grabbing the youngster's arm firmly, Scotty directed him to the nearest turbolift.

"Where are we going?" the boy demanded petulantly.

The lift door opened and they entered. Once inside, the engineer tapped the controls and said, "Transporter room."

Then he turned to his companion. The youngster cringed at Scotty's stern expression, but to his credit didn't turn away.

"What's your name, son?" Scotty asked.

The boy seemed surprised by the question. "Adam," he sputtered.

"Adam," he began, "do you know who I am?"

The boy shook his head no.

"When you get back to the base, I want you to look up Montgomery Scott of the *U.S.S. Enterprise.*"

The boy tried to speak, but Scotty cut him off.

"There is nae time for questions, lad. I need you to do exactly as I tell ye. Understand?"

The boy nodded his agreement.

The turbolift came to a halt, the doors opened and Scotty escorted the lad out into the corridor. They turned left. After just a few meters, they came to the transporter room.

Its doors parted for them. Scotty pulled the boy inside.

"Have ye ever taken a transporter?" he asked.

"N—No," the youngster responded, looking around with some trepidation.

The engineer grunted. "It's perfectly safe, ye know."

"I know," the boy piped up. "It's one of the securest forms of travel ever." Obviously, he was repeating something he'd heard—in school, perhaps.

"Good," Scotty told him. "Now, if ye dinnae mind, I'd like ye to get on one of the transporter pads. Ye're goin' to have an adventure, Adam."

Though clearly still apprehensive, the boy stepped onto the transporter platform. Scotty took his place behind the controls. He tapped the intercom.

"Captain Scott to Ensign Hammond," he said, making a point of using his rank.

"Hammond here," came the reply.

"I have the boy in the transporter room, Ensign. But there's nae time to bring him to you. I'm prepared to transport both of us to the shuttle while ye're in flight."

The tension in Hammond's voice was evident even over the intercom. "Sir, I can't allow that. We'll wait for you here."

Damn, Scott thought. He was out of options. If the shuttle didn't take off, he would have no choice but to take the boy down to the shuttlebay and submit to failure.

That was when the *Yorktown* saved him. The ship went to red alert: flashing lights, klaxons, and all.

Scotty smiled. If the ship were a woman, he would have kissed her right then and there.

Hammond's intercom voice was taut with urgency. "On second thought, sir, I don't think there's time."

"I'll scan ye," Scotty offered, "and transport as soon as ye clear the ship."

"Acknowledged," came Hammond's reply.

"You're coming with me?" Adam asked from the transporter pad.

Scotty shook his head. "No, son, I'm nae. I need this ship for an important mission."

"Where are you going?" the lad wanted to know.

"I'm going to . . . to face the Romulans," Scotty told him, watching the boy's eyes go wide. "They have a friend of mine," he continued.

That's the first time I've told anyone else the truth about what I'm doing, the engineer thought.

Scanning his board, Scotty could see that the shuttle was clear of the ship.

"And, son," he said, smiling and meeting the boy's awestruck gaze, "I could nae have done it without ye."

Then Scotty energized the transporter. He reveled in the feeling of the sliding controls under his fingers. Better than those damned touch pads they use today, he mused.

A moment later, the lad vanished from the transporter platform in a blur of color and light.

He used the ship's sensors to confirm that the boy was safely on board the shuttlecraft. Then he headed out the door at a jog, ignoring the intercom's insistent chirping.

A few seconds later, he was back at auxiliary control. Sitting down at the control panel, he heard Ensign Hammond say, "Hammond to Scott. Hammond to Scott. Captain Scott, please respond."

Though it pained him to do so, he ignored the hail and got to work. It was a simple matter to halt the engine overload. Next, he locked out the shuttlebay, so that the doors wouldn't open when the maintenance shuttle approached—which Scotty calculated would happen in less than a minute.

Then he set to work releasing the ship from the tractor beam moorings. A simple feedback loop would—

The base commander's angry face appeared abruptly on the auxiliary control viewscreen. "Whatever you're doing, Captain Scott, I advise you to stop it immediately."

Scotty ignored the face and the voice and concentrated on the task at hand. He regretted doing this to Commander Nelson, who seemed to be a good man and deserved an explanation—but Scott couldn't possibly give him one right now.

As soon as the mooring tractor beams were off-line, he

grabbed a tool kit from the storage locker, gave silent thanks to the museum curators for their thoroughness, and sprinted for the shuttledeck. Inside, he wasted no time freeing the cloaking device from its display case.

The job took longer than Scotty had expected. He resolved to make it up in the installation.

Down in engineering, Scotty headed right for the dilithium reaction chamber. He installed the cloaking device in eight minutes, which was comfortably under the ten he'd planned. Of course, he'd done this sort of thing before. He was even able to make a few improvements in the makeshift circuit that connected the Romulan beasty to the ship.

Scotty didn't bother to test the cloaking mechanism as he ran for the nearest turbolift. If it didn't work, there was no time to tinker with it.

The turbolift ride was interminably slow, thanks to the original shipyard specs. Upgrading the turbolift drivers had been one of his first tasks on board the *Enterprise.*

When he reached the bridge, Scotty bolted for Sulu's station. He spared a glance at the viewscreen, which already held the base commander's angry visage.

"We scanned the ship," Nelson warned him, "and saw that you altered the engineering lockouts and the prefix code. I can tell you that whatever you're planning, it won't work. Captain Scott?"

Scotty laid in the course that he'd calculated on board his own shuttle, and hit the forward thrusters.

"You won't get ten minutes out of dry dock," Nelson told him, his voice taking on even more of an edge than before. "Our runabouts can easily overtake the *Yorktown.* You should know that."

Watching the board carefully, Scotty calculated that it would take another full minute to clear the dock.

"I can't allow this vessel to be taken," the base commander pressed. "Don't make me fire on the *Yorktown,* Captain. I'm asking you as a Starfleet officer to bring the ship to a stop and release all controls."

Nelson's voice changed in tone again, softening this time.

"Please understand that no one here holds you responsible for what you're doing. We want to help you."

Of course ye do, thought Scotty. And I'm the blasted Prince of Donegal.

He looked up from his controls to face the commander. "I regret that I canna comply with yer request," he apologized. "But ye have my word that I'll return the *Yorktown,* if it's within m'power to do so."

After all, losing a prized antique starship to a crazy old coot wouldn't be good for Nelson's career. If there was another way, Scotty told himself, he would have taken it.

Nelson's composure was slipping fast. "Is this how you want to be remembered, after all you've done?" he asked. "This is crazy!"

There, the commander had said it. Scotty knew it was the subtext of all the man's arguments.

Well, so be it, he thought. At that point, he wasn't sure he entirely disagreed with Nelson's assessment of him.

"I'm sorry, Commander," the engineer said. And he was.

All that remained was one more roll of the dice.

The commander let fly his last warning. "You won't get half a light-year out of the system."

Scotty half wished that Nelson was right.

Nonetheless, he pushed the button that would activate the cloaking device. Scotty could feel the slight shudder of the deck as the ship redirected a portion of its power to the alien machine.

Then a warning light told Scotty there would be no quick and easy end to this mission. The cloak was operational.

He took the ship to full impulse.

Scotty knew it would be a simple matter for Nelson's people to recalibrate the starbase sensors and penetrate the obsolete cloaking system. But in those few minutes, the shuttle would make it well out of sensor range.

Moments later, free of the base, he went to warp. The *Yorktown* leaped forward, as if remembering what it was like to be free.

The deed done, Scotty drew a deep breath and surveyed the bridge carefully. He knew that if he went back to the engineering station—*his* station—he would be able to touch the underside of the control panel and feel a gouge in the metal that predated even his service on the ship.

This place was the closest thing to home he would likely ever find in the twenty-fourth century. Looking at the bridge stations, he could imagine his friends at them— just the way it used to be.

The notion should have comforted him, but it left him cold somehow. Curious, he thought.

Shaking off the feeling as he would a highland winter, Scotty got up and headed for the turbolift. He didn't have time for such foolish musings. He had work to do.

Somewhere in Romulan space, there was someone who needed him. As he entered the lift, he vowed to keep that in mind. For now, Scotty's work would be his world.

And he'd leave the ghosts on the bridge to theirs.

CHAPTER 4

Governor Tharrus of Constanthus leaned back in his chair and eyed his chief of security.

"Yes, Phabaris?"

"The prisoners have been secured, Governor." The security chief said the words with obvious pride, having taken part in the arrest. "They are in the detention facility at the city limits."

Tharrus nodded. "Good."

The large, craggy-featured governor allowed himself a smile. He rarely displayed his emotions in front of a subordinate, but he felt the occasion was worth it this time.

This was a pleasure. A rich, well-deserved, eminently *profitable* pleasure. And it was his vigilance and careful planning that had made it all possible.

In the end, he'd achieved something that had eluded even the vaunted Tal Shiar—who for all their fearsome power had been helpless before the unificationist movement.

The unificationists represented the first real challenge to the Romulan political system in a hundred years or more. The fact that the Tal Shiar had yet to make a significant dent in the movement had been a huge embarrassment for both the elite intelligence organization and the Empire.

And the rebels' philosophical grounding in pacifistic Vulcan ideals only compounded the humiliation.

Though the unificationist effort had been growing on the homeworlds for some time, their arrival on Constanthus had been an unforeseen development—one that Tharrus and his operatives had been more than ready to act upon.

With a gaggle of them now in hand, the governor would be able to carry out their disposition entirely on his own—from their arrests to their trial, to their ultimate disposal. And once he had finished with them, he would announce that he had crushed the movement once and for all.

That, of course, wouldn't be true in the least. However, the central government wouldn't be able to refute his claims without conceding that the movement was larger in scope than they'd admitted.

He would grow in prestige. And prestige translated into power.

And when the unificationists reared their heads again on Romulus, as Tharrus had no doubt they would, those in the central government would be shown for the fools they were. After all, the movement had been crushed— how could they have let it rise up again?

Then an even greater opportunity might present itself. He might, by popular demand, obtain for himself a voice in the homeworld bureaucracy—a voice no governor before him had ever enjoyed.

It was a dream, to be sure. But not so distant or intangible a dream that his mouth didn't water as he contemplated it.

Tharrus said none of this to Phabaris. He had learned long ago to keep his own counsel. He was not so arrogant to believe that the Tal Shiar could not place someone close to him, or convert an apparently loyal officer into a traitor.

So the governor simply smiled and lifted his powerful body out of his chair. With a gesture, he indicated the door.

"Take me to them," he ordered.

The security chief nodded and headed out the door. Tharrus followed.

On the roof of the office complex, they boarded Tharrus's personal shuttle for the short ride to the detention facility. The pilot was already waiting for them.

As they slid over the rooftops of Auranthus, the governor was reminded once more that this was neither Romulus or Remii. He hadn't had the resources to make it look the part, nor had he expected any.

But that could change, he thought. The prisoners might be all he needed to *make* it change.

The flight didn't take long. Only a few minutes, really, before they arrived at the detention facility.

Looking down as the shuttle landed, Tharrus could see the enclosed courtyard with its warren of prisoner quarters at one end and its administration building at the other. He was proud of the modern materials and construction techniques used in the facility, which made it unique among outworld prisons.

Too often, planetary governors on the outlying planets

neglected their duties in the pursuit of posts on Romulus and Remii. But Tharrus had long ago rejected that sort of thinking, preferring to build his power in the outworlds themselves—and he wasn't the only governor who thought that way.

In a few short moments, the shuttle had landed on the roof of the administration building. Before heading down into the structure, Tharrus paused for a moment to consider the forty-odd unificationists who had assembled in the courtyard.

He wondered if they knew how short their future would be. After all, the governor prided himself on meting out swift and sure justice.

Because of that, virtually all sorts of crime took place less frequently on Constanthus than anywhere else in the Empire—the homeworlds included. That was something else he would be sure to point out when he announced that he'd captured the unificationists.

Taking the lift down through the building, Tharrus exited it on the ground floor. He headed immediately for the security gate and made his way into the courtyard, where several of his personal guards awaited him.

At his appearance, the traitors' heads turned. For the first time, he scrutinized them.

He wasn't sure what he had expected to see in the rebels, but he found himself surprised by their appearance. Basically, they just looked like Romulans.

Of course, the governor had known they weren't exactly Klingons. But he had assumed they would all have some indefinable quality that would set them apart from other Romulans.

Obviously, he'd been wrong. The rebels were young and old, males as well as females. He was looking at all the types of Romulans there were, a veritable cross section of the Empire.

This is the enemy? Tharrus thought. What kind of plague was this movement that it would affect so many different types of Romulans? And how might one fight it?

Brushing the thought away, he forced himself to contemplate more pressing matters. For now, his sole concern was making the most of the current situation. He would worry about what to do about the unificationist problem when he was running the Empire, he thought with a smile.

Taking a position in front of the prisoners, the governor addressed them. As tall and powerful as he was, he knew he had to be an intimidating figure—though as yet, none of the prisoners seemed particularly daunted by him.

"Traitors to the Empire," he bellowed. His voice echoed nicely in the courtyard. "I am Governor Tharrus. I rule this world for the greater glory of the Empire."

Tharrus waited for that information to register on their faces. Surely, when they knew with whom they were dealing, their fear would rise to the surface.

But nothing happened. They maintained their air of calm.

Well, the governor thought, that would end quickly enough.

"You have been officially charged with treason," he told them. "In four days, you will be tried and convicted for your crimes. As Romulans, you know the punishment for treason, and each of you will face that punishment. However, if any of you chooses to make a full confession now, I will see that his or her death comes quickly."

The traitors began shuffling in place and murmuring among themselves. Pleased to see growing tension in the crowd, Tharrus imagined it would be only a few moments before the first one broke and asked for mercy.

He waited. Few of the traitors were meeting his eyes. Instead, they wore a blank expression—one reminiscent of the pitiful Vulcans.

Many in the highest levels of the Empire believed there was something to gain by conquering the Vulcans, by taking their world and subjugating them. Tharrus did not share this view. To him, those who believed that foolishness were little better than these traitorous unificationists.

The Vulcans had lost the very essence of the two races' joint heritage, a glorious one that celebrated the achievements of those bold enough to take what they wanted. The Romulans, on the other hand, had forged an empire from their own courage. They'd been right to leave their weakling brothers behind, shedding them like old skin.

For the same reason, the subjugation of Vulcan would be wrong now—as it would surely dilute the Romulan ethic through constant contact with a passive, even timid culture.

The governor noted that one of the traitors, a middle-aged specimen, was watching him closely—almost studying him. The individual did not even have the true Romulan's heavy brow. Though many highly placed and honored Romulans had the smooth brows of their Vulcan ancestors, Tharrus had always seen that feature as a sign of weakness.

And yet, this pathetic, traitorous weakling had the gall to stare at one who ruled a world for the Romulan Empire.

Moving forward, fired by his frustration with the prisoners' reactions, Tharrus approached the smooth-brow. Phabaris and one of his personal guards followed him, staying close—as was their duty. The other prisoners parted before the governor, but the middle-aged one stood his ground.

He seemed impassive. Almost disinterested, Tharrus observed.

When he reached the traitor, the man maintained his infuriatingly calm expression. His only gesture was to raise an eyebrow, as if appraising the governor. As if sizing him up, as one might do to an adversary of equal standing.

Tharrus could feel the blood rush to his face. He was tempted to order the traitor's death on the spot. Resisting the impulse, he reminded himself that the prisoner would die soon enough. For now, the governor would have to content himself with pointing out the pitfalls of such behavior.

He addressed the smooth-brow. "What is your name, traitor?"

"I am called Selek," the Romulan replied evenly.

"Do you wish to confess your crimes, Selek?"

The prisoner shook his head. "No, I do not."

Tharrus struggled to keep his anger from overflowing. He would not be provoked by this arrogant weakling.

"Confession will assure you a quick and painless death," the governor reminded him. Then, making no effort to hide his contempt, he added, "Surely, as a student of the Vulcans, you can see the sense in avoiding unnecessary discomfort. You might even inspire some of your friends here to do the same. Such behavior would spare them a very unpleasant future."

But the prisoner didn't take the bait. "I see no logic," he answered, "in confessing to crimes I have not committed. Like everyone here, I only seek knowledge."

Sneering, Tharrus used the voice that had made hardened soldiers cringe before him. "You dare claim your treason is no more than a quest for knowledge? You would consort with our enemies and destroy the purity of the Romulan way of life by polluting it with weakling philosophies. You are the worst kind of criminal."

The prisoner spoke as if they were having a polite conversation at the Praetor's dinner table. "The Empire cannot rule by crushing all opposing philosophies and ideas. All living things must grow and change. If the Empire insists—"

The governor lashed out with the back of his hand, which made a most satisfying contact with the prisoner's face.

As the smooth-brow's head turned from the force of the blow, Tharrus heard the hiss of his guards drawing their weapons. He motioned for them to hold their fire and waited to see the traitor's reaction.

The middle-aged Romulan recovered quickly from the assault, which by all rights should have felled him. Worse, he had fixed that impassive gaze on Tharrus again. And once again, he considered the governor with a raised eyebrow.

Anger raged inside Tharrus, but he kept it in check. Didn't the prisoner realize how close he was to death?

It wasn't apparent from the look on the Romulan's face. Unless, of course, he foresaw his fate and was simply not bothered by it.

Then the rebel compounded his arrogance. As a final insult, he turned the other side of his face to the governor, as if presenting it for another blow.

A challenge? Tharrus thought incredulously.

But even as his fury threatened to blot out all reason, Tharrus reined himself in again. He would not be baited in front of his own men, or in front of the other prisoners.

"You seek to secure yourself an easy death by taxing my patience," the governor concluded. "A pathetic attempt. I will be presiding over your collective trial personally. And I will pronounce your sentence myself."

With that, he turned away from the prisoner and led his men out of the detention area. As he left, he could feel the traitor's stare on his back.

He resolved not to give the weakling unificationist another thought. Soon, all the prisoners would know a fate that every sane Romulan rightly feared.

Tharrus shook himself mentally. He was a planetary governor of the Romulan Empire, and soon he might be more than that.

Nevertheless, as he departed the courtyard, he couldn't help but feel he'd just lost something to the prisoner. Something *important.*

Proconsul Eragian stared at his data screen in silence for a moment before he spoke. As usual, Lennex had done an excellent job collecting and providing him with intelligence.

"My compliments," he said dryly, glancing at the Tal Shiar officer standing beside him. It seemed Lennex was *always* standing beside him.

The Tal Shiar nodded once. But he didn't respond verbally. He wasn't one to exchange mere pleasantries, after all.

Unfortunately, Eragian mused, most of the reports before him revealed increasing tension in the outer worlds of the Empire. Two instances of outright insurrection, for instance—quickly put down, but disturbing nonetheless.

Nor did it end there. There were also a great many other incidents. Dangerous individuals and political groups were daring more and more open criticism of the Empire and its policies.

And then there was Tharrus.

The proconsul's eyes narrowed, giving his reflection in the monitor an even more predatory look. "I have never given much thought to this outworld governor. I find it irksome to have to think of him now."

Lennex shrugged, his blunt, rough-hewn features giving away nothing. "In apprehending these unificationists, Governor Tharrus has accomplished something even the Tal Shiar have failed at. It would be foolish not to give the devil his due."

"Tharrus has merely had a stroke of good luck," said Eragian, trying to dismiss the problem. "He will not know how to capitalize on it."

"Is that an opinion?" Lennex inquired. "Or do you speak from knowledge of the man?"

Answering a statement with a question—a typical response, thought the proconsul. A Tal Shiar response.

Eragian knew that Lennex had spent most of his life in the service of the Empire. In several different capacities, the man had proven himself to be cunning, aggressive, and very good at his job.

That was one reason he had been accepted into the Tal Shiar, the secret police of the Empire. The other was an ability to remain circumspect. Though he was willing to offer counsel, Lennex confided in no one—not even a proconsul for whom he had served as advisor for the past fifteen years.

As a high-ranking official in the Tal Shiar, Lennex was entrusted with secrets even Eragian would never even glimpse. And if necessary, he would carry those secrets to his grave.

What's more, the proconsul had no illusions about the

man's loyalty, despite their long association. Lennex would have served any government official to whom he was assigned. If the proconsul fell out of power tomorrow, Lennex would no doubt counsel his successor just as readily.

"Knowledge," Eragian countered, "is your province, Lennex. So tell me—what should I expect from this upstart Tharrus?"

The Tal Shiar shrugged. "A certain determination. A penchant for survival. And a cleverness, unfinished as it may be, that would not be out of place on the floor of the Senate."

The proconsul cursed beneath his breath. It seemed he had no choice but to resign himself to the situation. "Then he'll seek to make something out of this? To gain a name for himself?"

"More than likely," Lennex replied. "As you know, his sort hungers after power the way Ferengi hunger after latinum. And now, he has the means to satisfy his hunger. Tharrus will keep the prisoners—I have no doubt of that."

"And try them himself?" Eragian asked, not at all happy at the prospect.

"Yes, Proconsul. He will attempt to demonstrate, to the people if no one else, that he is every bit as effective as the homeworld leadership."

Eragian didn't conceal his resentment. "You almost sound as if you approve of him, Lennex."

As usual, the Tal Shiar was unmoved by the proconsul's pique. "Not at all," he responded. "As I said, I merely give him his due. What's more, if he does not falter along the way, he will probably succeed in gaining some portion of his objectives.

"Of course," he went on, "from the Empire's point of

view, his actions will be deplorable. Clearly, the Tal Shiar are the ones best qualified to obtain information from the prisoners. By shutting us out of the process, Tharrus is showing that he is more interested in his own gain than in crushing the unificationist movement once and for all. His first allegiance is not to the Empire—and that is dangerous."

"The question then," said the proconsul, "is what do we do?"

For the briefest moment, Lennex let his feelings register on his face. For perhaps the first time since Eragian had known him, the man let slip that he was uncertain about something. Finally, Lennex shook his head.

"I do not believe there is an easy solution, Proconsul. If you eliminate Tharrus or order him to turn over the prisoners, the leaders of many of the outer worlds would see that as a threat to their power."

"But the planetary governors serve the Empire," Eragian protested.

"True," Lennex remarked. "But they also want to protect their provinces and their own influence. And the outer worlds are becoming very well represented in the Senate, Proconsul—as you yourself have no doubt observed."

Eragian knew his advisor was right. Things had changed a great deal in the Empire, just in his own lifetime.

A generation ago, all citizens had taken their orders solely from the hierarchy on the Romulan homeworlds. Now, the number of Romulans who lived on colony worlds rivaled the number that lived on Romulus and Remii.

In large part, the Romulan dream of conquest had been fulfilled. However, the growing Empire constantly found new difficulties maintaining order in an increasingly fractured sphere of influence.

More and more, each of the outer worlds was coming to consider its own self-interest as well as the interests of the Empire. As proconsul, Eragian often found himself in the uncomfortable position of living with compromises that his predecessors would have scorned.

But such was the price of victory and the price of conquest.

Where will we be a generation from now? Eragian wondered. Where will we be when there are many more Romulans living on the colony worlds than on the home-worlds?

Where will the allegiances of those Romulans lie? And where will we be if any of the native inhabitants of the subjugated worlds ever win their bids for full citizenship?

Two decades ago, such an idea would have been un-thinkable. Two decades from now, who could tell?

"Do you know the story of the Rodarh'vna?" the proconsul asked.

Lennex shook his head. "No, though I have heard of it. A children's story, is it not? An old one, I believe."

Eragian shook his head. "More like mythology."

Lennex's face remained blank. The proconsul was not surprised by the officer's lack of education in the more obscure aspects of their Romulan cultural heritage. The Tal Shiar were generally concerned about more tangible things.

"The Rodarh'vna," the proconsul explained, "was a mythical, two-headed flying creature. A predator so fierce that no other living creature could face it and live. However, the Rodarh'vna was also a very stupid creature.

"One day, a great hero named Gaian faced the crea-ture. He did not fight, because even as great a warrior as he would not stand a chance against the beast. Instead, he told the Rodarh'vna's two heads that they were each other's greatest enemies, finally convincing them to battle one another to the death."

Eragian smiled thinly. "For me, that story has always been a warning—to be wary of those who would set the Empire against itself for their own gain. Tharrus is one who would do this, but he is not the only one. As the Empire grows, it produces more and more of them every day. And it will take more than strength to defeat those forces. It will require considerable cunning as well."

"The challenge," said Lennex, "is to recognize the opportunity to apply that cunning."

The proconsul nodded grimly. "Yes. And when it comes, to act."

CHAPTER 5

Picard stood in the shuttlebay, flanked by Data, Troi, Geordi, and Doctor Crusher, and waited for the shuttle from the *Zapata* to make its approach. He could already see the craft through the open bay doors.

"Sorry, sir," came a voice from behind him, echoing in the enclosed space.

He turned and saw Riker crossing the bay in long strides. Darting the first officer a look, the captain received an apologetic shrug.

"A course correction," Riker explained.

Picard let the man off with a nod. On a ship this big, something always seemed to come up—even when a dignitary of sorts was about to board the *Enterprise.* And it was the first officer's job to take care of such details.

At any rate, the admiral would never even notice Riker's late arrival. His craft was only just now nearing the forcefield that held in the shuttlebay's oxygen atmosphere.

The slight sound of crackling energy told the captain that the shuttle was making contact with the field. In a moment, it was through. It glided across the bay and gently landed on the deck.

Picard approached the sleek craft, reaching the door just as it opened. An ensign stepped out first, then reached back inside for Admiral McCoy.

The admiral accepted the assistance only long enough to descend to the deck. Then he shook off the ensign's arm.

"Dismissed," he growled.

"Aye, sir," the ensign replied quickly.

The captain had met Admiral McCoy once before, shortly before the launch of the *Enterprise*. Then, as now, Picard was struck by how frail the man looked. Of course, simply reaching such an advanced age was a remarkable achievement in itself.

However, as a boy, the captain had studied the adventures of the admiral and his well-known comrades. A part of him still found it difficult to accept that McCoy was mortal.

Nonetheless, the evidence was right there before his eyes. The admiral was thin, almost painfully so, with downy white hair. His gait was slow and deliberate.

Only his eyes seemed untouched by time. They were bright, alert, and clearly focused—at the moment, on Picard.

"Admiral," said the captain, "welcome to the *Enterprise*."

McCoy took the captain's hand and shook it with a reasonably firm grip—which obviously came at the cost of some effort to the man.

"Thanks," the admiral replied. "I wish I could say I

was happy to be here, but under the circumstances . . . well, I'll just say I'm glad the situation is in your hands, and not someone else's."

Picard nodded. "I appreciate your confidence." He gestured to his officers. "May I present my senior staff. My first officer, Commander William Riker."

Riker inclined his head slightly and said, "Admiral." He didn't offer his hand, however—an astute and sensitive move on his part. No doubt, he had seen the effort McCoy had applied to return the captain's handshake.

Moving down the line, Picard indicated Deanna next. "Ship's counselor Deanna Troi."

This time, McCoy took the initiative. Reaching for the Betazoid's hand, he raised it to his lips and kissed it in gentlemanly fashion. "A pleasure to meet you, Counselor."

"Thank you, Admiral." She smiled at the gesture.

A moment later, the captain would have introduced Beverly. However, McCoy had taken her hand before Picard could say anything.

"Doctor Crusher," he said, "it's good to see you again."

"And you, Admiral," the chief medical officer replied.

"You know each other," the captain observed.

Beverly nodded. "Yes, from my tenure at Starfleet Medical."

"Of course," Picard remarked.

"I'm just sorry I couldn't keep her there longer," the admiral complained, already moving on to Geordi.

"My chief engineer," said the captain. "Lieutenant Commander Geordi La Forge."

"Admiral." Geordi smiled. Like Riker, he didn't extend his hand.

McCoy nodded to him. "La Forge."

"And finally," Picard finished, "Lieutenant Commander Data."

"Admiral," said the android. Then he turned to the captain. "The admiral and I have met before as well, sir."

"Have we?" McCoy interjected. "When?"

"Several years ago," Data told him. "I gave you a brief tour of the *Enterprise,* prior to its launch."

The admiral considered the android for a moment. "So you did, son. You're the artificial Vulcan," he said. Then he turned to Picard. "What's next, Captain?"

"We'll arrange for your things to be taken to your quarters," Picard assured him. "You then have the option of retiring there for a rest, or joining us in the ship's Ten-Forward lounge."

When the admiral spoke, his voice took on a slight edge. "Captain, I came here to participate in a mission, not just to show Starfleet colors. I'd like to be included in your strategy sessions."

"You will be," Picard promised.

"Then," asked McCoy, "what would we be doing in the ship's lounge?"

For a moment, the captain didn't understand what the admiral was getting at. "We would relax," he said finally.

"Relax?" McCoy snorted. "There's too much work to do. I'd like to know what state your plans are in for getting Spock out of that Romulan rats' den."

Suddenly the truth was painfully clear to Picard. He cleared his throat.

"Admiral, at the moment there *is* no plan—other than to follow Starfleet orders and take up a position near the Neutral Zone, where we will pursue a diplomatic liaison."

"Diplomatic?" McCoy railed suddenly, making no effort to control the tone or volume of his voice. "For God sakes, man, we don't have *time* for diplomacy. Spock is at the *mercy* of those people!"

The admiral was nearly shouting by the time he finished, as the captain and his officers noted uncomfortably. Picard would not allow such a display to continue on board his ship. He would have to put a stop to this immediately.

"At the moment," he began, "there is no danger—"

"No danger?" McCoy cursed beneath his breath. "How can you say that? Spock's in a great deal of danger."

"I was about to say," the captain replied, "that there is no danger to Federation interests or security. And until—"

"And until Spock becomes a security disaster, we don't have to do anything to help him." The admiral was ranting out loud now, having given up any pretense to officer's decorum.

Picard managed with effort to keep his own voice steady. "I am not proposing to abandon the ambassador to his fate—but I am saying we must be cautious."

McCoy harrumphed loudly. "Captain, I'm not sure I'm on the right ship. You are the Jean-Luc Picard who beat back the Romulans during that Klingon civil war, aren't you? The fella who invented the Picard maneuver? Who busted up the conspiracy when those parasites invaded Starfleet Command? And unless I'm mistaken, didn't you go to Romulus yourself once, ready to pull Spock out by the ear?"

The older man brought his face to within inches of the captain's. "And now you're hemming and hawing over a simple rescue operation."

"Admiral," Picard said, "there is nothing simple about the rescue of an important Federation official from a heavily guarded position in hostile territory—where our very appearance would constitute an act of war. And allow me to point out that rescue may not be an option, which is something the ambassador himself must by now understand.

"At the moment, my primary duty is to try to negotiate for the prisoners' release, and to monitor the situation— to see that Spock's true identity is not revealed. We have a very delicate situation on our hands—one where we must weigh and balance a great many issues and interests."

Instead of bowing to Picard's logic, McCoy virtually exploded.

"Captain," he seethed, "I was weighing and balancing before your father was in diapers—and I've learned one thing. The longer you wait to get into a tough situation, the harder it is to come away in one piece."

For the first time, Picard let some of the anger he was feeling seep into his voice. "Admiral, I'll take into account whatever advice you care to give me on this mission. But I categorically refuse to be rushed into any action that will endanger the Federation, this ship, or its crew.

"I hope you and I will be in agreement when we reach the Neutral Zone," he added. "But in the event we are not, I will nonetheless continue to follow orders—and to act in accordance with the principles of sound command judgment."

The admiral glared at him for a moment, to the point where the captain feared he might endanger his health. Then, muttering to himself, the man turned and made his way toward the exit.

Unfortunately, Picard had the feeling this conversation

wasn't quite over. At least, not as far as Admiral McCoy was concerned.

Spock brought himself out of his meditation period early, but there was no choice. They had less than four days before the trial. He and his charges had much to do in that time.

Standing up in his solitary quarters, he noted that his five remaining homeworld followers were spread among the new students. That was good, he mused.

He and his most experienced pupils would need to work very hard together in the time they had left. And before they could begin that work, he would have to convince his new students to take a path they would no doubt resist.

Yes, the six of them had much to do.

We should be seven.

The thought came unbidden, but he did not resist it. Sel'den's death was an unfortunate, illogical waste. The young Romulan had been a gifted student who too often did not see his own potential.

However, Spock knew that Sel'den had been his most devoted follower. In fact, the Vulcan had entertained the hope that Sel'den would be able to continue his work in the future.

It occurred to Spock that he had never mentioned these plans to Sel'den himself. He had never even expressed his satisfaction with his student's progress.

Of course, now that Sel'den was dead, it was pointless to concern himself with regrets. Still, the Vulcan found his mind returning to the idea that he had been in error. That he had failed to communicate his approval of the young Romulan's accomplishments.

It was a mistake that Spock's own father had made—

an odd failing in a diplomat. Logic dictated that proper communication was essential to any relationship. The Vulcan was determined not to make the same mistake again.

Leaving his quarters, Spock noted that their captors had been fairly generous in the accommodations they'd given them. Of course, this would not have been possible if the facility were filled with actual criminals.

Though most of the prisoners shared living space, the cells were small but adequate. And there were even a small number of single enclosures.

Most important to Spock's work, the students of Surak were free to roam the compound's central courtyard during the day—though under the watchful eyes of the armed guards stationed on the walls.

Unfortunately, there was only one entrance to the compound, and the Vulcan had seen that it was well guarded—so well guarded, in fact, that their captors could afford to give their prisoners the appearance of freedom within the prison walls.

Making his way past other cells and into the courtyard, Spock stepped out into the sunlight. He noted how his comrades' heads all turned in his direction. It was clear to him that they revered him.

Part of the reason was the Romulan cultural bias toward social hierarchy. As a Teacher, he was automatically accepted as their leader.

The Vulcan accepted their reverence even as he recognized that he did not deserve it. As Surak had said, Teachers did not give knowledge and wisdom; they merely guided those who sought those things for themselves.

Eventually, Spock hoped, their reverence would become additional motivation to receive what he had to impart to them. In this endeavor, time would be their worst enemy.

Very quickly, the Vulcan obtained the attention of all of his assembled students. They came to him and considered him in silence.

Spock knew he would have to proceed thoughtfully. What he had to say to his students would surprise and unsettle many of them. Thus, he chose his words with care.

"I have meditated on our situation," he told them, "and I believe that we can accomplish much in the time we have left. If we apply ourselves, we will remain undefeated in our quest for enlightenment.

"But we have much to discuss," he went on, "and much to learn. Our course of study will be necessarily abridged—"

"Course of study?" came a surprised voice from the crowd.

Spock turned his attention to a young Romulan of perhaps twenty-five years—not much older than Sel'den. But that was where his similarity to the Vulcan's late student ended. The Romulan made no effort to hide his anger as he approached the Teacher.

"Yes," Spock maintained. "Our course of study."

The Vulcan watched the Romulans before him muttering among themselves. Of course, he had expected it.

As the youth approached, Spock noticed that his five students from Romulus had moved closer as well, as if to protect him from a threat.

"Is that all your logic can offer us now?" the young Romulan asked, belligerence in his voice.

"What is your name?" the Vulcan inquired.

"Skrasis," the youth said. "And you have not answered my question."

Spock considered his charge for a moment. He looked past the anger, past the fear, and saw resentment in the man's soul. Skrasis had been expecting something more from him.

"We are four days away from trial," the youth pointed out, "which means we may be five days from a terrible death. And all your philosophy can offer us is a course of study?"

An older Romulan separated himself from the crowd which had gathered around them. It was Belan, the Vulcan noted.

"Teacher," Belan said softly, "do not judge Skrasis harshly. It is only that we had hoped for a . . . solution to our problem."

Spock nodded to show he understood. "Unfortunately, there is no logic or philosophy that will allow us to avoid our fate. We are prisoners of the Romulan government, without weapons or means of escape.

"Surak teaches us that life is by its nature finite, and therefore precious. All of us are fated to die. We accept that fact and continue to live. To do anything else is to deny the gift of life."

The Vulcan's words had a calming effect on his followers. Clearly, they saw the logic in accepting their future. All of them except Skrasis, who was unconvinced.

"Teacher," the youth countered, "even though death is inevitable, we usually expect life to last more than a few days. What good will knowledge do us if we will be dead so soon?"

Spock focused his full attention on Skrasis. "The question," he said, "is not what we will gain from the quest for knowledge—because the search is its own reward. The question is how we choose to spend the time we have left.

"Until we die, we all remain the masters of our lives. I choose to spend that time learning. And I welcome all others who make the same choice."

Silence fell over the assembled students. None of them moved, the Vulcan noted with satisfaction.

Turning again to Skrasis, he saw the look of defiance on the young man's face. Still, Skrasis remained with the others, willing to hear more of Surak's wisdom.

That was good, Spock thought. Skrasis was prepared to let his assumptions be challenged. That was the beginning of education.

Thinking that the young Romulan would be an interesting student, the Teacher began the afternoon's lesson.

CHAPTER 6

Sitting in engineering, Scotty passed the time by inspecting his cloaking device. It resided just where he had installed it, on the dilithium reaction chamber.

Of course, it looked a little different now. In addition to its basic components, it sported all the new add-on modules he'd constructed out of equipment scavenged from the *Yorktown*.

The Romulans had abandoned most of the cloaking technology behind the device after the *Enterprise* stole this prototype. That was a mistake, Scotty thought.

With a little ingenuity, he'd been able to increase the power of the device drastically, and all without taking the thing off-line. Also, he'd been able to eliminate most of the trace energy discharges that had rendered the thing susceptible to Starfleet sensors. With the way she was working now, the improved cloak would almost certainly ensure him safe passage out of Federation territory.

Now there was just one more piece of business before

he could head for the Romulan Neutral Zone. And a very important piece of business at that.

Once, a long time ago, he and his friends had tried to operate a starship with a skeleton crew, using a centralized computer control system he installed himself. That was on the refitted *Enterprise* 1701.

Unfortunately, the vessel was incapacitated by a single volley from an underpowered Klingon Bird-of-Prey. And when push came to shove, the centralized computer control system overloaded, leaving the ship a sitting duck.

For years afterward, Scotty had blamed himself for the destruction that followed, thinking that his automated system had failed because it simply wasn't good enough. However, he had known even then that he'd been pushing twenty-third-century technology to the limit.

A vessel meant to be crewed by 430 people just couldn't cut it with a crew of five. Or, in this case, a crew of one.

Likewise, Scotty knew that he was pushing the *Yorktown* computer to its limits now—even though he was asking it to do little more than stay on course. Very shortly, all that would change. He would be asking a lot more. But, this time, he had some twenty-fourth-century technology to back him up.

And according to his control panel, which was lighting up on the other end of the room, the biggest component of that technology had just made itself available.

Swiveling in his chair, Scotty hit the switch that opened the shuttlebay. Then he left engineering control and headed for the shuttledeck at a trot.

He arrived at the shuttlebay control room just as the doors were opening. Through them, he could see the *Romaine* hanging in space. The shuttle had been called the *Goddard* when Captain Picard gave it to him, but the engineer had rechristened the ship—naming it after a lovely lass he had known. The shuttle's autopilot had brought it obediently to the rendezvous point, but Scotty would have to handle the rest of its journey.

Taking the controls, he locked the *Yorktown*'s tractor beams onto the smaller vessel. Then, watching through the control room's transparent-aluminum window, he guided the shuttle inside with well-practiced hands.

Once the *Romaine* was where he wanted it and the bay was secured, Scotty shut the doors and waited several painfully long seconds for the chamber to repressurize. The warning light finally shut off.

At last, Scotty entered the shuttlebay. Striding across the deck, the engineer noted the contrasts between the shuttles the *Yorktown* normally carried and the *Romaine,* which was built more than a century later.

On the outside, the improvements were subtle. The modern shuttle had more curves and rounded surfaces and a decidedly streamlined look. Of course, Scotty knew that the real differences ran much deeper.

Entering the shuttle, the engineer made his way to her control console. "Computer," he said, "activate Constitution-class command interface."

The operation, which established a link between the shuttle's computer and that of the *Yorktown,* took less than a second to complete. Scotty had designed the computer interface from memory, and he was pleased by how well he had done.

Still, he made a few quick modifications now, based on what he had observed in his short time on board the *Yorktown.* Pronouncing the interface complete, he got up and headed for the bridge.

For each day of its nearly thirty years of active space duty, the *Yorktown* had required a full crew to run her effectively. In a few minutes, from the bridge, Scotty would slave the starship's primary functions to the shuttle's computer, which would handle them all with plenty of processing power to spare.

Then he would establish access to the shuttle's computer via the *Yorktown*'s bridge stations. At that point, he would have full control over a vessel that had once been the pride of Starfleet. And it would only be possible because of a shuttle that was smaller than a cadet's stateroom.

Entering the bridge, Scotty found it didn't have quite the same effect on him this time. The initial surprise was gone, he supposed. And besides, he didn't have the time to wax nostalgic.

Of course, he still felt the ghostly presence of his friends around him. But now they seemed to hover in the background, cheering him on.

Taking Sulu's position at the helm, Scotty routed all ship's functions to the shuttle. He was about to complete the last part of the process, transferring control of the shuttle to the starship's bridge, when the proximity detector flashed on his board.

"Computer," Scott said, "identify the vessel now in sensor range."

"Working," the computer replied. "Vessel is the *U.S.S. Intrepid,* Galaxy-class. Thank you for your inquiry and enjoy your starship adventure on the *U.S.S. Yorktown.*"

Damn, Scotty thought. They must have been scanning for his energy signature. Checking his sensors, he saw the ship approaching fast. It had just come into sensor range a few seconds earlier, and it was already almost on top of him. What's more, the ship was on an intercept course.

"Well, that's it, then," Scotty told himself.

If the phasers were on-line and the photon torpedoes

were loaded with antimatter—neither of which was the case—he might have thought about putting up a fight and trying to escape. It would have been a long shot, but he would have had a chance.

As it was, he was out of luck.

After all, as fine a vessel as the *Yorktown* was, she was no match for a modern starship. Hell, she couldn't outrun even a fast shuttle these days.

Still, out of sheer stubbornness, he continued to try to complete the command setup before the *Intrepid* came into weapons range. Scotty could see the light on Uhura's station indicating that the *Intrepid* was trying to hail him, but he couldn't stop his work to answer the call.

Finally, the circuitry diagram on his monitor went from red to green. He had control of the shuttle and the shuttle had control of the ship. All functions were available through the helm.

Scotty felt a flush of pride at his accomplishment. Even at over a century old, the ship was a powerful force, and he'd found a way to harness it. However, it didn't look like he was going to get a chance to put her capabilities to the test.

"Computer, what is the status of the *Intrepid?*" Scotty asked.

"Working," the computer told him. "The *Intrepid* is hailing this vessel and focusing its tractor beam."

Scotty felt the thump through the ship as the beam latched onto the *Yorktown.*

"Tractor engaged," the computer added helpfully. "Thank you for your inquiry and enjoy your starship adventure on the *U.S.S. Yorktown.*"

It's done, Scotty remarked inwardly. *I'm* done.

"Computer, put the *Intrepid* on the main viewscreen."

Even as he spoke, the engineer found it hard to admit defeat. Had everything he'd done been for nothing?

Clearly the *Yorktown* wouldn't be moving another light-second under his control. That meant his attempt to rescue Spock ended here as well.

And perhaps worst of all, he would never get a chance to reprogram that damned tourist-friendly computer voice.

The *Intrepid*'s captain came on screen. Gray-haired and ruddy, the man looked about fifty-five to sixty, which meant he was well into his Starfleet career.

He wore his experience easily, obviously comfortable with the fit. Scotty didn't think there would be any tricking this man or charming him, or appealing to him. This was a fellow who knew his duty.

"Captain Scott, this is Captain Terrance Riley of the *U.S.S. Intrepid.* I have orders to apprehend you and take the *Yorktown* in tow. Please release the controls of your ship."

Riley's tone was deadly serious. "Make no mistake, Captain, I will fire on the *Yorktown* and disable her if necessary."

Scotty heard every word the man said. Yet part of his mind was one hundred years in the past.

It can't be, he thought. *There must be dozens of them in Starfleet.* Still, the engineer was sure he could see a resemblance.

"Captain," Scotty began, "I am prepared to cooperate with ye fully. But I have one request."

Riley let his impatience show. "Captain Scott, I'm afraid I can't allow you to set terms. Your surrender must be immediate. Please do not test me, sir."

The engineer sighed. He had to make his move quickly—or not at all.

"Captain Riley . . . are ye related at all to a Starfleet officer named Kevin Riley?"

For a moment, Riley's face betrayed his surprise. Then he looked downright uncomfortable, and Scotty was sure he was right.

"My family has no bearing on the matter at hand, Captain Scott. You have stolen Starfleet property and are in violation of at least a dozen Federation laws and Starfleet regulations. I must insist—"

"Son or grandson?" Scotty asked.

The man paused. "Kevin Riley was my father," he replied.

It fit, Scotty thought. Kevin Riley must have had a son relatively late in life. Now, the boy was fully into middle age.

"He was a lieutenant when he served on board the *Enterprise* under Captain Kirk," Scotty noted.

Riley's face was stony. "I'm aware of that, sir."

"I was his supervisor in engineering," Scotty added. "Did ye know that as well?"

The captain nodded. "My father told me a great deal about the *Enterprise* . . . and about you, sir." He added the last part almost reluctantly.

Riley frowned. "Please understand, Captain Scott. You're putting me in a very awkward position. I can't let you go, no matter what you've done for the Federation or what you did in the past for my father."

Scotty smiled broadly.

"Lad, I'm nae asking you to do anything but talk to me, in private—for a few minutes at most. I'll beam over to yer ship. And once we've spoken, ye may do with me and the *Yorktown* what ye wish. As an officer, I'm just asking for a few minutes of yer time."

Captain Riley hesitated as he mulled over the proposition. Watching the doubt play over the man's features, Scotty felt sorry for him. Yet again, the engineer regretted what he was about to do.

At last, Riley came to a decision. He looked like a man who had set a course he knew he would regret.

"I'll have you beamed directly to my ready room," he said.

"Thank ye, Captain," Scotty replied.

The transporter took him just a few seconds later. The meeting was brief, and Scotty did virtually all of the talking. He simply told Riley the truth.

As he spoke, Scotty avoided mentioning Kevin Riley's name or their service together. But then, he didn't need to. Hell, it was only because of his relationship with the elder Riley that the younger one was even listening to him.

To his credit, the captain remained attentive to Scotty's story throughout. He didn't interrupt him even once. But when it was over, his expression was as stony as before.

Scotty cursed inwardly. He was on the verge of losing everything—on the verge of losing Spock.

"Captain," he started again, "did yer father ever tell ye about the time he shut off the *Enterprise*'s engines? As we were in orbit around a class-M planet?"

"Yes," Riley answered, his face a mask. "He was under the influence of a mind-altering compound at the time."

"Aye, most of the crew was by then," Scotty remarked. "It was nae Kevin's fault, but the ship was minutes away from burning up in the planet's atmosphere." He leaned forward. "Did yer father mention it was Ambassador Spock who saved him and the entire ship? That he came up with an intermix formula, and a cold-start procedure for the engines?"

"Yes," Riley said again.

"And did yer father happen to mention that he felt a debt to Spock? A wee bit of gratitude for all he'd done?"

Riley exploded, his face the color of blood. "Dammit, Captain, you have no right to ask me this!"

The engineer met the man's anger dead-on. "Ye're right, lad. I have nae right to ask what I'm asking—but I've got nae choice. Unless ye help me, a good man'll die—a man I owe my life to many times over. A man yer father and hundreds of others owe their lives to as well. Now, the Federation canna do anything to help him, we understand that. But *I* can—if ye let me."

For a long moment, Captain Riley stared at him in silence, the decision weighing on him. Finally, with a pained expression, he nodded.

"All right," the captain said. "I'll come up with a way to sort it out in the logs."

Scotty wondered how the man would explain that a Galaxy-class vessel lost a ship more than a century old. Of course, he didn't ask. Riley knew well enough what kind of risk he was taking without being reminded.

The man tapped his communicator badge. "Captain Riley to transporter room one. Prepare to beam Captain Scott back to the bridge of his ship on my command."

Standing up, Scotty regarded the captain kindly. "I'm truly sorry to be askin' this of ye. If there was another way, I would surely take it."

For the first time, Riley smiled. It made the resemblance to his father that much greater.

"Good luck, Captain Scott."

"Thank ye, lad."

"Energize," said Riley.

The next thing he knew, Scotty was back on the bridge of the *Yorktown*. Turning to the viewscreen, he watched the *Intrepid* warp away.

If he ever survived this mission, Scotty resolved, he'd look up Captain Terrance Riley and tell him a few stories about his father.

That was, of course, after he returned the *Yorktown* to Commander Nelson and apologized to Ensign Hammond for stealing the vessel on her watch. Sighing, he thanked the Great Bird of the Galaxy and his lucky stars for taking him this far.

Then he got back to work.

First, he ran a quick diagnostic on the new computer interface, which checked out fine. Then he laid in a course for Constanthus at warp factor eight.

But his labors were far from finished. He still had to release the safety interlocks on the phaser banks and power them up. And when that was done, he would have to bleed off antimatter from the engines for the photon torpedoes.

There was still a lot to do. As he headed for the turbolift, Scotty decided that he would start on the phaser banks and then work on the torpedoes as the phasers charged. . . .

CHAPTER 7

As Spock approached his followers, he raised his hand in the traditional Vulcan greeting. "Live long and prosper, students of Surak."

As a group, they returned the salute. "Peace and long life," they responded.

Before Spock could begin the day's lessons, Belan stepped forward. The Constantharine addressed him.

"Teacher," Belan said. "Please excuse my interruption, but we have not yet dealt with the fact that there is a spy among us. Ganos detected his transmission, remember, before he was cut down by the governor's soldiers."

Spock raised an eyebrow. By the look on Belan's face—a look that was shared by a number of the students, he noted—the Teacher could see that the Romulan was troubled by the idea.

Spock reminded himself that he was not dealing with Vulcan students. These people were Romulans, their passions very close to the surface, and they were only beginning their efforts to embrace the principles of Surak.

"How do you propose to determine the identity of this infiltrator?" the Vulcan asked.

Belan had an answer ready. "I propose we question each member of our group, both those from the home-worlds and from Constanthus—with the exception of you, of course. Certainly, logic would provide a method of questioning that would yield the desired results."

Spock shrugged. "I could use the Vulcan mind meld to determine the identity with certainty. Would you have me do that?"

Apparently, Belan hadn't considered that approach. However, he was quick to accept it.

"Yes, if necessary," he replied.

The Teacher nodded. "To what end?"

At that point, Belan faltered—as if the reason were obvious, but he hesitated to name it. "We seek justice," he said finally.

Young Skrasis stepped forward to join Belan. "Surely, logic allows us to seek retribution for what was done to us."

"No," Spock replied. "Logic tells us that each of us is responsible for our situation, in equal measure. Each of us made a decision to violate the laws of the Romulan Empire in our quest for knowledge. We freely chose this path, knowing what the consequences would be if we were caught.

"Now we face the justice of the Romulan Empire." He paused. "Would you have us mete out the same style of justice to the Romulan agent among us? An individual who no doubt serves his or her society with dedication and conviction?"

The Vulcan waited. He surveyed the faces of his followers as they grappled with what he had said.

They were Romulans, so there was a measure of resistance. But they were also his students. He was confident that logic would prevail. And to help it along, he raised his voice again.

"Before beginning any course of action," he instructed, "we must ask ourselves if it serves any useful purpose. In this case, revenge would serve no purpose at all."

Skrasis remained unconvinced. "But the spy is still among us," he pointed out. "Our every move is very likely being reported."

"And what would the infiltrator have to report?" Spock asked. "That we are discussing the wisdom of Surak? That would only serve our purpose—to spread Surak's wisdom throughout the Empire. Thus, our captors would become our messengers. Logical, is it not?"

Skrasis shook his head. "The Romulan soul—and our joint heritage—cries out for retribution. To ignore that would be to deny who we are."

The Teacher saw that Skrasis had made his point with the others. The students were waiting for their mentor's reply.

"It is illogical," he agreed, "to deny one's nature. However, the intellect is also part of that nature. Surak teaches mastery of the intellect over passion. As his followers, we do not seek to subvert the impulse for retribution, or for that matter, any other impulse. Instead, we seek to ensure that emotions are not the guiding principles in our lives.

"Reason must prevail. The principles of logic must apply. Otherwise, it is impossible to advance—as either a single being or a society. In the present case," he concluded, "we would only lose by seeking revenge on our betrayer. And instead of furthering our cause, we could very well destroy our own legacy."

At that, even Skrasis was silent.

It began with young D'tan, one of the unificationists who had traveled with Spock from Romulus. He raised his hand, offering the Teacher the Vulcan salute.

Then another student did the same, and another. It was the Vulcan equivalent of applause, and it quickly engulfed all of his charges.

Skrasis was the last to respond. But in the end, he raised his hand as well.

The Vulcan felt a rush of pride—a natural response which it would have been illogical to deny. He had reached all of those before him, even the difficult Skrasis.

It was a satisfying moment. And it was made more precious because he would enjoy so few of them before the Romulan sentence was carried out.

Nodding almost imperceptibly to his students, Spock raised his own hand to return the salute.

Scotty sighed.

"The *Yorktown* is now crossing the Romulan Neutral Zone," the computer said in its familiar, agonizingly friendly tone. "Thank you for your inquiry, and enjoy your starship adventure on the *U.S.S. Yorktown.*"

Montgomery Scott looked at the viewscreen and felt nothing but tired. He knew the news should have filled him with excitement, fear, anticipation—all of the things that he had felt when he made the same trip into these waters in the past.

But now, he only felt the aches and pains of four hours of work on the weapons systems. In the end, of course, it had been worth it. He had the phasers back on-line and seven fully charged torpedoes at the ready.

The ship was really up to speed now. He enjoyed full control of the helm, full power to all of the main systems including weapons. And the computer on board his shuttlecraft was doing virtually all the real work of running the ship, rivaling the efficiency of the original *Enterprise* with a full crew.

All he had to do was give the orders.

The fact was, his adventure was going better than it had any right to. Scotty knew it was luck that had gotten him to this point unscathed. Luck and an improved cloaking device, with which the ship could go virtually anywhere in the Empire unnoticed.

Of course, the hardest part was yet to come, and it had nothing to do with high-tech tinkering. He still had to locate Spock on a planet full of Vulcanoids, beam his friend up to the ship, and escape—after probably setting off every alarm from Romulus to the Neutral Zone.

Grabbing the forward edge of the helm console for support, Scotty pulled himself up out of his chair. Then he headed for the turbolift, all the while brushing off the accumulated dirt and grime he'd collected on his uniform.

It was no use. He would need a new one.

Of course, that was easily enough accomplished. The uniform he wore now was one of a half dozen he had borrowed from ship's stores. It was the traditional red tunic and black slacks he'd worn a lifetime ago, which hadn't seen active duty in nearly a century—much like Scotty himself.

He couldn't help feeling a little embarrassed in the antique outfit—as if he were trying to pass himself off as a teenager at a school dance. But then, he had to wear *something,* didn't he?

Back in his quarters, he shucked the soiled clothes,

forced himself to take a quick shower, and put on a fresh uniform. Dressed and ready, Scotty finally allowed himself to fall into bed. If the computer woke him up with an emergency, as he had programmed it to, he wanted to be able to move on a moment's notice.

Fortunately, the call didn't come for hours. And when it did, Scotty was already beginning to drift back toward consciousness.

"Mister Scott," the computer said, "a Romulan vessel has been identified by long-range sensors. If there is any other information you require, do not hesitate to ask. And enjoy your starship adventure on the *U.S.S. Yorktown.*"

Rising from the bed, Scotty resolved not to jump to any conclusions. Unless a vessel was purposely looking for him and knew that he was using an old-style Romulan cloaking device, he doubted the *Yorktown* could have been detected.

And even if someone *were* looking for him, they'd have to pass pretty close to pick him up. Otherwise, the cloak would conceal him. Given the size and relative emptiness of this sector of space, the odds were vastly on his side.

In any case, he would know soon enough whether he had been—or would be—seen. Hitting the corridor at a trot, he headed for the turbolift.

When he came out onto the bridge, there was no sign that anything was wrong—except for the blinking proximity indicator on the helm console. Heading for Spock's science station, Scotty tied the viewer into the long-range sensors.

Sure enough, there was a ship out there. Judging by the power curve, it was pretty damned large, probably a warbird. A dangerous vessel, to be sure, and more than a match for the century-plus-old *Yorktown*.

However, it was only dangerous to vessels it could detect. And so far, there was no indication it had detected the *Yorktown.*

Using the ship's computer and sensor logs, Scotty extrapolated the Romulan vessel's course and heading. It appeared to be a standard patrol pattern. At its closest point it would come within about half a light-year of the *Yorktown*—a comfortable distance.

What's more, the Romulans were moving quickly. He doubted that the *Yorktown* would be in close sensor range for more than a few seconds.

It could've been much worse. But still, he watched the ship very carefully on the science station viewer.

When he saw the Romulan slow down and then come to a stop, he thought it might have been a glitch in his sensor array. But when the vessel changed its heading, he had to at least concede the possibility that he had been spotted.

"The Romulan vessel is initiating an intercept course," the computer informed him. "If you require any—"

"Computer," Scotty interrupted, "initiate a new course perpendicular to the Romulan vessel's. Warp factor eight."

"Initiating now," the computer answered. "Thank you for your request. And enjoy—"

"Status of Romulan vessel?" Scotty demanded before the computer could say anything else.

"Romulan vessel is altering course to match. Thank you for your inquiry and enjoy your starship adventure on board the *U.S.S. Yorktown.*"

And then Scotty understood—his luck had finally run out.

Standing up, he faced the main viewscreen. He would meet his end on his feet, he vowed. Having confronted the Romulans more than once in the past, he had learned at least one thing about them—they did not take prisoners.

Montgomery Scott was a Starfleet officer on a Federation starship, deep inside enemy space. As old as it was, the *Yorktown* was of no value to the Romulans. Scott didn't imagine they would hesitate for a second before blowing the old girl to atoms.

Well, they wouldn't take him without a fight. "Computer, drop cloak," he commanded, knowing it was pointless now to direct any energy to it. "Full power to shields and weapons systems."

He and the *Yorktown* might just give the Romulans a surprise or two.

"Shields and weapons at full power," the computer replied. "Thank you for your request and enjoy your starship adventure aboard the *U.S.S. Yorktown.*"

"Aye," was all the reply Scotty could muster.

"If this is a joke . . ." the Romulan commander said to his sensor operator.

The officer was nervous and completely earnest in his response. "No, sir. It is a Federation starship. And according to our computer models, it is at least one hundred years old."

The commander walked forward to get a better look at the sensor screen. He wanted to confirm the information with his own eyes.

"Has it been upgraded?" he asked. "New weapons? Power systems?"

The sensor operator shook his head. "No, sir. Sensors indicate it meets the original specifications for that type of vessel. The only modification seems to be the presence of a cloaking device. One of Romulan design."

Curious, the commander thought.

The officer continued. "It is a modified version of the device used during the same era as the vessel. The modifications are quite good, however. If I had not been monitoring the sensor input manually as we approached—"

"Yes, yes," the commander said impatiently. "What I want to know is what it is doing in our space. Could that vessel be any threat to this ship?"

The reply came from his tactical officer, who was clearly unimpressed.

"Commander, that vessel would not be a threat to an underpowered scout ship. I am targeting it now. If you like, we can destroy it with a single burst."

The commander thought for a moment, then shook his head. "No, not yet. First, I want someone to tell me why an antique Federation starship with a crew of one has invaded the Romulan Empire. Anyone?"

The entire command crew was silent.

"As I thought," the commander remarked. "Then what we have here is a mystery. And I have no particular fondness for mysteries. If there is an explanation, I will have it."

He turned to his communications officer. "Report this to Central Command," he instructed.

"As you wish," the officer replied.

Next, he turned to his helm officer. "Take us to towing range. Maximum power to defensive shields. And keep weapons locked on target—just in case."

The warbird had remained motionless for some time. Now it came closer, looming fearfully large on the main viewscreen.

Scotty didn't understand. The *Yorktown* had been well within the warbird's weapons range for more than five minutes. Yet in all that time, the Romulan had made no move against her.

He'd hesitated as well. After all, he couldn't fire first. To do so would breach Starfleet's rules of engagement, and that was a regulation Scotty was not prepared to violate—especially when it would mean the immediate destruction of his ship.

Scanning the interior of the warbird, Scotty was amazed at the magnitude and complexity of it. The thing was several times the size of the Galaxy-class *Enterprise* commanded by Captain Picard, and Picard's ship was more than double the size of the *Yorktown*.

Finally, the Romulans hailed him. When he answered the hail, an angry-looking individual in a commander's uniform appeared on the viewscreen.

"Federation starship," he intoned, "you are in violation of Romulan space and the Treaty of Algeron. What is your explanation?"

Scotty stared at the screen for a moment, unsure of what to do next. Clearly, the truth wouldn't be appropriate here. So, at a loss for what to say, he said nothing.

The Romulan commander considered him for a moment. "I will have my answers, human. Lower your shields and prepare to be boarded. Do so immediately or I will blow you out of space."

Scotty knew he had no choice but to comply. Still, he took the time to purge all information about Spock from the data banks of both the *Yorktown* and his shuttle. That done, he lowered the *Yorktown*'s shields—and felt the Romulan tractor beam latch onto her.

Only then did Scotty realize something quite remarkable had occurred. No, two things. One, he was still alive. And two, the *Yorktown* was still in one piece.

He never would have thought it possible.

On the other hand, the galaxy had changed quite a bit since his time. And at that moment, Scotty had to admit, some of the changes were for the better.

CHAPTER 8

Picard leaned back in his seat and considered the bridge's main viewscreen, where he'd asked Worf to bring up a long-range sensor grid. There were several red blips moving across the thin green lines of the grid.

Each blip, the captain knew, represented a Romulan warbird.

It was no surprise to him to see that the Romulans were still patrolling the far side of the Neutral Zone. What *did* surprise him was the number of vessels assigned to that function.

"Curious," Picard said, stroking his chin with the knuckle of his forefinger.

Riker, who was seated beside him, turned to the captain. He looked suspicious. "There should be more of them, shouldn't there?"

"There should," Picard agreed.

He would have turned to Counselor Troi, who was seated on his other flank, but there was no point in doing so. They weren't even close enough for a visual yet, much less for her to gauge the Romulans' emotions.

Instead, the captain addressed Data, who was stationed at Ops. "Commander, put together whatever information you can access and come up with a reasonable hypothesis. I want to know why—"

His command was interrupted by the subtle *shoosh* of the turbolift doors. Picard didn't have to crane his neck to see who had come in. He could tell by the caustic mumbling, and the looks of discomfort on the faces of his officers.

Admiral McCoy had emerged onto the bridge.

"—why these Neutral Zone patrols look sparse," the captain finished.

"Aye, sir," replied the android, and set to work.

"Sparse?" echoed the admiral, as he descended to a position in line with the command center, alongside Riker. His eyes narrowed, deepening the elaborate crow's-feet at their corners, as he took in the graphics on the viewscreen. "What's sparse?"

Picard sat up in his chair and turned to face McCoy. "The number of warbirds along the border," he explained evenly. "If we can determine the reason for it, we might be able to use it to our advantage."

The admiral harrumphed. It was not a compliment. "Idle speculation," he commented. "A waste of time, if you ask me." He eyed the captain from beneath bushy white brows. "What are we doing to help Spock?"

Picard could feel a considerable heat climb his neck and rise into his cheeks. He did not normally tolerate that tone on his bridge. Not even from a higher-ranking officer.

However, he reminded himself, McCoy *had* served on

the original *Enterprise*—and he was desperately trying to rescue his friend. As a result, the captain felt constrained to stretch the rules a bit in this case.

"As it happens," he informed the admiral, "I have already begun working toward Ambassador Spock's release." He glanced over his shoulder at Worf, whose stolid figure loomed behind him at the tactical station. "Any response from the Romulans yet, Lieutenant?"

The Klingon grunted. "None, sir."

"Well," said McCoy irascibly, "I'll just wait here till we get one. That is, if Commander Riker'll be good enough to give me his seat."

Picard exchanged a glance with his first officer. Rising, Riker indicated the empty seat with a gesture. "All yours, sir," he told the admiral.

As McCoy sat down, he muttered something beneath his breath.

"Did you say something?" the captain asked him.

The admiral turned to him. "I said, in my day they served coffee on the bridge. And I could sure as shootin' use a cup right now."

Picard sighed and appealed to Riker again. With an expression of forced tolerance, the first officer headed for the replicator.

"And I want it hot," McCoy added.

The captain nodded obediently. "Of course, Admiral. As you wish."

Spock watched the shadowy faces of his students as they anticipated the ending to his lesson in the security of his quarters. "And so," he said, "it is clear that the way of Surak is preferable to a life of passion."

For a moment, he allowed the words to sink in. Then he awaited questions.

On Romulus, those questions had often been long in coming. His students there had been inclined to ponder their lessons at length.

Obviously, that would not be the case here on Constanthus, he thought. Not as long as Skrasis was among them.

Responding to the youth's upraised hand with a nod, the Vulcan awaited Skrasis's onslaught. What's more, he wasn't disappointed.

"If a system is intrinsically superior," the youth said, "does it not make sense to spread it?"

"It does," Spock agreed. "After all, that is what we are doing here. We are encouraging the spread of Surak's wisdom. Or his system, if you prefer to think of it that way."

But the Vulcan had a feeling Skrasis meant more than that. As it turned out, he was right.

"But the teaching method is slow," the Romulan observed. "And if there are benefits to be derived from such a system, is it not better to spread it quickly?"

Before Spock could answer his question, Skrasis beat him to it.

"It would seem it is. And the quickest way of all," he finished, "is through force. So, then, is it not appropriate to use force as well as the teaching method to spread the word of Surak?"

The Vulcan sighed. Though possessed of a keen and analytical mind, Skrasis accepted nothing at face value.

In this, he was different from D'tan, who had come with Spock from Romulus. In fact, aside from their intelligence and youth, the two had virtually nothing in common.

D'tan soaked up his lessons as the desert plains of Vulcan soaked up water during the rainy season. He accepted virtually everything he was told and had memorized nearly all of Surak's writings—a formidable task that few raised on Vulcan even undertook.

Skrasis, on the other hand, questioned everything. Even the most basic tenets of Surak's teachings, at times. It was his way to test a thing over and over again before allowing himself to rely on it.

What's more, Spock welcomed the youth's questioning. And not just because it helped to illuminate the issues at hand.

As the time drew near for their trial and execution, he had sensed growing unrest in his charges. Fear, anxiety, and frustration were all natural reactions for an emotional people facing death. And even the relatively disciplined and motivated unificationists were susceptible to these strong emotions.

The Vulcan had long ago made peace with the possibility of his own death. Having experienced the phenomenon, it no longer carried the same weight with him.

However, his students did not have the benefits of his lifetime of study and personal experience. For them, the lessons provided a distraction—and Skrasis's questions only increased their value in that regard.

"However," Spock explained, "your proposition contains a contradiction, Skrasis. The principles of Surak are based on personal choice and an avoidance of violence. One cannot accept these principles and condone the use of violence to spread them."

The youth wasn't ready to relent. Not yet. "But the use of force in this case would serve the greater good. As you have also taught us, the needs of the many outweigh the needs of the few. Or the one."

The Teacher should have been appalled to hear his own words used to defend such unethical practices. Yet he was pleased.

Clearly Skrasis had internalized Spock's lessons. Even when he did not quite believe his own position, he held it out for inspection anyway—no matter how harsh a scrutiny it was likely to receive.

And that was the essence of Surak's legacy.

The Vulcan eyed his student. "Even if we assume the Vulcan way would be superior for all sentient creatures, surely there would be those who would resist, those who would not submit no matter what the price."

Skrasis said nothing.

"Presumably," Spock continued, "these individuals would have to be eliminated."

The youth shrugged. "In the beginning, perhaps. But the greater good would still be served. Imagine a galaxy governed by intellect, pure logic. A galaxy without war, or crime, or senseless violence."

The Vulcan tilted his head, demonstrating his skepticism. "Except for that violence perpetrated by the administrators of this superior system."

"But in the end," Skrasis persisted, "you would have a generation of beings who knew nothing but the way of logic. Ultimately the need for all violence would disappear."

The other Romulans assembled there had long ago become spectators, watching the Teacher and his young student in their verbal confrontation. Now, they were all looking at Spock for his answer.

"What you propose," the Vulcan said, "has been tried many times in history. One example of it would be the Romulan Empire itself."

Obviously, this was something that Skrasis had not considered. The youth's face betrayed his surprise.

Spock went on. "Like many empires great and small before it, the Romulan Star Empire believed it had a superior system. From its earliest days, violence was used to firmly establish its power and to maintain loyalty to the state. And more than one generation grew to maturity knowing nothing else. Yet, as we can see, unrest persists.

"Insurrection. Purges. These are clearly a part of the fabric of Romulan society. And still, there are those who risk death simply for the knowledge of another way of life. Many of them are in this room. Many more are outside, in the courtyard."

The Vulcan could see Skrasis absorbing the new information, turning the idea over in his mind.

"Surak teaches us to find order in chaos," Spock pointed out. "He does not teach us to try to eliminate chaos or impose order onto it. And the reasons are not simply ethical, because a complex system—whether a biological entity, or a society, or even a language—must remain diverse. It must remain open to change or it will die."

He took in all his listeners at a glance. "Infinite diversity in infinite combination is at the heart of Surak's philosophy. An ordered galactic civilization, even if such a thing were possible, would fail to thrive. And inevitably, it would decay."

For the first time since Spock had encountered Skrasis, the youth was completely and utterly silent, lost in the thoughts the Vulcan had planted. Allowing this silence to linger, Spock found himself actually looking forward to Skrasis's reaction.

In the end, however, the silence was broken not by

Skrasis, but by Belan. The older man entered hastily, apologizing for the intrusion.

"Teacher," he said, "a word with you on an important issue?"

The Vulcan nodded his assent.

"A group of us has given our situation careful thought," Belan informed him, "and though we are honored by your instruction, we have chosen a different path."

Spock looked at him. "I see," he replied.

Belan looked back over his shoulder to make sure there were no guards within earshot. Then he turned to the Vulcan again.

"We are planning an escape, Teacher. I have come to ask all present, and for you as well, to join us."

Spock frowned ever so slightly. "You must know," he said, "that your chances of success are slim indeed. All who try will almost certainly perish."

By the determined look on Belan's face, he could see that the Romulan had already considered this.

"We accept the risk," Belan told him, "and the odds against us. If we live, our efforts will have been vindicated. If we die, our deaths will point up the absurdity and waste of the Romulan system. However, if we do not try, we will die anyway, and then our deaths will serve no meaningful purpose."

He met the Teacher's gaze. "It is just not our way, to wait for death. It may be weakness on our part, but we cannot deny who we are. We must meet our fate head-on."

Ultimately, the Vulcan could not argue with Belan's logic. He had made the point himself to Skrasis moments ago. Infinite diversity . . .

"How do you intend to prevent the infiltrator from alerting the authorities to your plans?" Spock asked.

Belan shrugged. "Admittedly, a problem. However, we are asking that none of us remain alone for any period of time. It will be impossible for the spy to signal anyone if he or she is constantly in the company of others. Of course, we would not presume to ask you, Teacher—"

"Unnecessary," the Vulcan interrupted. "I will comply with your request."

"But you will not join us?" Belan asked.

Spock shook his head. "Like you, I must be true to my own nature."

Belan turned to the others in the room. "Any who wish to link their fortunes to ours, come now. We have preparations to make."

For a moment, no one moved. Then two of the Romulans who'd been listening to the Vulcan got up to join Belan. Both of them were Constantharines.

But neither of them was Skrasis. The youth remained seated, meeting neither Spock's gaze nor Belan's.

The Vulcan stood to face Belan and his two compatriots.

"Live long and prosper," he told them. "May you find what you seek."

The three of them returned the gesture. "Thank you," Belan replied.

"You have a single-mindedness that I have experienced before," Spock observed. "You refuse to accept your fate even when it is inevitable. That is an almost human quality."

Belan studied his teacher, as if to find clarification in the Vulcan's face. "Is that a criticism, Teacher?"

Spock almost smiled.

"No," he assured the Romulan. "It is not."

* * *

105

This time, when Eragian went over the day's briefs, he looked for news from Constanthus. Surprisingly, there wasn't any.

Most of what he perused was mundane—reports on minor military victories and resource allotments. The proconsul was about to shut off the screen when the last item caught his eye.

He read it again, more closely. Then he turned to Lennex, who had been standing by in his silent and disciplined way.

"Why was I not informed of this immediately?" the proconsul asked, pointing to the item.

The Tal Shiar looked at him. "It did not seem to merit special attention," he explained.

Eragian was genuinely surprised. "A Federation starship crosses the Neutral Zone—with a Romulan cloaking device aboard—and that does not merit special attention?"

The tone of the proconsul's voice would have cowered most other officers, but Lennex was unflappable. "Your Eminence, the ship is at least one hundred years old, as is the cloaking device. It had no crew, only a single addled and middle-aged human. Neither he nor the ship ever posed a threat to our security. What's more, the warbird commander is preparing to interrogate him, after which he will dispose of the ship—and most likely, the human as well."

"The human is said to be a Starfleet officer," Eragian pointed out. "Have you checked his service record?"

The Tal Shiar shook his head. "He was not identified, either by name or by image."

"And you tolerated that lack of information? I'm surprised," said the proconsul.

"As I indicated," Lennex repeated, "I did not deem the matter worthy of special attention."

Eragian cursed inwardly. It was a common failing among the Tal Shiar to adopt a narrow focus when dealing with other races. After all, as the guardians of order and orthodoxy, they were primarily concerned with security within the Empire.

Naturally, this pitted them most often against other Romulans. In his position as proconsul, Eragian had to pay equal attention to enemies within and without the Empire.

Staring at the image of the human on his screen, Eragian stroked his chin. "There are nothing but questions here."

And the proconsul knew there would be no quick answers. But he hadn't risen to the exalted rank of proconsul without fine-tuning his instincts. And right now, those instincts were telling him that this human was important.

Hitting a padd on his desk, Eragian signaled one of his junior officers. "Alert Commander Hajak to prepare the *Vengeance,*" he directed. "I am traveling to the outer worlds today."

"Do you have a specific destination in mind?" asked the officer, over the intercom link.

"I will be visiting Outpost . . ." Eragian quickly scanned his memory for the one nearest to the site of the Starfleet officer's capture. "Outpost Number Forty-Eight," he said finally.

He turned his attention to Lennex again. "See that the prisoner is not harmed, and that he is transferred to the outpost. And get me all the information you can about his vessel."

Nodding succinctly, Lennex left the proconsul's office. Eragian didn't doubt that the Tal Shiar officer would ferret out every bit of data available on the starship. Sitting back in his chair, Eragian entertained the prospect of visiting a bleak, primitive outpost which could hardly have been farther from the splendor of Romulus.

He hoped the human was worth it.

CHAPTER 9

Picard was growing weary of McCoy's company. *Painfully* weary.

Playing host to the old gentleman was fraying the captain's nerves, which might be put to other and better uses. At the moment, the man was standing among the aft stations, harassing the officers posted there.

Out of desperation, Picard turned to Worf and asked the Klingon the same question he'd asked of him a half-dozen times already.

"Any word from Romulus, Lieutenant?"

The Klingon grunted. "None, sir. Perhaps if I were to—"

He stopped in midsentence and looked at one of his monitors. Smiling grimly, he turned to the captain again.

"I have received a response, sir. The Romulans have granted us a secure link to their governmental center."

"With whom will I be speaking?" asked Picard.

Worf consulted his monitors, his dark eyes moving

beneath even darker brows. Finally he obtained the information he needed and looked up.

"The respondent is a proconsul named Eragian."

The captain had never heard of the man. But then, his knowledge of Romulan politics was fairly limited. And except for the Senate, the hierarchy seemed to change quite often.

"All right," he told Worf finally. "Proceed, Lieutenant."

In the next moment, the viewscreen filled with the image of a lean and wolfish countenance. It was a look not uncommon among prominent Romulans. However, in this case, it was especially pronounced.

For some reason, Picard had the feeling that the Romulan was on his way somewhere—that he'd remained only long enough to take part in this conversation. But of course, it was only a feeling.

"I am Proconsul Eragian," the Romulan said by way of a greeting. "And if you command the *Enterprise,* you must be—"

"Jean-Luc Picard," the captain interjected, preferring to supply his own identification.

Eragian measured him with his gaze. "Yes, of course. And what is the occasion that has prompted this communication?"

Picard prepared himself. It was time to lay his cards on the table—at least, those he was willing to show.

"The Federation," he said, "is aware of the capture of some forty Romulan unificationists on Constanthus. As a strictly humanitarian gesture, I have been empowered to take them off your hands."

A smile played at the corners of the Romulan's mouth. "A humanitarian gesture?" he echoed. "I fear you've lost me, Captain."

"Allow me to explain," said Picard. "As the Federation sees it, your empire is in a no-win situation. If you keep the prisoners, they become symbols of oppression to all those who already sympathize with their movement. If you kill them, they become martyrs, and the pot of discontent gets stirred even more quickly. But if you turn them over to us . . ."

"I see your point now," Eragian replied—though of course, he must have seen it right from the beginning. "If I release the prisoners, they will be seen as exiles. Examples of Federation weakness, who couldn't make it in the Empire."

"Precisely," the captain confirmed. "Not that it will provide a long-term solution to the unificationist problem, but at least it will buy you some time to think of one."

The Romulan tilted his head. "Then you believe this . . . *unification* movement . . . will be an ongoing difficulty for us? Even with this group gone?"

"I do," Picard told him.

That much was the truth. What came next was the lie.

"Nor is Vulcan any happier about it than the Romulans are."

Eragian's eyes narrowed ever so slightly. "What has Vulcan got to be unhappy about . . . if I may ask?"

"Perhaps I misspoke," the captain said. "Certainly, a few individual Vulcans are in favor of unification. However, most believe that their society will be corrupted by an influx of Romulan ideas and want no part of it. Hence, the dispatch of the *Enterprise.*"

"In other words," the Romulan commented, "this is an embarrassment to your side as well as mine."

"Yes," Picard answered. "And my job is to eliminate it—preferably *before* it gets out of hand." He paused for effect. "What I am offering," he emphasized, "is a graceful way out of this mess. If I were you, Proconsul, I would give it some thought."

Eragian seemed to be doing that already. Finally he said, "I will take it under advisement, I assure you. We will speak again, Captain. Eragian out."

A moment later, the image on the viewscreen reverted to the grid they'd seen before, with its red blips moving slowly from one quadrant to the next.

Picard frowned. It wasn't easy to tell what effect his advice had had on the proconsul. However, he was reasonably confident that he'd made some headway.

The captain had barely completed the thought before he heard an exclamation from the vicinity of the aft stations. Turning, he saw Admiral McCoy glaring at him.

"Dammit, man," the admiral rasped, making his way around the sweeping curve of the tactical station. "Are you out of your mind?"

Again, the captain thought. On my bridge. In front of my officers.

Picard could feel a gout of anger rising in his throat. With an effort he fought it down.

"If you have something to say to me," he responded, "I'd suggest we discuss it in my ready room." Then, before McCoy could suggest otherwise, he turned to Riker. "You have the bridge, Number One."

His executive officer nodded sympathetically. "Aye, sir."

The captain led the way into the familiar confines of his ready room, took a seat behind his desk, and waited patiently for the admiral to join him. He didn't look at McCoy until he'd shuffled in and the door had closed behind him. Then he raised his eyes to meet the admiral's.

CROSSOVER

"Now," said Picard, "what is it you wished to tell me?"

McCoy cursed lavishly beneath his breath. "My question," he declared, "is why you don't know these things for yourself. I mean, you've dealt with the Romulans before, haven't you? You've seen what they're like?"

The captain felt his lips compressing into a thin, hard line. "And your advice?" he prodded as gently as possible.

That brought forth another string of curses. "My advice," the admiral hissed, "is not to trust those bastards. Dollars to doughnuts, they'll find a way to stab you in the back—unless you stab them first."

Picard leaned forward. "What, exactly, are you suggesting? That I carry out this negotiation without speaking to the Romulans?"

McCoy's face reddened. He came forward until he was standing directly in front of the captain.

"What I'm suggesting," he snapped, "is that you do what you set out to do—help Spock. And the only way to accomplish that is to go in there and get him out."

The captain stared at him. "In other words, you'd like me to take on an entire enemy fleet, not to mention whatever defenses they enjoy on Constanthus, without any regard for diplomacy."

"In other words," the admiral replied, "you're damned right. In fact, I—"

McCoy was cut short by a sharp *bleep* from the ship's intercom system. "Picard here," the captain replied.

Data's voice filled the ready room. "Sir, I have obtained some information concerning Romulan ship movements, which may shed light on the inadequacy of their numbers at the Neutral Zone border."

"Go ahead," said the captain.

"In tracking their engines' ion emissions," the android

113

explained, "it became clear to me that a large number of their vessels have been deployed to a particular sector of the Empire."

"I see," Picard acknowledged. "And why that sector in particular?"

There was a brief pause. "I do not know, sir," Data admitted. "However, I will continue to attempt to find out. In the meantime, I will make this information available to your terminal, so you may consider it at your leisure."

With the admiral around, the captain didn't expect to *have* much leisure. Still, he thanked the android for his thoughtfulness—after which Data signed off.

In the silence that followed, McCoy glowered almost accusingly at Picard. "Ship movements," he muttered. "And this patty-cake you're playing with the Romulans." He sighed. "I expected more from you, Captain."

Without waiting for a reply, the admiral turned his back on the captain and headed for the door, which opened obediently at his approach. Picard bit his lip as he watched McCoy walk out onto the bridge.

It was difficult enough dealing with the Romulans in so delicate a matter. Dealing with the admiral only increased the captain's difficulties.

He wondered who at Starfleet Command had believed McCoy would be an asset on this mission.

Scotty turned at the sound of footfalls. Standing, he looked out across the energy barrier separating his cell from the ship's corridor outside it.

A moment later, he found himself face-to-face with three Romulan officers. The one in the middle was the commander he had seen on the *Yorktown*'s viewscreen.

Of course that had been hours ago, before the Romulans had beamed him onto their ship and brought him to their brig. Obviously they didn't know how to treat a guest. A Starfleet captain would never have kept him waiting so long.

The delay was probably purposeful. Give the human time to think, he mused, and he'll be that much more eager to talk when the time comes.

The commander took a step forward, until his face was half a meter from the engineer's. "I will have my explanation now, human," the Romulan told him.

Scott returned the commander's unblinking stare, and his scowl as well. "I have nothin' to say," he replied.

"If I were you," the commander advised, "I would reconsider." He frowned and started again. "You are alone on a ship that is a century out of date. And yet you dare to enter Romulan territory. Tell me why."

Scotty tried to size the commander up—to divine his intentions. Why hadn't he destroyed the *Yorktown* on the spot? Was it simply to be sure the human wasn't a threat before disposing of him?

He repeated his earlier remark. "I have nothin' to say."

"You must be mad, even for a human," the commander spat.

Suddenly, Scotty had an idea.

If nothing else, it might buy him some time. And though the engineer wasn't sure it would do him any good, he knew he had to hold on as long as he could. After all, as long as he lived, Spock still had a chance.

"You'll nae win," Scotty snarled. "Nae as long as I draw breath."

"Win what?" the commander asked, his brow furrowing. "We are not at war, your people and mine. At least, we weren't until you made your pathetic incursion into our space."

Leaning toward the commander suddenly, Scotty was gratified to see him flinch—despite the barrier between them. "Dinnae think ye can pull the wool over my eyes, ye treacherous Romulan pig."

Hyperventilating, he could feel the color rising in his cheeks. He imagined that he was quite a sight. By the look on the commander's face, he was right.

"I see what ye're trying to do," he growled, adding an uncontrollable blink in one eye, for effect. "Ye scheme yer little schemes, and ye think the Federation will be yers for the taking. Even if the fools at Starfleet canna make out what ye're up to, *I* can. And I'll nae rest until I destroy every last one of ye!"

Obviously repelled by the display, the Romulan withdrew a few paces to confer with his officers. Finally, he came to a conclusion.

"Interrogate him," said the commander. "Find out if he has some hidden purpose, or if he really is as crazy as he appears. If he turns out to be insane in truth, you may put him out of his misery—and mine."

Though he maintained his manic expression, Scotty blanched inside at the prospect. He knew he wouldn't last long at the hands of a Romulan interrogator.

And then something incredible happened. The voice of a Romulan officer came from the room's intercom system.

"Commander," the voice said, "we have new orders regarding the prisoner."

"What new orders?" the Romulan demanded.

"He is not to be harmed, sir."

"What?" The commander was livid now.

"Sir, the orders come directly from Proconsul Eragian himself. We are to bring the prisoner and his vessel to a station in this sector. Eragian is en route and will deal with the matter personally."

The commander grunted. Turning to Scotty, he managed a resentful sort of smile.

"So there is something more to your story, human. Whatever it is, I can assure you the proconsul will find it out."

Scotty didn't reply. He was too lost in his own thoughts. However, that only seemed to annoy the commander further.

"Watch him carefully," the Romulan said. Then he departed, his officers falling into line behind him.

As he watched them go, Scotty wondered what the Romulan proconsul could possibly want with him. Had the Romulan hierarchy somehow connected his appearance to the unificationists . . . or to Spock?

The engineer doubted it. If they'd made that connection already, they'd have no need to question him. Yet the proconsul was sufficiently interested in him to come personally.

He couldn't see why—at least not yet. But as he sat down again in his cell, he had the distinctly unpleasant feeling that he'd soon find out.

CHAPTER 10

Spock looked up from the circle of his students and saw Santek's approach. The Romulan raised his hand in the traditional Vulcan salute. Though Santek's control was good, Spock could see that he was apprehensive about something.

"Teacher," he said, "I apologize for disturbing you during a lesson, but I must speak with you."

The Vulcan had wondered about Santek's absence. A good student, the man had been with him almost since the beginning of his work on Romulus.

Spock nodded, though he already had an idea what the Romulan would say. "Please, speak."

"Teacher," Santek sighed, "I regret that I will not be able to continue my studies. You have honored me with your instruction, and I beg your forgiveness if I have disappointed or failed you."

The Vulcan considered his student a moment before

answering. In that time, D'tan rose to his feet and approached Santek.

"You dishonor your teacher," said D'tan. "You, who have been with us from the beginning." The youth was clearly angry and had forgotten his control.

Despite D'tan's age, he had always been a serious and earnest student. His emotional display genuinely surprised Spock, even more than Santek's decision to join the escape attempt.

From the moment Belan had informed the Vulcan of the escape attempt, the number of Romulans who had chosen to terminate their studies and join Belan had grown steadily. And the number of students remaining had decreased proportionally.

"You betray all the Teacher has taught you," D'tan said, furious now. "You betray the wisdom of Surak."

Spock was certain that in another moment D'tan would strike Santek. And if Santek's expression was any indication of his state of mind, he would reply in kind.

Madness.

"Enough," the Vulcan announced.

Immediately, the two Romulans regained their composure. Spock addressed Santek.

"You do not need my forgiveness," he said.

D'tan began to speak, but the Vulcan silenced him with a gesture.

"You have chosen your path," he told Santek. "It is only logical that you follow your nature. And it is *you* who have honored *me* with your study."

Raising his hand, he added, "Live long and prosper."

The Romulan's face betrayed his surprise. At a loss for words, he simply nodded, turned, and left.

The Vulcan turned his attention to D'tan, who had by then regained control of himself.

"I beg forgiveness, Teacher," said the Romulan, keeping his voice calm and even—though it obviously took some effort. "I allowed my passions to guide me."

"We find ourselves in difficult times. Do not think of it again," Spock advised him.

D'tan shook his head. "I do not understand, Teacher. How can you allow your students to forget all we have labored to acquire? Is not such behavior wasteful and therefore illogical?"

The Vulcan made a subtle gesture of dismissal with his hands. "It is impossible to teach those whose minds are elsewhere," he said. "A student's path must be freely chosen."

Through the mask of D'tan's control, Spock could see the war of emotions within him. It was easy to understand. The boy would soon be facing death, and everything he had come to believe was being tested.

The Vulcan himself had come to find recent events . . . unsettling. He had always believed that the only difference between the Romulans and his own people was education. From a scientific standpoint, that was very nearly true.

However, under extreme pressure, Santek had shown that his nature was still distinctly Romulan. He'd been unable to submit to his fate, however logical the submission.

D'tan, when pushed to his limits, had lost control as well. Perhaps even the best teaching could not erase the lessons of a lifetime—or plumb the mysteries of a person's nature.

If that were true, then what of his efforts on Romulus? What could the future hold for the unification movement to which he and his students had labored to give life?

Indeed, what could the future hold for those awaiting their deaths here on Constanthus?

Spock scanned the faces still attending him. And he wondered.

Despite his outburst, D'tan remained determined to continue his studies. But was it because he believed in them—or was he motivated more by his loyalty to his teacher?

How many of the others who remained were staying for the same reason? How many of them felt the call of their inner selves and denied it for Spock's sake?

With these questions in mind, the Vulcan addressed his remaining charges. "How many others wish to end their study, as Santek has? There will be no censure for those who choose this path."

He waited.

None of the Romulans before him moved or spoke.

Then one of them got up and approached the Vulcan. She lifted her hand in salute, turned, and retreated toward the group planning the escape.

Another student followed, and then another, each of them offering the Vulcan salute before leaving. None of them spoke during the grim procession—at least, not with their voices.

In the end, there was only the Teacher and twelve others—four of whom, including D'tan, had accompanied him on his journey from Romulus. And then one of these four students approached him.

Minan had been among the first Romulans to become a student of Surak. And now she was the last to leave. Spock noted that her control was impeccable as she faced him and raised her hand.

"Thank you, Teacher," she said. A moment later, she was gone.

Among the eleven students to remain was Skrasis. Yet this did not surprise the Vulcan. The youth had great potential.

Unfortunately it would go unfulfilled. Regrets, of course, were not logical, but Spock made no effort to correct the thought.

All of the remaining eleven looked at him expectantly, as if their teacher could explain the recent turn of events. But, in this instance, Spock had no solace to give them.

He himself was too troubled by what had just taken place. Nearly three quarters of his original body of students had abandoned their studies.

Granted, some of them were still quite new to the principles of logic. Yet the Teacher knew he had made his case well. And he knew as well that it was right to continue his efforts, even in the face of death.

Spock saw the truth in these thoughts. Yet it seemed the truth was somehow inadequate now. It was not logical, but so it was.

"I suggest we meditate individually," he said, "so that we may consider today's lessons in the depth they deserve."

His followers nodded their assent. As they left for their quarters, the Vulcan watched them go.

Though he had called the break for the benefit of his students, he needed the peace and certainty of meditation as much as they did. No . . .

More.

Hunched over on the floor of his cell, Scotty peered once again past the energy barrier that penned him in— essentially the same sort of barrier he'd seen in his confinement on the warbird. Satisfied that his guards weren't around, he resumed his attempts to pry loose a bulkhead plate in the cell's back wall.

His tool in this effort was a metal eating utensil which the Romulans had given to him with his meal a half hour before. Hardly the picture of efficiency, they hadn't bothered to check on him since. He doubted they would even notice the utensil was missing when they picked up the remains of his uneaten lunch.

Certainly, the personnel on this station had their flaws—perhaps because the place was such a dead end for them. But then they were no more imperfect than the station itself.

This was an older facility and—Scotty guessed—a relatively unimportant one. Some of the construction techniques and pieces of equipment he had seen on his brief walk through the corridors predated even the Romulan technology he'd encountered on the *Enterprise.*

That meant the station was very likely even older than he was. And would probably be here after he was gone, the engineer groused.

Truth to tell, it depressed him to meet his end in such a sloppy operation. All the more reason to keep at what he was doing—to continue in his attempt to pry up the bulkhead plate—and not think about the consequences.

Scotty grunted as he applied some elbow grease. Fortunately, the plate was already loose and was located on the back wall—the warmest of the three available to him.

That meant there was a relatively high concentration of antiquated circuitry behind the plating. And if he could gain access to it, he might be able to get out of here.

Then, even if he couldn't quite escape, he might be able at least to throw the Romulans a curve. Perhaps disable an important system. It might help him later on.

Abruptly he heard the sound of footsteps. Slipping the utensil into his boot, he stood up to face whoever was approaching.

As it turned out, it was only one of his jailers. By the look on the Romulan's face, he had something to say—for a change.

"You will see the station administrator in a little while," he said. "He will interrogate you. He wanted you to know."

Scotty didn't say anything. He just curled his lip at the Romulan.

The guard shook his head at the human's idiocy. Then he turned and departed the way he'd come.

As soon as he was sure the Romulan was gone, Scotty cursed beneath his breath. Here he'd thought he was to be handled with kid gloves until the proconsul arrived. Obviously, someone had had other ideas in the meantime.

If you couldn't trust a Romulan bureaucrat, he thought with disgust, who could you trust?

He had only minutes left before he was ushered out of his cell. At the rate he was going, it would take hours for him to work his way behind the bulkhead panel.

And once they brought him to an interrogation room, the engineer held no illusions about his prospects of escape—no matter what shape the station was in.

In the academy, Scotty had had a grizzled old instructor who taught a course in survival techniques. The old man had said, "If you are under interrogation by an advanced race, I have one piece of advice for you: talk. Tell them anything and everything they want to know."

At the time, there had been audible gasps of surprise from everyone in the class, including Scott himself.

"But, sir," a cadet had asked, "what if that costs lives?"

The instructor had answered without thinking. "There is nothing you can do about that. If you've been captured by someone like the Klingons, you no longer have any control over the situation. No matter how tough you are—or *think* you are—you will eventually tell them what they want to know.

"If you do it without subjecting yourself to debilitating or even lethal torture," the man had said, "then you will be preserving a valuable Starfleet asset: yourself. If you remain alive, then there is the possibility of escape or a negotiated release. But if you allow yourself to be killed protecting secrets you are going to give up anyway, you will not have done Starfleet, or yourself, any favors."

A shocked silence had descended over the room as the students absorbed the professor's surprising—but coldly logical—advice.

After a long moment, Scotty's own hand had gone up. "But, sir," he'd asked plainly, "how would we live with ourselves afterward?"

For the first and only time since Scotty had known him, the old man had been speechless.

Right now, the memory offered the engineer no comfort. He had no illusions about his own ability to withstand the calculated precision of a full-bore Romulan interrogation.

Not as Montgomery Scott, anyway. Not as the clear-thinking, often ingenious officer who'd come within a hair of making it to Constanthus.

No, if he was going to be of any use to his friend Spock, he was going to have to present a different persona to his interrogator. After all, the act had worked on the Romulan warbird commander. Why not trot it out again?

Hell, it was just about the only card he had left.

* * *

Spock knew that the time was very near. Of course he had not been a part of the escape plans, nor had he spoken about them with Belan since the Constantharine excused himself from his studies.

However, he had overheard enough of the discussions to know the basic scheme—another product of the hybrid's improved hearing. It would take place during the afternoon mealtime, when the soldiers delivered food to the unificationists through the only entrance into the compound.

The Vulcan himself had seen the soldiers' vulnerability during these intervals. Undoubtedly, they had come to view the unificationists as pacifists, and they had become more and more lax in their attention to the minutiae of security. Though not covered in the teachings of Surak, Spock's Starfleet training required him to make such observations.

At the moment, there were two groups of prisoners, one on each side of the entrance. Each group was assembled as if it were engaged in academic dialogue on the principles of logic—something it had done day after day, in the same place at the same time.

As a result, doing it now would arouse no suspicions. It was a precaution that was both logical and practical.

In fact, the Teacher was impressed with the entire plan. It was an admirable effort. Unfortunately, it also seemed doomed to failure.

Clearly, the first phase would have a good chance of success. Spock had no doubt that his former students would be able to overpower the guards who entered the compound and make it into the command center of the detention complex.

After that the prospects were much less certain. The

prisoners would be entering a highly fortified facility that was no doubt full of soldiers and security systems.

The chances of getting out of the complex were virtually nonexistent. But then, those involved in the escape attempt already knew that.

"Teacher," came a voice from beside him.

He turned and faced D'tan. Looking down at his charge, one of eleven in a semicircle before him, Spock realized that he had for a few moments allowed his mind to wander during a lesson. It was something he had never done before. In fact, until now, he would have called it a purely human tendency.

Odd, the Vulcan thought.

"Teacher, shall we conduct the class inside today?" D'tan asked, in recognition of what would soon take place.

Spock considered the question for only a moment. "No," he replied.

D'tan looked pained. "But, today, we would no doubt find it an atmosphere more conducive to study," the youth pressed.

According to the strictest principles of logic, D'tan was correct. Nevertheless, that was not what the Teacher intended to do. The conflict between the two should have concerned him, but it did not.

Addressing his students, he said, "Today we will continue our studies where we are. We will bear witness to all that we see. And we will remember."

Complete stillness descended over his followers. They looked to Spock for an explanation of his decision. But for the second time in as many days, he felt inadequate to the task.

Today he would not be their teacher. Instead they

would learn from their former comrades out in the courtyard—those who had set a different course for themselves. Spock sighed, wondering what he himself might learn.

As he observed Belan and the others waiting for their moment, he noticed his students rising and forming a line to either side of him. After a moment or two, he realized what they were doing.

In Surak's time, they were known as lines of witnessing. On his immediate left was D'tan, and on his right was Skrasis, each at the head of a queue.

The old and the new, the Teacher thought. It was fitting.

As on ancient Vulcan, he and his students would bear witness to the events that would follow. They would recall these events for others who wished to know of them, for as long as they lived.

Though pleased to see the old tradition surviving so long after Surak practiced it, and so far from the burning sands of his homeworld, Spock was uncomfortable in the role of leader just then. Surely, Surak had not known the sort of doubt he felt, as he attended what would come.

He did not have long to wait. As usual, the guards were extremely punctual.

Four of them pushed out the cart that contained the prisoners' food, while a total of eight others watched the prisoners themselves.

As usual, the rebels approached the food cart from all sides. It was then that the Vulcan realized something was wrong.

The soldiers were unusually alert, watching the prisoners more carefully than at any time since Spock and his followers were brought into the compound. Subtle signs of tension in their posture told the Teacher that they were on guard.

The only explanation was that the spy had somehow informed his superiors, despite their precautions.

For a moment, Spock was certain that Belan would realize his plan had been discovered and call off the attempt. Either the Constantharine saw the signs as Spock did and chose to ignore them, or missed them entirely in his preoccupation. In either case, the subject was soon rendered moot.

Being closest to a soldier, Belan was the first to strike. He lunged for the guard's weapon, at the same time calling out to his accomplices to do the same. Almost simultaneously, the rest of the prisoners in Belan's group converged on the remaining soldiers.

As Belan struggled with his guard, he struck him in the side of the neck, using a technique that predated the exodus of the Empire's founders from Vulcan. And though the blow was primitive by current Vulcan martial arts standards, it was nonetheless effective.

When the Romulan crumpled to the floor, Belan grabbed his hand weapon. Within seconds, all of the guards were similarly accosted.

Spock noted that Santek had also secured a weapon. So had Minan, both of them employing fighting techniques that the Vulcan had taught him. And though the soldiers resisted, each of them was soon lying on the ground, disarmed and presumably at least temporarily disabled.

It was then that their captors made their move. Soldiers appeared suddenly all along the wall that ringed the compound—armed with disruptor rifles.

Others appeared behind the Teacher and his students. Their weapons, Spock noticed, were set to kill. He sighed.

For at the same time, the soldiers on the walls went about their grisly work. The hum of disruptor fire grew loud, like a swarm of angry insects. Dark blue chaos walked on long legs across the courtyard.

Belan had been the first to arm himself. He was also the first to fall—with a disruptor blast in the center of his back.

Another of the prisoners was cut down, and another. Their comrades returned the guards' fire—or tried to. But not a single one of their weapons worked.

What's more, Spock knew why. They had been deactivated by the guards in anticipation of the attack.

Within seconds, only four of the twelve armed unificationists remained standing. Three of those were brought down at once by another disruptor barrage. Santek was the last to fall, shaking his weapon above his head in a final act of defiance.

In the wake of the slaughter, there was a moment of complete and tangible silence. Though it lasted only a fraction of a second, it seemed much longer. The Vulcan didn't wonder at the discrepancy.

Then as quickly as they appeared, the soldiers withdrew from their positions. Surveying the scene, the Vulcan noted that besides the twelve armed prisoners, an additional two had been struck down.

Spock was the first to move, walking purposefully toward the carnage. He knew that having dispatched the threat, the soldiers would not retrieve the bodies or the useless weapons. Not right away, anyway. Instead, they would be left as reminders to the rebels who remained.

Even as the Vulcan approached his fallen students, he could see that none of them was stirring. None of them had survived. Apparently, the soldiers were as deadly as they were precise.

Still there was work to do.

Standing over Belan's body, Spock raised his hand and offered the Vulcan salute. A moment later, he could sense that the surviving unificationists had assembled behind him.

Spock did not have to turn around to know that they had joined him in his tribute to their fallen comrades. There would be no more lessons today. For now, they would only grieve.

Even as his mind laid out the elements of the mourning ritual, the Vulcan knew there was a larger lesson in the bodies of those before him. He only hoped he had the wisdom to uncover it.

CHAPTER 11

Planetary Governor Tharrus watched the data screen with unblinking eyes.

"How many dead?" he asked.

"Fourteen," came Phabaris's clipped reply.

"Any casualties among our soldiers?" the governor asked.

The security officer shook his head. "Only very minor injuries. Nothing requiring treatment," he reported.

Tharrus grunted. His soldiers had performed well. All of the prisoners armed with the deactivated weapons had been killed, with only two incidental deaths.

And the survivors had learned a much-needed lesson. Of course, had all of them participated, or had they enjoyed even a remote chance of success, the governor never would have allowed the attempt.

On reflection, it surprised him that the pathetic philosophers had gone through with their plan. It showed they still had some teeth—that there was some Romulan left in them despite everything.

In any case, there were more than thirty of the unificationists left. It was an acceptable number for the upcoming trial.

Tharrus took a moment to congratulate himself on keeping his operative in place through it all. The Tal Shiar would no doubt have recalled the agent as soon as the initial arrest was made.

But then, the Tal Shiar did not understand the value of information as the governor did. That was why he had been able to infiltrate the unificationists, whereas the homeworld organization had failed.

Fascinated, Tharrus took a closer look at the data screen. In the closing seconds of the incident, its recorder had swept over all of the surviving prisoners—including the cowardly bunch of unificationists who had chosen not to make the attempt.

For a moment, the recorder had lingered on them. They were watching the scene with the same maddening, impassive expressions the governor had seen them wear in person.

They had watched their braver friends perish, yet their faces betrayed nothing of what they must have been thinking. No doubt, the cowards envied the dying—for they were escaping the trial and the lingering death that came with it.

That kind of thinking was of concern to Tharrus. He could not allow any further nonsense, certainly nothing that would jeopardize the trial.

If the remaining traitors sought another escape attempt as a way to court death and cheat their fate, that would put him in an awkward position. The trial was to be broadcast throughout the Empire. The recognition it would bring was vital to his long-term plans.

Speaking of which . . .

He turned to Phabaris. "Has there been any official response to our communiqué to the homeworlds?"

"No, Governor," the security officer replied.

That didn't make sense. Romulus was certain to be furious at the announcement that Tharrus was handling the business of the traitors on his own.

He had not released the information until just the day before—specifically to reduce the central government's options. Not that it could do much without losing support in the outer systems. But the governor had expected a reply at the very least.

He thought for a moment, then made his decision. There would be no surprises—not from the prisoners or anyone else.

"Ready your staff," he told Phabaris. "I'm moving the trial up a day. The traitors will face their fate tomorrow."

Walking the corridors of his outpost, Administrator Barnak resolved to have the matter of the human settled before the proconsul arrived. He knew full well that this was not exactly in the spirit of Eragian's orders, but he would do it anyway.

After all, Barnak was already at an age when it was generally considered too late for a major promotion. He knew that this might be his last opportunity to do something that would be noticed by the central government.

If he failed, and damaged the human in the process, he would certainly incur the proconsul's wrath. But if he succeeded, his impertinence would no doubt be forgotten. It was a chance he would take.

Besides, he was determined not to fail.

A moment later, he reached the door of the interrogation room. The administrator motioned for the two guards posted at the door to follow him inside.

He found the human seated on a chair in front of the table in the center of the room. As they entered, he looked up at them.

And immediately, a scowl formed on his face. He glowered at Barnak and his guards with hate in his eyes. It was a dangerous look, thought the administrator. A peculiarly Romulan sort of look.

The human stood slowly, maintaining his scrutiny of Barnak as he did so. It was then that the administrator noticed the officer's clothes. Though familiar, they did not look like the Starfleet uniforms he had seen in reports.

Then Barnak realized what was wrong. The uniform was Starfleet, all right. But it was very old.

That was curious. Both the human's uniform and his ship were from another era. Perhaps he really *was* mad.

For a moment, the administrator thought the human would attack them. He certainly looked as if he wanted to.

Barnak could sense his guards—his two best—tensing beside him, preparing themselves to react if the prisoner made an aggressive move. But the human didn't attack. He merely continued to glare at his captors.

Not entirely mad? the administrator wondered.

"I am Administrator Barnak," he said. "I would like to ask you a few questions." His tone was serious, but not threatening. Certainly it was not meant to antagonize—not yet, anyway.

But antagonize it did. Suddenly going red in the face,

135

the human snapped, "I have nothing to say to the likes of ye, Romulan!"

Barnak ignored the outburst, keeping his own tone even and inflectionless. "You have invaded Romulan space. You have made your hostile intent extremely clear. Yet, we are treating you with all the courtesies required by the Treaty of Algeron—which, I will point out, you yourself have broken."

He paused. "Perhaps this incident was a mistake, in which case we could arrange your release with your government. But I can do nothing for you unless you cooperate."

The human remained defiant. But underneath the defiance, Barnak detected something else at work. He was no expert in non-Romulan body language and responses, but he would have sworn he saw something behind the human's eyes. The only word that came to mind was . . . intelligence.

The human may very well have been mad, but he wasn't stupid. The administrator could see that.

Nonetheless, when the human spoke, it was with the same active disdain he had displayed since Barnak entered the room.

"My mother didnae raise any fools, Romulan. Ye'll nae more let me go than I'll grow wings and fly out of here."

The administrator eyed the man. "I am an officer of the Romulan Empire. My word is my word."

The prisoner was unimpressed. "Yer word means nothing to me, ye pointy-eared barbarian. Yer Empire is a lying, thieving band of bullies, and I'll nae kneel before ye."

Feeling his own anger rise within him, Barnak allowed some of it to seep into his voice. "All we are asking is simple cooperation," he insisted. "Our governments are not at war—yet you invade us and dare to insult the Empire. You will answer my questions, or you will answer the proconsul's—and his are not likely to be so polite."

In response, the human did something that completely surprised the administrator. He laughed.

"Are ye threatening me?" he asked. "Are ye playing Good Romulan, Bad Romulan?" the human railed.

Barnak was silent for a moment. He was growing impatient with this exercise.

Forcing down his anger, he sat at the table in front of the Starfleet officer. His guards remained standing beside him.

Looking up at the human, he said, "Please, have a seat."

To his further surprise, the prisoner sat down immediately. For the moment, he wore a calm expression, except for a maddening twitch in one eye.

"I would like to begin again," Barnak told him. "Perhaps you will explain to me how it is that you are the only crew member aboard a century-old starship, and how you are wearing a uniform at least as old?"

The human mirrored the administrator's reasonable tone. "I have come from the past," he whispered, "to defend the Federation against the blight on the galaxy that is the Romulan Empire."

Barnak grunted softly. "Yet it is you who attack us."

The human waved his hand dismissively. "I know yer plans," he breathed in an almost conspiratorial way. "And I'll nae let ye take the Federation without a fight."

Watching the man's eyes closely, Barnak could see that same flash of something. Intelligence? Recognition? He once again had the feeling that the prisoner was somehow toying with them.

But to what end? He would surely know that anything

hidden on his vessel would be found, and any secrets would be revealed in a formal interrogation.

What would be the purpose of a charade that merely postponed the inevitable? Unless . . . the key was in the postponing.

The administrator frowned, disappointed. This had not worked out the way he had planned. Still, there was no harm done. The prisoner was undamaged, as ripe as ever for Eragian's plucking.

"I am afraid," Barnak announced, "you leave me no choice but to end this interview."

The human's mouth twisted. "Romulan bastard," he spat.

The administrator didn't understand the reference. But he understood from the man's tone that it was meant as an insult.

Resolving not to be baited, Barnak began to stand. But before he was out of his chair, the human's hand shot out and grabbed the Romulan's uniform at the throat.

Pulling himself close, the prisoner regarded Barnak with his now familiar sneer. "Yer mother's a Klingon," he snarled.

Reacting more to the insult than to the pitiful display of aggression, the administrator shook free of the human's hand and stood—drawing his sidearm in the process.

With the disruptor aimed directly at the prisoner's head, the Romulan reached for the trigger with his firing finger. But in the fraction of a second before he could fire, he was reminded of Eragian's instructions.

The prisoner is to remain undamaged. Otherwise, Barnak knew, whoever had damaged him would be damaged in turn. Exquisitely so.

With an effort, the administrator put away his weapon,

then motioned his guards to do the same. Apparently, he'd been wrong about the human. Only a madman would court death the way he had, for no apparent gain.

Barnak smiled a thin, grudging smile. "That concludes our interview. I regret that I have other business to attend to." He glared at the human. "But do not worry. If you are withholding something from us, the proconsul will extract it from you. The time may come when you regret not having spoken with me."

And with that, he left the room.

The first time Worf noticed the intermittent energy pulses on his long-range sensor monitor, he believed they were caused by a natural phenomenon. His best guess was that they'd come across a pulsar, positioned somewhere in Romulan space.

However, after he'd observed the pulses for a while, he began to wonder if he hadn't discovered something else entirely.

That was when he put the ship's computer on the case. Before long, an answer came back. The pulses didn't seem to be generated by anything natural, the computer advised him.

More than likely, they represented some sort of *message.*

But what was it? Who had sent it? And for what purpose?

Again, he set the task before the ship's computer. As it began its translation protocol, the Klingon tapped his communications badge. A moment later, he received an acknowledgment in the form of Picard's voice.

"Yes, Lieutenant. What is it?"

Worf told him about the pulses. And by the time he was

done, the computer had finished its work. The answer to his questions stood in small red letters on the otherwise dark monitor screen.

It wasn't good news. Not at all.

"Lieutenant? Are you still there?"

"I am, sir," the Klingon replied. "Unfortunately, our rescue mission just became a good deal more complicated."

CHAPTER 12

Picard leaned forward in his chair at the head of the long, polished table that dominated the observation lounge. Riker, Troi, Geordi, Worf, Data, and Doctor Crusher looked back at him from their customary seats.

Admiral McCoy was there as well, of course, at the far end of the table. Though the captain had been tempted to leave him out of this, he ultimately had no recourse but to invite him.

"So," said Picard, glancing from one face to the next, "it seems we now have more than one hostage situation to address."

"More than one?" Troi echoed.

The captain nodded. "Montgomery Scott—another of the admiral's old comrades—seems to have been lost in Romulan space. That's the message Mister Worf received just a little while ago—from Captain Scott himself, apparently, via a series of energy pulses."

McCoy's brow furrowed as he absorbed the news. After all, he had served with Scott on the original *Enterprise.*

"How the devil did *Scotty* get into Romulan territory?" the admiral rasped.

"I wondered that myself," said Picard. "As a result, I did some checking with Starfleet Command—which provided some rather interesting information."

Picard went on to describe the "liberation" of the *Yorktown.* By the time he finished, there were more than a few expressions of admiration around the table.

"Impressive," said Crusher.

Picard agreed. "Few men could have gotten that ship into action in so brief a time," he commented. "Captain Scott, it seems, is one of them."

"You can say that again," McCoy muttered, barely loud enough to be heard.

Riker's eyes narrowed. "This isn't just a coincidence, is it? He must have gotten wind of Spock's capture and set out to rescue the ambassador on his own."

The captain nodded. "That's what Starfleet Command believes as well."

The admiral harrumphed. "At least *someone* showed they had the guts to get Spock back," he remarked pointedly.

Picard darted a glance in McCoy's direction. He would not take the bait, he told himself. He would *not.*

"What are our orders, sir?" asked Data.

The captain turned to him. "Our orders are largely the same as before. We are to negotiate for Ambassador Spock's release." He paused, gathering himself for what he knew would not be a pleasant announcement. "Captain Scott's situation must be regarded as secondary," he finished.

"Secondary?" blurted the admiral. "Of all the—!"

"We are here to address a threat to the Federation," Picard pointed out, maintaining an even keel. "In other words, the capture of Ambassador Spock. What has happened to Captain Scott is unfortunate—but we cannot allow our personal feelings to cloud our objective."

"Then why bring Scotty up at all?" McCoy spat.

The captain fixed him with his gaze. "Because he may be tortured. And if so, he may talk. Thus far, the Romulans don't know what they've got on Constanthus. But soon, they may."

"All the more reason to go in there and get the both of them out," the admiral argued.

Picard shook his head. "That is not the approach with the greatest chance of success. Nor will I risk the *Enterprise* on such a venture."

"I agree," said Riker. "We can't put the whole ship in jeopardy." He leaned toward the captain, a light in his eyes. "But, sir . . . what about a shuttle?"

The captain was surprised by Riker's suggestion. Nonetheless, he didn't reject it out of hand. At least, not quite.

"A clandestine mission," Worf remarked, putting a finer point on it.

"Yes," Picard agreed. "And a dangerous one, to be sure."

"I'd like to try it, sir," said the first officer, "despite the danger. I know it won't be an easy matter to retrieve Captain Scott from wherever they're holding him." He grinned bravely. "But then, I like a challenge."

"I'd like to go, too, Captain," Geordi chimed in. "I guess I've got a soft spot for the man. And, hell—if it were *me* out there, I know he'd be among the first to come chasing after me."

The captain frowned. No doubt, the engineer's assessment was an accurate one. Still—

"Sir?" interjected the counselor. She smiled wistfully. "Captain Scott came to mean something to me as well. If I can be of any use on this kind of mission . . ."

Before Picard could answer, Worf uttered a Klingon curse. For the sake of propriety, the security officer had apparently limited himself to one of the milder variety.

"I cannot say we were the best of friends," Worf elucidated. "However, I know what the Romulans will do to such a man. I cannot stand by and allow them to work their tortures on him."

"But if they *have,*" said Crusher, "he's going to need a doctor."

Data leaned forward. "I too would like to see Captain Scott restored to more familiar surroundings. I believe my skills would be an asset to whatever team you select."

Picard held up his hand for silence. He hadn't expected such a response. Apparently, Scott had made quite an impression during his short stay on the *Enterprise.*

"I'm certain Captain Scott would be gratified to see how highly you think of him," he said. "However, risking even a shuttlecraft—"

"—would not be much of a risk at all," the Klingon pressed. "After all, Captain Scott is being held in a lightly fortified sector of the Empire—nothing at all like Constanthus. And according to his message, his prison is a rather dilapidated one."

"Which means we could get in there and get him out pretty easily," Geordi noted.

"Sounds good to me," said McCoy.

Picard stiffened. "There is still a considerable risk," he reminded the others. "And I will not gamble my entire complement of senior officers on one throw of the dice."

"But you *will* gamble *some* of them," McCoy insisted.

The captain sighed. He weighed the chances of success against the rewards of failure. And finally, he made his decision.

"Against my better judgment," he remarked, "I will allow a rescue attempt." He turned to his first officer. "Commander Riker, you will be in charge. You'll be accompanied by Commanders La Forge and Data. And by all means, Will, come back safely."

Riker inclined his head. "Thank you, sir. We'll do our best."

Picard looked to Troi, then Worf. "As for the rest of you, I appreciate your eagerness and your courage, but I need you more here on the *Enterprise.* Mister Worf, you will take over Mister Data's examination of Romulan ship movements. Dismissed."

The Klingon looked as if he was about to say something, but thought better of it. Instead, he merely frowned and headed for the exit.

So did everyone else. Everyone except the captain and Admiral McCoy, that is. It was clear to Picard that *their* discussion was only just beginning.

Once they were alone, facing each other across the length of the long, polished surface of the table, McCoy leaned back in his chair. His blue eyes gleamed beneath his feathery white brows.

"You know what this does?" he asked. "Scotty's capture—and this rescue mission?"

"I thought you were in favor of it," the captain noted.

The admiral grunted. "I *am* in favor of it—but it ups the ante, dammit. If the Romulans realize the Federation's sent a team to get Scotty out, they're going to take it personally. You can count on that. And it's going to make them a whole lot less eager to negotiate about *anything.*"

"Including the release of the unificationists," Picard suggested.

"That's exactly right," McCoy confirmed. "They'll shut up tighter than a Venus flytrap with a big ol' beetle in its mouth."

A colorful image, the captain had to admit. "Your point?" he asked.

McCoy stood up and jabbed a bony finger at the younger man. "My point," he snarled, "is you're going to have to find a way to speed things up."

"With regard to Ambassador Spock," Picard said evenly.

"That's right," the admiral agreed. "Play another angle, maybe. In fact, I've been thinking about this, and I've got a scheme in mind already. All you've got to do is carry it out."

"Really," commented the captain. Under the circumstances, it was difficult for him to keep the sarcasm out of his voice. "Perhaps you'd like to share it with me."

As Picard listened, McCoy did just that. But there was one problem with his plan.

"It won't work," the captain told him.

The admiral's brows met over his nose in an expression of pique. "What do you mean it won't work? How do you know until you've tried?"

"It's too risky," Picard said. "Too reckless. We're dealing with a very delicate problem here—and one with sweeping implications for the Federation. This is no time to conduct an experiment in gamesmanship."

McCoy planted his gnarly hands on the table before him. "Dammit, man, don't you see? Extreme situations call for extreme measures. That's the way we always did it on *our Enterprise!*"

As the captain rose, he felt the blood rushing to his

face. Pushed over the edge, he found himself raising his voice until it seemed to fill the entire lounge.

"It might help," he snapped, "if you remembered that this is *not* your *Enterprise*. We do things differently around here. And as long as I am in command of this vessel, we will *continue* to do them differently."

The admiral's eyes screwed up tightly. "Then you leave me no choice," he grated, trembling with fury. "From now on, Captain, you are no longer in command of the *Enterprise!"*

Picard blinked, scarcely able to believe his ears. "What?" he said.

"You heard me," McCoy barked. "I gave you a chance to act like a captain and you threw it away."

"I did nothing of the sort," Picard maintained.

But it was clear to him that the admiral wasn't listening. He was too intent on making his point.

"I can't force you to obey my orders," McCoy continued, his mouth twisted in anger, "but I can sure as shootin' make sure *someone* does. That's one of the benefits of being an admiral, for God sake."

The captain shook his head. He hadn't expected anything like this. Even now, it didn't seem real.

"Effective immediately," said McCoy, "I'm relieving you of your command. You're restricted to quarters, Picard."

The captain shook his head. He couldn't allow this to happen. He had to take hold of events before they whirled out of control.

"No," he demanded, "listen to me. I am not rendering these decisions arbitrarily. I speak from long years of experience."

"No longer than mine," the admiral seethed. "And

what's that got to do with it, anyway? Jim Kirk was smarter than both of us when he was in command of the *Enterprise,* and he was barely out of the Academy."

"All right, then," Picard told him, ignoring the comparison. "Forget how long I've been doing this. Think of the officers we're sending out in that shuttle. Think of the lives you're playing fast and loose with."

McCoy's nostrils flared. "I *am* thinking of lives," he replied, his anger boiling over. "I'm a doctor, dammit. I've never thought of anything *else.*"

"Then act like it," the captain told him. "Give up this . . . this plan of yours."

"Not a chance," the admiral insisted. "To save a patient, you've got to act quickly sometimes. You've got to make choices. And you've got to live with the choices you make." He stuck his thumb in his chest. "This is a choice I can live with."

Picard bit his lip. This jousting was getting him nowhere. If he couldn't put a cap on his anger, he would lose everything.

Taking a deep breath, he forced himself to think rationally. To appeal to McCoy's better judgment.

"I beg you to reconsider," he said. "Romulus is a strict hierarchy, after all. Once you ignore that fact, you're asking for trouble. And with the stakes so high—"

"I told you," the admiral advised him, unrelenting in his stubbornness. "I've already given this plenty of thought. Now it's time to act."

He started toward the door. Without thinking, Picard grasped him by his spindly upper arm—an action he immediately regretted.

McCoy's eyes blazed. "I have no desire," the man said in a low voice, "to throw you in the brig, Captain. But if you make it necessary, I'll do just that."

Picard released him. He had never before felt so helpless. There had to be a way to get through to him—to make him understand.

"Admiral," he pleaded, "you are going to get someone killed. How can I make you see that?"

McCoy didn't answer. He simply turned and exited the observation lounge, leaving the captain alone.

Behind his back, Picard could hear the admiral address Lieutenant Worf. "Open a channel for me," the older man snapped.

The Klingon hesitated, no doubt wondering why McCoy was giving such an order. Finally he asked, "Where is the captain?"

"Forget the captain," the admiral ordered. "You'll answer to me now."

Silence.

Picard knew that Worf would not simply obey McCoy's directives—not without some explanation. After all, personal loyalty meant even more to the Klingon than his duty to Starfleet.

Sighing, the captain exited the lounge. All eyes were drawn to him—Worf's in particular.

"You have received an order," he told the Klingon, the apology in his voice belying the harshness of his words. "You will follow it, Lieutenant."

"Well?" said McCoy. "Are you going to open that channel or not?"

Worf scowled, obviously still uncomfortable with the situation. But this time he did as he was told.

"To what location?" he asked.

The admiral darted a glance at Picard. "To Constanthus, Mister Worf."

As the Klingon complied, albeit reluctantly, the captain

crossed in back of him and made his way to the turbolift. Nor, when its doors opened, did he look back.

He simply stepped inside and let the doors whisper closed again. For the first time in years, someone else was in charge of the *Enterprise*.

CHAPTER **13**

Lieutenant Goodwin turned and saw Commander Riker enter the shuttlebay with Commanders La Forge and Data close behind him. He bit his lip and concentrated on running the shuttle *Justman* through some last-second diagnostics.

"Mister Goodwin," said the first officer.

The lieutenant sighed, raised his head, and saw the frown on Riker's face.

"Aye, sir?" he replied, wincing at the catch in his voice that made him sound like someone much younger than his twenty-eight years.

"I alerted you that we needed a shuttlecraft nearly five minutes ago," the first officer told him. His voice was gentle but firm. "Don't tell me you're still running diagnostic routines."

"Actually," said Goodwin, "I am, sir."

Riker's frown deepened a little. "It shouldn't take more than a minute to get a shuttle ready for departure,

Lieutenant. What have you been doing for the last five minutes? Reading a library file?"

There was a murmur of well-intended laughter from the other crew people on the shuttle deck. Goodwin couldn't help smile a little himself.

"Well, sir," he said, "it wouldn't have taken quite so long if we'd started with the *Justman*. As it was, we started with the *Hawking.*"

"And?" the first officer prodded.

"There was a minute inconsistency in the matter-antimatter mix. I didn't want to send you out in a vehicle with an even remotely unstable power source."

Riker's frown faded a little—but not completely. "I appreciate your concern, Lieutenant. But it still shouldn't have taken so long to get a second shuttle ready."

Goodwin nodded. "I agree, sir. But the *Justman* is actually the *third* craft we've had to check out."

The first officer looked at him. "The *third?*"

"Aye, sir," said the lieutenant. "You see, we looked at the *Magellan* next. And everything looked pretty good until we got to the end of the diagnostic routine. That's when I spotted some feedback in the sensor array. It probably wouldn't have made much difference, to tell you the truth, but—"

"But Mister Goodwin is more attentive to detail than most shuttle deck technicians," Commander La Forge interjected. "And a good thing, too. That kind of feedback is tough to spot, but its effects can be devastating."

"True," remarked Commander Data. "If our sensor array failed us at a crucial moment, perhaps as we—"

"Please," said Riker, holding up a hand for emphasis. "I get the idea."

"In any case," Goodwin continued, glancing one last

time at his control panel, "the *Justman* seems to check out fine. I'll have no trouble turning her over to you, sir."

The first officer looked relieved to bring the conversation to an end. "Thank you, Lieutenant. And forget what I said about the library file. It seems *I* was the one who was out of line."

Goodwin blushed. He'd never been able to handle praise very well, especially in public. "That's quite all right, sir."

Switching from diagnostic mode to operations, he reflected on how glad he was not to have disappointed his superior after all. On his last assignment, the lieutenant recalled, he'd started out on the wrong foot and never gotten off it.

But he'd heard good things about the *Enterprise,* and Captain Picard in particular. Hoping like crazy, Goodwin had requested a transfer. And to his delight, the captain had approved it.

The way the lieutenant looked at it, he owed a lot to Captain Picard. He was glad to serve under a man who was as compassionate as he was forceful. And he was sure it was no coincidence that Commander Riker displayed those qualities as well.

"I'm opening the hatch door now," he reported. "You can step in any time you like."

A moment later, the door to the *Justman* slid back, revealing the interior of the vehicle. Without hesitation, Riker entered. His companions were right on his heels, every bit as focused as their commanding officer.

As soon as they were all inside, the door slid forward again, concealing the trio within. In accordance with Starfleet procedure, that function had been performed from inside the shuttle.

The next step was to part the large duranium bay doors that separated the crew from open space. Goodwin tapped the appropriate pads.

Automatically, a pair of forcefield generators—one on either side of the opening—created an almost invisible, annular barrier. Otherwise, the atmosphere in the bay would have rushed out helter-skelter into the void, taking Goodwin's crew people and most of the equipment along with it.

"Clear for departure?" asked Riker, his voice coming through over the shuttlebay's intercom system.

Goodwin could see the first officer at the helm controls, through the vehicle's forward observation port. He nodded.

"Clear for departure, Commander."

As if in acknowledgment, the *Justman* lifted slightly off the deck and moved forward toward the energy barrier. Fortunately, the barrier was designed to resist only atmospheric pressures, not the kind of force exerted by a type six Starfleet shuttle.

As a result, the craft simply knifed through the energy field. A moment later it was free of the ship and the field had closed again in its wake.

Goodwin smiled. The *Justman* was on its way.

But that didn't mean he was about to relax. Not when the *Hawking* had that matter-antimatter glitch and the *Magellan* was plagued with sensor feedback.

One never knew when the captain was going to need another shuttle placed into service. But whenever that was, the lieutenant wanted to be ready.

He was just closing the outer doors when a voice flooded the shuttlebay. "Commander Riker? You still there, man?"

Goodwin didn't recognize the voice. It seemed to

crackle with annoyance, as if it couldn't wait to find fault with something. It was just the sort of tone his old commanding officer used to take.

He shuddered at the thought. There was no way Captain Ben Abdul could've come aboard without his knowing about it . . . was there?

Shaking off his trepidation, he replied, "Commander Riker is gone, sir. He and Commander Data and Commander La Forge have taken off already." He cleared his throat. "Is there anything I can help you with, sir?"

The intercom system conveyed a sound of disgust. "I guess not, Lieutenant. All I wanted to do was let them know what's happened up here—that Captain Picard's no longer in charge and such."

Goodwin felt the information go through him like an electric shock. Captain Picard . . . no longer in charge?

"But then," the voice went on, "they'll find that out soon enough. McCoy out."

In the empty silence that followed, the lieutenant looked around at his fellow crew members. They seemed just as puzzled as he was.

"McCoy?" he muttered. *"Admiral McCoy?"*

The bent, frail-looking, white-haired old fellow who'd come aboard en route to the Neutral Zone? *That* McCoy?

"But what happened to Captain Picard?" asked Ensign Perry, a slim brunette.

Goodwin shook his head. "I don't know," he admitted. But the lieutenant made it his business to find out.

Proconsul Eragian stood with his hands clasped behind his back and surveyed the bridge of the Federation starship. As his aides went over each station with the utmost scrutiny, he shook his head.

"Leave it to Starfleet to cobble together such a confusing amalgamation of equipment," he mused. "Such an outright *mess."*

At his side, Lennex nodded in agreement. But he added no comment of his own.

Typical, thought Eragian. Probably, the Tal Shiar was busy contemplating the implications of the Starfleet captain's offer. Free the unificationists indeed. Even if it were within his power—which it wasn't at the moment—the proconsul would hardly entertain such a notion.

Still, a way to capitalize on the human's arrogance might yet occur to him. Eragian was glad he had left the matter open for further discussion. He might even find a way to use it as leverage against Tharrus.

For now, however, he had other things on his mind. A puzzle, as it were. The puzzle of this ship.

The registry on its hull had suggested this was the *Yorktown*—a Constitution-class vessel employed more than a century ago, according to the intelligence Lennex had garnered on it.

At the same time, the plaque beside the turbolift, translated for him by his own ship's computer, indicated that the bridge came from a vessel called *Enterprise.*

Obviously not the Galaxy-class *Enterprise* currently in service, but a predecessor—though Romulan records showed that at least two of those predecessors had been destroyed. One of them, apparently, had been a victim of the great military victory at Narendra III, still commemorated as a holiday among his people.

But by far the strangest part of the puzzle was the one that had spawned his interest in the first place—the cloaking device that had been discovered in the engineering section. It was one of the original modules developed on the homeworld, it seemed, long before they perfected cloaking technology.

Of course, it had since been upgraded, and by someone who knew what he was doing. But its rudimentary construction was still eminently recognizable.

How had the Federation gotten its hands on it? None of the records Lennex had obtained could give him an answer. But then even a Tal Shiar couldn't access quite everything in the imperial data banks.

Unfortunately, this vessel would be of little or no use to them from a tactical standpoint. He had a hard time believing that it bore any real resemblance to the Starfleet ships in use today.

However, here it was. Someone had gone to the trouble to construct it. And beyond that, someone had used it to cross the Federation Neutral Zone.

Of course, there was speculation that the one who had performed that feat was demented. A madman, the report said, who had somehow had the gall and the great good luck to steal a Federation starship, only to be caught by the ever-vigilant imperial border patrols.

A madman with the talent to run a fair-sized, space-going vessel all on his own. Eragian had heard of idiot savants capable of such things among his own people— but this was the first he'd heard of a human with such capabilities.

Eragian approached the red-orange railing that encircled the command center and ran his fingertips along its surface. Even the materials used in the structure seemed outmoded, somehow. Antiquated.

"A middle-aged human on an antique vessel," he said out loud. "A mission that defied all logic. And yet, a mission—whatever it was—that came dangerously close to succeeding."

Again Lennex was noncommittal. No help there,

thought Eragian. Clearly the Tal Shiar thought his time was being wasted.

The proconsul sighed. He was certain there was something missing here—some bit of information he lacked, which would have imposed sense on the situation. But what could it be? Where might he find it? Frustrated, Eragian rapped his knuckles sharply on the railing.

"Proconsul?" said a voice.

He turned and saw one of his aides approaching him, data padd in hand. The man's name was T'racc. Though one of the youngest in Eragian's technical entourage, he was also one of the brightest.

And the one with the finest grasp of protocol as well, the proconsul reflected. Nodding once, he gave T'racc permission to speak.

"We wondered how the vessel's command functions could have been operated by a single individual," his aide explained. "Now we know."

He handed Eragian his padd, with his analysis on its tiny data screen.

"It seems many of these functions—those which could be handled automatically, at least—were slaved to a smaller vehicle in the ship's shuttlebay. I believe it is called a shuttlecraft."

The proconsul considered the graphic representation of T'racc's analysis. The human had been clever—devilishly clever.

But he had a question. "What prevented him from using the computer aboard the starship for this purpose?" he inquired.

His aide answered without hesitation. "The computer aboard the shuttle is more advanced than the one on the starship."

That piqued Eragian's interest. "Is it really? Then the

shuttle might have originated with a different vessel entirely—one significantly closer to the cutting edge of Federation science?"

T'racc nodded. "So it would seem, Your Eminence."

The proconsul grunted. Could this be the clue he'd been hoping for? Or just another question to set beside all the others?

His meditations were cut short by the approach of a second aide. This one—a man named Orath—was considerably older than the first.

Once, like T'racc, Orath had been eager to show off his brilliance. Now in a more advanced stage of life, he was content simply to do his job.

Fortunately for him, he was still very good at what he did. Otherwise Eragian might have taken offense at the man's lack of initiative.

"You have something for me?" he asked Orath.

The man nodded. "I do, Your Eminence." He said the words with a measure of satisfaction. "There is an energy leak in the vessel's warp engine."

"An energy leak?" the proconsul echoed. "Is it dangerous?"

That seemed to have gotten Lennex's attention. He looked on silently, but with interest.

Orath shook his head. "I do not regard it as such, for the time being. However, if it becomes any worse, you may wish to consider an early departure."

Eragian muttered a curse. "Can't the leak be repaired?" he asked.

"It can," Orath replied. "However, it may take some time to do so, and I do not wish to see you placed in any peril."

It was the correct answer. Orath had become a master of correct answers, it seemed to the proconsul.

On the other hand, an engine leak was an engine leak. Even Eragian knew how unpredictable such things could be.

He frowned. "Very well," he said reluctantly. "Make arrangements for my immediate return to the *Vengeance.*"

Unexpectedly, T'racc piped up. He was standing behind Orath, peering at the information on the older man's padd. "Your Eminence, may I see Orath's data, please?"

The older aide was not pleased by the younger one's impertinence. However, Eragian was curious as to what T'racc might have seen. So was Lennex, by the look of him.

"By all means," the proconsul responded. "Orath, if you please."

With obvious distaste for the situation, Orath handed T'racc his data padd. The younger man took a moment or two to study the thing, then murmured something beneath his breath.

"Speak up," Eragian instructed. "What is it?"

T'racc looked up at him. "Proconsul, this is not an accidental leak. At least, as far as I can tell."

Eragian returned the man's gaze. "Not accidental?" he repeated. "Are you saying the human sabotaged this ship before he was taken from it?"

Lennex's interest seemed to be increasing.

T'racc shook his head from side to side. "No, Proconsul. Not sabotaged it—simply created an energy leak which would direct a pulse out into space."

Eragian felt the hairs on the back of his neck begin to rise. "And why would he wish to do that?" he asked.

But even before T'racc provided the answer, the proconsul came up with it himself. Nor did it please him immensely.

"I believe," said the younger aide, "it is an attempt to communicate with someone in the Federation."

Finally the Tal Shiar spoke up. "What makes you say that?"

T'racc paled. Lennex seemed to make him nervous.

"Certainly," he replied, "that theory would be supported by the direction in which the energy is leaking—though it would require a more thorough examination to determine if there is a code involved."

The Tal Shiar turned to Eragian. "Perhaps an investigation is in order."

But the proconsul shook his head. He didn't need to conduct an investigation. He could feel the truth of the matter in his bones.

"More than likely," he said, "T'racc is right. The energy leak is a means of sending a message to the Federation. A call for help, perhaps."

It made Eragian angry that no one had detected it before. He glared at Orath. "Return to the *Vengeance,*" he snapped. "And send someone else in your place—someone who shows some intellectual curiosity."

Orath swallowed. "Yes, Your Eminence." He bowed his head and backed out of the proconsul's presence. The turbolift doors whispered open behind him, offering him a refuge which he no doubt gladly accepted.

Eragian turned back to T'racc. "You've done well," he told the younger man. "Now do something more."

"Anything, Your Eminence."

"See to it that the human's activities are curtailed until I transport to the surface—which will be in a matter of minutes."

"Of course," said the younger man. He removed his personal communications device from his belt and made contact with the ground installation.

161

In the meantime, the proconsul seethed. Finally he had obtained the clue he'd been searching for—the key that would allow him to understand this entire affair, in due time.

"The human, the one called Scott, is not at all what he seems," Lennex noted. "It was one thing to commandeer an ancient starship and try to take it behind Romulan lines. But to devise such a clever way of calling for assistance . . ."

Eragian nodded. "A demented being could not have accomplished that. Hence, the human was only *pretending* to be mad. What's more, he will regret that pretense as soon as I have a chance to interrogate him."

"Proconsul!" called T'racc.

Eragian turned, surprised at the lack of deference in his aide's voice. But when he actually saw T'racc, he began to understand it. The man looked positively ill.

"What is it?" asked the proconsul.

T'racc shrugged helplessly. "The . . . the human," he stammered. "He's *gone.*"

His anger mounting even higher, Eragian whipped out his own communicator and established contact with the base. He would soon straighten this out.

"Commander Barnak!" he spat.

A moment later, the base commander responded, his voice tremulous. "I don't know what to say, Your Eminence. The human was under the watch of—"

"Then T'racc is right?" the proconsul bellowed. "The human managed to escape?"

"No, Your Eminence. Not *escape,*" Barnak insisted. "He is still somewhere on the base."

Lennex darted a look at Eragian. "Taking notes on the outpost's defensive capabilities, no doubt."

The proconsul could barely contain his fury. "I want

you to find him, do you hear me? Find him and contain him, or you will wish you'd never been born!"

"Yes, Your Eminence," the base commander assured him. "It is only a matter of time before we—"

Suddenly, Barnak stopped. Eragian could hear someone else speaking in the background. Immediately thereafter, there was a considerable amount of shouting.

"What's going on down there?" he demanded.

"Proconsul," said the base commander. His voice sounded frantic, strained. "Sensors show that one of our transport vessels has broken orbit without authorization—and is leaving at maximum speed."

Eragian couldn't believe it. He terminated the communication and initiated another one—this time, with Hajak, the commander of the *Vengeance.*

"This is the proconsul," he raged. "Bring me and Commander Lennex aboard—now!"

In a matter of seconds, he found himself on the warbird's bridge, the Tal Shiar still beside him. He turned to Hajak, who had risen from the center seat to attend them.

Eragian made a gesture of dismissal at the viewscreen, which showed him some arcane technical graphic. "There's a transport vessel that's just broken orbit. I want you to pursue it."

Hajak nodded and barked some orders. Immediately the bridge crew set to work. Before the proconsul could take up a position in front of the viewscreen, its perspective changed—displaying an image of the departing transport.

The *Vengeance* was a good deal faster, Eragian assured himself. The human would not get away, despite everything.

"I want the pilot of that vessel taken alive," he warned

Hajak. "He owes me an explanation—and a great deal more."

"I understand perfectly," Hajak replied.

As usual, there was a note of confidence in his voice—an air of efficiency. At least someone in my employ knows what he's doing, the proconsul remarked inwardly.

As a youth, Eragian had hunted scavenger birds with a pet hawk. He recalled vividly the way the scavengers had fled their pursuers, seeming to tremble in midflight, as if they could foresee that their efforts would end in failure. And of course, they always did.

To the proconsul's eye, that was the way the transport ship looked now. Tremulous, afraid. Caught in the grip of increasing despair. The human had almost slipped their grasp—but in the end, he would fall well short.

"Target the transport's warp drive," Commander Hajak instructed calmly.

"Warp drive targeted," came the reply from his weapons officer. "Photon torpedoes ready."

"Fire," said the commander.

As Eragian watched the viewscreen, he saw the transport ship wracked by a barrage of photon torpedoes—all of them focused on the portion of the vessel where the warp drive was most vulnerable. He smiled as the transport dropped out of warp.

"Good work," he told Hajak.

The commander inclined his head. "Thank you, Your Eminence."

That's when the transport blew up, in a massive conflagration of matter-antimatter pyrotechnics. The shards of the vessel's hull went careening in all directions, including right at the viewscreen.

The proconsul realized that his mouth was hanging open. He shut it, then cast a glance over his shoulder at

Hajak. The commander had gone white as a mollusk shell on the shores of the Apnex Sea.

"I said I wanted him *alive,*" Eragian snarled.

Hajak shook his head disbelievingly. "I do not understand, Your Eminence. Those torpedoes should not have caused an explosion. They should have disabled the warp drive, nothing more."

"Then you miscalculated," Lennex concluded.

"No," said the commander firmly, whirling on the Tal Shiar. He turned back to the proconsul. "There was no miscalculation, Your Eminence. If the transport blew up, it was not our doing."

Eragian eyed the man, gauging his certainty. Hajak didn't flinch. Not an iota.

The proconsul turned again to the viewscreen, where the fragments of the transport vessel were still tumbling through space unhindered. Perhaps the commander was correct, he conceded.

Perhaps the human saw that he would be caught and interrogated, and escaped the only way he could—by destroying himself. It made as much sense as any other explanation.

But this wasn't over yet, Eragian resolved. It was not even *close* to being over. The human himself might have escaped, but his secret would be unearthed—even if he had to bring the full resources of the homeworld's information network to bear on the problem.

Clearly they knew what he looked like. They could create a composite image from witness accounts. And he'd shown up in a Starfleet uniform. That meant there was a good chance of their matching him with a Starfleet personnel file.

"Commander Hajak," Eragian intoned.

"Your Eminence?" responded the commander.

"Open a secure channel to the homeworld," the pro-consul instructed.

As Hajak moved to comply, Eragian took another look at the viewscreen and grunted. He would get to the bottom of this, he promised himself. And then he would find a way to turn that knowledge to his advantage.

CHAPTER 14

As McCoy got his old bones comfortable in the command center, he could feel Counselor Troi's scrutiny. Turning to his left, he saw that she wasn't exactly the picture of confidence. In fact, she looked a little green around the gills.

But then, she hadn't heard the admiral's conversation with Picard in the observation lounge. She'd had no reason to expect anyone but her captain to assume the center seat.

"You're surprised," McCoy noted.

The counselor nodded. "Yes, I am."

"Don't be," the admiral told her. "Captain Picard and I had a little disagreement, that's all. I'll be in charge around here until we've pried Spock loose from that den of vipers."

Tapping his communications badge—a gesture he'd never quite gotten used to—McCoy looked up at the intercom grid hidden in the ceiling. He tried to imagine the *Enterprise*'s crew looking back at him.

"This is Admiral McCoy," he intoned. "Until further notice, I will be replacing Captain Picard as commander of this vessel. I expect you to respond to my orders just as you would respond to his. That'll be all."

Troi didn't say anything in response—not at first, anyway. But that changed after a minute or so.

"Admiral McCoy," she said, "you are well within your rights to take over command of the *Enterprise*. However, I sense a certain . . . impatience on your part, which may be impairing your ability to think clearly."

McCoy grunted. "Little lady, I haven't thought clearly in a great many years. And what does Starfleet do?"

He let the question hang provokingly in the air. She shook her head, not sure how to respond to him.

He put his hand over hers in an effort to reassure her. Unfortunately, it didn't seem to have any immediate effect.

"I'll tell you what they do," he went on. "They refuse to let me retire. And then, to add insult to injury, they make a blasted admiral out of me." He smiled at her. "So if you're not pleased with my state of mind, take it up with them. They obviously know a lot more than they're telling either one of us."

The counselor shook her head. "Sir, this is not a joke. It's been a great many years—" Abruptly she stopped.

The admiral could feel his spine stiffen at the suggestion that his age was a hindrance to him. "Yes?" he prodded.

Troi frowned. "I didn't mean to offend you," he said. "But it *has* been a long time since you served on a starship. Captain Picard has been doing it almost every day for the last thirty years."

"These are people I'm all too familiar with," McCoy returned. "And they've got my friend, for God sake. I'll be drawn and quartered before I let someone like your captain—"

Worf cut him off before he could finish. "Admiral McCoy," he said, "I have obtained a communications link with Constanthus."

The admiral turned to the main viewscreen. It was showtime.

"Who are we dealing with here, Lieutenant?"

"You will be speaking with Governor Tharrus," Worf told him.

It gave McCoy a strange feeling to be conversing with a Klingon this way, on the bridge of a Federation starship. But times had changed, hadn't they? And he was proud to say he'd helped change them.

"Governor Tharrus it is, then," the admiral remarked. "Let 'er rip, Lieutenant."

A moment later, the governor's image filled the viewscreen. As far as McCoy could tell, Tharrus was a typical Romulan administrator—dignified, wary, and not half as smart as he thought he was.

"Greetings," said the admiral, sitting up as straight as he could in the captain's seat. "My name's McCoy. Leonard James McCoy."

The governor inclined his head ever so slightly. "Tharrus, governor of Constanthus. And the reason for your communication?"

The admiral grunted. Ol' Tharrus believed in getting right to the point, didn't he? Not unlike a certain Vulcan of his acquaintance.

"The reason I called," McCoy explained in his most deliberate back-country drawl, "is to see if we can't work

something out with regard to those raggedy unificationists you're sitting on."

The governor's eyes narrowed at the admiral's use of
the unfamiliar idiom. "Is it not customary to carry on
negotiations with the homeworld?"

"We tried that," McCoy admitted. He was reluctant to
get caught in a lie so early in the game. "Some proconsul
said he'd take some time and think about it. You know
what that means, don't you?"

Tharrus was too cautious to go into detail on an
unsecured channel. After all, McCoy reflected, the governor still didn't know where this conversation was headed.

"I have some idea," Tharrus answered.

The admiral told him anyway, for the sake of clarity.
"What it means," he remarked, "is it could take years to
resolve this mess." He smiled his most disarming smile.
"I'm no spring chicken, Governor. I don't have that much
time to see an end to this."

Tharrus looked at him. "Are you suggesting an alternative to negotiation with the homeworld?"

Now they were getting somewhere, thought McCoy. He
shrugged.

"You're the one who captured the rebels," he said. "It
makes sense to me you'd be the one to decide their fates."

The admiral leaned forward in a conspiratorial kind of
way. It was the way his father used to lean forward in Ed
Baxter's barber shop, back in Georgia, when he wanted to
get the attention of the other gentlemen waiting for their
haircuts. And invariably, he did.

"Governor," McCoy began, "what I'm saying is I'd like
to deal directly with you. I'd like to present you with . . .
let's call it an opportunity."

"An opportunity," Tharrus echoed flatly, without inflection.

"Just what I said. A chance for you to improve your position in the empire—without making martyrs out of the rebels." He paused. "You *do* want to improve your position, don't you?"

"Go on," said the governor.

"I'll do that," the admiral agreed. "Because, to tell you the truth, it would make *me* look good if I could get those unificationist folks out safely. It'd give me . . . oh, I don't know. Some kind of legacy, something for people to remember me by."

McCoy had never spouted such a load of hogwash in his life. But he knew his Romulans.

Tharrus might not be showing it, but he was drooling over the possibilities for material advancement—possibilities he probably hadn't thought of until the admiral pointed them out. As far as McCoy was concerned, he had the governor right where he wanted him.

"Here's what I'm proposing," the admiral continued. "Essentially it's the same thing we offered the proconsul—except he's got nothing to gain by it."

He described the offer Picard had tendered Eragian. However, in this version of the transaction, Tharrus would get credit for extracting the empire from its pickle. And Eragian, by contrast, would be made to look like a fool.

The idea seemed to please the governor. McCoy actually saw a smile pull at the corners of his mouth, which was more than he'd hoped for.

"So what do you say?" asked the admiral. "Have we got a deal?"

Tharrus thought about it. "I will consider it," he responded at last, "and return your communication when I have an answer for you."

"Fair enough," said McCoy. "Just don't take too long,

now. I mean, it'd be a shame if the proconsul surprised us all and acted on our offer."

The governor's smile became more pronounced. "I assure you," he replied, "I will not waste any time in this matter."

And with that, his image vanished from the viewscreen, to be replaced by the starfield that had preceded it. An abrupt departure, McCoy mused. But then, the Romulans had never been sticklers for good manners.

Turning in his seat, he noticed that Counselor Troi was looking at him again. She didn't look any less concerned than she was before.

The admiral chuckled. "Don't have a canary, Counselor." He leaned his head closer to hers. "Y'see," he said, "when it comes to Romulans, the direct approach is usually the best approach. Appeal to a Romulan's baser instincts and you can't go wrong."

"Sir," she replied, "that is not—"

McCoy held his hand up for silence. "Trust me on this," he insisted.

But far from giving him her trust, Troi got up and left the command center. He watched her circumnavigate the tactical station and approach the turbolift, then enter it as the doors parted.

When they closed, the admiral stopped watching and returned his attention to the viewscreen. But he could feel the tension the counselor had left in her wake. The chill, for lack of a better word.

What's more, the admiral understood the feeling. To Troi and the other bridge officers, he was an intruder. An invader. An unknown quantity, to whom they felt no particular loyalty.

But that was their problem. They'd have to deal with it, or find themselves replaced as their captain had been.

After all, this wasn't a blasted cadet training mission. As Picard himself had pointed out, people's lives depended on what they did here. And McCoy wasn't going to let anyone deter him from doing what he had to do.

An admiral? Tharrus wondered.

Did the humans care that much about the fate of a few Romulan traitors? Enough to involve such a high-ranking officer in the negotiations?

Apparently so. The question was *why*.

Tharrus had never had any direct experience with the Federation before, but he had studied it via public records. And the one thing he'd learned was that it hated to involve itself in the affairs of others—a function of basic cowardice, no doubt.

Yet this admiral was going to great lengths to insert himself into a Romulan matter. It could mean only one thing. The Federation had more at stake in this than it wished to let on.

Hitting the comm panel in front of him, the governor sent for Phabaris. When the security officer entered the room, Tharrus turned to him.

"Research the personal history of Admiral Leonard James McCoy," he instructed. "Search every data bank in the Empire, but find out why he is so concerned about the fate of our prisoners. I want an answer, you understand?"

Phabaris nodded. "Yes, Governor. I will see to it immediately."

A moment later, the security officer was gone. Tharrus leaned back in his chair.

Before the conversation with the human, Tharrus had known that the rebels were valuable. But now he had the distinct feeling they were even more valuable than he had imagined.

Riker placed his hand on Data's shoulder. The android turned to look up at him, a question on his face.

"Yes, sir?" he asked.

The first officer smiled. "My shift," he explained.

Data's brow creased. He looked puzzled.

"I do not believe so, Commander. Unless there is something wrong with my internal chronometer—an unlikely circumstance, as you are no doubt aware—your shift begins in slightly more than seven minutes."

"True," Riker conceded. After all, the android was never wrong when it came to things like that. "At least, that was the plan. But I'm exercising my right to *change* the plan."

"In other words," muttered Geordi, from a reclining position further back in the shuttle, "Commander Riker wants to be the one at the helm when we go in for the rescue attempt."

"Ah," said Data. "In that case, the helm is all yours, sir." Making sure the shuttle was on course, he abdicated the seat he'd been occupying and moved into the one next to it.

"You were supposed to be sleeping," the first officer reminded Geordi as he swung into the pilot's position.

The engineer grunted. "You were supposed to wake me when we came within a million kilometers of the outpost."

"Which we have yet to do for another several seconds," Riker countered. "Now, if you're done being insubordinate, Mister La Forge, I think you should take this opportunity to wake up. Our objective is almost in sight."

The first officer took a breath and concentrated, focusing all his attention on his controls. So far, everything looked pretty much as he'd expected—at least to the long-range sensors.

Riker glanced at the android beside him. Data could easily have handled this fly-by, of course. After all, he had the top pilot's rating in Starfleet. So did Geordi, for that matter.

But the first officer was better than both of them. And if anything unexpected reared its ugly head, Riker wanted to have his most skilled personnel on the job. Namely, himself.

"I'm taking her down to three-quarters impulse speed," he announced. "Mister La Forge, if you'll be so kind as to man the transporter . . ."

"I'd be glad to," came the reply.

Glancing over his shoulder for just a moment, the first officer watched Geordi move to the shuttle's compact, two-person transporter unit. Then he turned back to his own controls.

Riker listened for the engineer's report. It wasn't long in coming.

"Ready, sir," Geordi told him.

"Acknowledged," said the first officer.

Their strategy was a simple one. They would pass by the outpost where Captain Scott was imprisoned—for it couldn't be anything more than an outpost out here, so far from the Romulan homeworld—and beam him up.

Then they would take off again. If all went well, they would be heading for the Neutral Zone before Scott's captors had any notion he was gone.

"Approaching the outpost," Data remarked. "Sensors show an orbiting vessel that could be the *Yorktown*. This would seem to confirm our conclusion that Captain Scott is being held by the outpost's—"

He stopped in midsentence. Riker knew from experience that that was not a good sign.

Turning to the android, he asked, "What is it, Data?"

Still intent on his monitor panel, the android frowned ever so slightly. "Commander, there is also a Romulan warbird in orbit around the planetoid on which the outpost is situated."

The first officer cursed beneath his breath. A *warbird*. No doubt the homeworld's response to the incursion of a Starfleet vessel into Romulan space.

Its presence would complicate matters somewhat. Still there was a chance.

"Have they spotted us yet?" he asked Data.

The android checked his instruments. "I do not believe so, sir."

"Must be operating on passive sensors only," Geordi contributed.

"However," Data went on, "even if that is the case, they will detect us in no more than four and a half minutes. I base that estimate on Starfleet assessments of Romulan sensor capacities."

Riker nodded. "I see." He bit his lip. "Data, can you tell me where the warbird's positioned with regard to the outpost?"

"Yes," the android informed him.

Again it took him a second or two to assimilate the information on his monitors. That wasn't nearly as long as it would have taken a human to do the same job.

"The warbird appears to be on the opposite side of the planetoid from the ground installation," Data reported. "From our angle of approach, it is located just over the northern horizon."

"Good," said the first officer. "Then with a relatively small adjustment, we can place the planetoid between us and the warbird—and still have line-of-sight access to the installation."

Data looked at him. "That is correct, sir."

"In other words," Geordi interjected, "if we're careful, we may be able to use the planetoid itself for cover, and get close to the outpost without the warbird's knowing about it."

Riker turned in his chair. "Exactly," he confirmed.

"But getting in is only *half* the problem," the engineer pointed out. "Even if we can do that—and sneak Scott out—they're eventually going to realize he's gone. And when they do, they'll have a warbird to sic on us."

"And a shuttle can't outrun a warbird," the first officer conceded.

"Not as far as I can tell," Geordi agreed.

Riker eyed him. "In that case, we'll have to find another way to elude it. Or hope that one presents itself."

"Then we will proceed with the rescue attempt?" the android inquired.

"We will indeed," the first officer assured him.

Neither Data nor the engineer gave Riker an argument. Despite their apparent misgivings, they wanted to retrieve Captain Scott as much as he did. Otherwise, they wouldn't be here.

Riker made the course adjustment. It took them out of their way and delayed their arrival at the planetoid, but it was necessary if they were going to keep the warbird in the dark.

Then they made their way through the planetoid's star system. By the time they'd crept within forty thousand kilometers, the maximum rated range of the transporter unit, the first officer could see the planetoid through the observation port in front of him.

It was a dead gray rock, devoid of even an atmosphere.

The place was basically featureless, except for the Romulan installation that clung to it like some kind of artificial octopus.

"There it is," said Riker. "Fortunately, a place that old isn't likely to have the sensor capacity to detect us at this range—even if we were expected. Scan it for human life signs, Data."

The android complied. Unfortunately, it seemed, they'd hit another snag.

"What now?" asked the first officer.

"There appears to be some sort of magnetic shield around the central portion of the installation," Data told him. "No doubt, a measure designed to prevent just the sort of rescue attempt we had in mind."

"You can say that again," Geordi chimed in, from the rear of the shuttle. He shook his head. "Of course, we've still got a card to play. We can use the remote control bands to beam down and penetrate the shield on foot— since the outer limits of the place are unshielded."

Riker nodded. "That's what we'll do, then."

Fixing the controls on autopilot, he got up from his pilot's seat and headed for the compartment where the phaser pistols were stored. Touching his hand to the padd beside the compartment door, he opened it.

There were four racks full of phasers inside, a dozen in all. They would only need three of them. Taking one out, he handed it to his chief engineer.

"This limb we're out on is getting narrower and narrower," Geordi remarked. "Pretty soon, there won't be enough left of it to support a decent leaf."

"Could be worse," the first officer observed as he offered Data another of the phasers. The android, who had also gotten up from his seat, accepted it dutifully.

178

"How do you figure that?" asked the engineer, responding to Riker's comment.

"We may have underestimated the sensor range on that warbird." The first officer made sure the weapon was set for a nonlethal intensity. "In that case, there'd be no limb left at all."

CHAPTER 15

Alone in his quarters, Picard stared out the observation port at a vista of Romulan stars. Somewhere out there, across the imaginary border of the Neutral Zone, three of his people were risking their lives to rescue one of the most inspirational figures in the history of the Federation.

Captain Scott was more than just a brilliant engineer, of course. He was a member of a legendary crew that symbolized all that was good about the Federation, a standard for others to aspire to.

But men like Riker, Geordi, and Data had value as well. He would hate to think he had simply thrown them away in the pursuit of a hopeless cause.

The captain felt his jaw clench. If their mission had been fraught with danger before, it was now doubly so. He had an awful feeling they would all come to regret Admiral McCoy's actions.

And there was nothing he could do about it. Nothing at

all, except monitor communications through his personal terminal and hope for the best.

He cursed beneath his breath. If there was some way he could contribute—some way he could help steer them all to safety, despite the admiral's ill-advised machinations.

But how?

Abruptly, a series of chimes insinuated themselves into his consciousness. There was someone at the door, Picard realized.

Turning toward it, he said, "Come."

A moment later, the door slid aside and revealed the muscular physique of his Klingon tactical officer. Worf peered at the captain from under the bony protrusion of his brow ridge.

"Sir? I have accumulated additional data on Romulan ship deployments."

The gleam in the Klingon's eyes told Picard there was something particularly interesting about the information Worf had gathered. It was gratifying to him that Worf had come to him with the news, rather than to McCoy.

However, he was no longer in command. "Have you apprised the admiral of this information?" the captain asked.

Worf grunted. "I told him that I had it. However, he did not seem very interested. I was advised to . . ." He frowned. ". . . *File* it."

Picard nodded. "In that case, Lieutenant, have a seat."

The Klingon moved to a chair on the other side of the room. Momentarily putting aside his concern for Riker and the others, the captain gave Worf his undivided attention.

"Apparently," the tactical officer began, "the sector of space to which the Romulan ships have been sent is bounded by the border opposite the Neutral Zone. They share this border with a race called the Stugg."

Picard grunted. "The same Stugg who cut off relations with the Federation recently, for no apparent reason?"

"It would appear so," Worf replied. "A formidable people, according to all records of our dealings with them. However, they have never succeeded in unifying themselves sufficiently to pose a threat."

"Either to the Federation or anyone else," the captain added. "So why would the Romulans have committed so many of their vessels to Stugg space?"

The Klingon scowled. It was obvious that he hated the idea of admitting his ignorance—but he had no choice.

"I do not know," he said finally. "But I would *like* to."

Picard nodded. "Continue to keep an eye on the situation, Mister Worf. Perhaps the Romulans—or even the Stugg—will do something that will illuminate their motives for us."

The tactical officer inclined his massive head. "Aye, sir." And without further ado he rose and made his exit.

The captain watched the door slide closed behind Worf, then turned again toward the view through his observation port. Like Worf, he wished he knew more about what was going on out there.

But as always, the stars weren't about to make his job any easier for him. Again, he cursed—this time, out loud.

As long as the *Enterprise* was someone else's to command, he could only watch—and wait.

Riker looked around at his new surroundings. A moment ago, he'd been standing on the shuttle, waiting for Geordi to complete the transporter protocols. Now he was in the middle of a narrow, eerily lit corridor, somewhere in an outer arm of the sprawling Romulan installation.

Data was right beside him. Like the first officer, he held his phaser in his right hand and his tricorder in his left. Each of them wore a remote transporter control band as well. Together, they scanned for approaching Romulans.

There weren't any. At least not within a hundred meters or so.

Under normal circumstances, even an antiquated sensor array would have picked up their transport to the surface. However, Geordi had managed to locate a blind spot in the system.

As luck would have it, it allowed them to beam down just outside the magnetic shield. But then, if they were *really* lucky, there wouldn't have been any shield to begin with—or any warbird, for that matter.

A moment later, Geordi materialized as well, equipped as they were. He looked at them meaningfully.

"Anything?" he whispered.

"Nothing so far," Riker told him, sotto voce.

He gazed at the stretch of corridor that led toward the center of the installation—where they would undoubtedly find Captain Scott. After all, it wouldn't have made any sense to erect a shield around part of the outpost and then hold him somewhere else.

It would have been easier if they could have pinpointed Scott's location here. However, the magnetic shield confounded the short-range sensors as thoroughly as it did the transporter function.

"Come on," the first officer breathed.

He led. The others followed, exhibiting a wariness he found comforting. With Data and Geordi to watch his back, Riker knew he could concentrate on what was up ahead.

They passed through the shield without incident. In the back of his mind, the first officer had wondered if it might not serve as some kind of internal security net, in addition to its other functions. Apparently, that wasn't the case.

For several long, tense minutes, they continued their progress along one corridor after the next, deftly approaching the center of the place by the most obscure route possible. Then their tricorders picked up a couple of Romulans cutting across their path.

Retreating to the closest intersection, they concealed themselves until the Romulans had come and gone, their steps echoing resoundingly. Noting on his tricorder that the pair was no longer a threat to them, Riker gave the signal to resume their journey.

A short time later, they entered what looked like a detention area—though the cells they could see were quite empty. However, Scotty couldn't be far now.

The first officer checked his tricorder for human life signs. Strangely, he couldn't find any. He shook his head. How could that be?

Looking up, he saw that Geordi and Data were just as puzzled as he was. Could they have missed something? Where in blazes was Captain Scott?

Suddenly, the android's head snapped about. Taking his cue from Data, Riker made a sign for quiet.

The android gestured to indicate something up ahead of them. Most likely, the first officer thought, another couple of guards passing by. He listened intently, but didn't hear anything.

He was just about to ask Data what he'd detected when the android's head snapped around again—this time in the opposite direction. Then it happened a third time. And a fourth, in quick succession.

By then, Riker could feel the blood pumping in his neck. There was something going on, and he didn't like it. Taking the initiative, he brushed past his companions and stuck his head out into the corridor.

The next thing he knew, there was a blinding flash of bluish energy—a flash that might have caught him square between the eyes if Data hadn't hauled him back out of harm's way. As it was, the beam glanced off the wall behind him and filled their hiding place with azure light.

The first officer swallowed. "Thanks," he whispered.

"You are welcome," the android whispered back.

"We're surrounded," Geordi observed. "Aren't we?"

"Yes," Data told him. "All avenues of egress are blocked."

The engineer turned to Riker. "Your call, Commander."

The first officer sighed. If the Romulans were onto them, there wasn't a large chance of their getting away.

On the other hand, the idea of being taken prisoner wasn't much to his liking—especially after what he'd heard about the way these people treated unwanted guests. Riker tightened his grip on his phaser.

"Follow me," he rasped.

Diving out into the corridor, he rolled as he hit the floor and came up firing. He stayed in one place just long enough to see one of the Romulans fall, then rolled back in the other direction and tried it again.

Of course, he had some help at that point. He didn't have to look back to know that Data and Geordi were right behind him, giving the Romulans all they could handle. Energy beams lanced past him in both directions.

Somehow, none of it managed to hit him. And in a

matter of seconds, their adversaries were lying stunned at the end of the corridor.

Unfortunately, that wasn't the way they wanted to go, seeing as how it led deeper into the installation. But as his father had told him more than once, beggars couldn't be choosers.

"This way," he said, beckoning to the others—and headed in the direction of the fallen Romulans. Maybe they'd get out of this yet.

Then he heard the sound of footfalls behind them. Glancing over his shoulder, he saw that another pack of pursuers had caught up with them. Cursing, he turned to fire back at them.

This time, he wasn't so lucky. A dark blue beam caught him in the shoulder and spun him around. A second one swept his leg out from under him. The last thing he remembered was twisting awkwardly in the air and wondering how much it would hurt when he finally landed.

Beverly Crusher had seen people storm into her office in sickbay before, usually out of anxiety over one of her patients. But Reg Barclay had never been one of them.

The tall, thin engineer was normally the timid type. Crusher had seen him mope around for days rather than pose a question about some trivial matter that was nagging at him. But not this time.

Either his personality had done a one-eighty, or what he had on his mind wasn't trivial.

"Doctor?" blurted Barclay. "Is it true?"

Crusher studied him from behind her desk, but couldn't find a clue as to what he was talking about. "Is *what* true, Reg?"

"Is it true that we're leaving for Romulus?" he asked.

The doctor couldn't help smile. "I doubt it," she told him. "I'm sure someone would have let me know about something like that."

The lieutenant looked as if he desperately wanted to believe her. "Are you sure?" he pressed.

Crusher nodded. "Pretty sure."

Barclay heaved a sigh. "That's a relief," he told her. "I guess Nevins didn't know what she was talking about."

"Nevins?" the doctor echoed. "In security?"

The engineer nodded. "There's a lot of talk in security these days. Come to think of it, in engineering, too. Lots of . . . er, rumors flying around."

Crusher sighed. "About Admiral McCoy, you mean."

Barclay looked apologetic. "Uh-huh. People say he's . . . well, reckless. That he's treating the mission as if it were a game. And it's scaring people—a lot, in some cases."

The doctor leaned back in her chair. Reg was right. She'd heard the whispers every time she negotiated a corridor.

People were afraid, all right. Afraid and confused.

"I guess they don't know what to expect of him," Barclay continued. "They don't know what he'll do next."

Crusher grunted. "And he's probably older than anyone they've ever known. That scares them, too, I'm sure."

The engineer regarded her honestly. "I'll tell you what, Doctor—it scares *me.*" He paused. "If you ask me, I'd rather have the captain back."

Crusher looked up at him. "I understand, Reg. Believe me, I do."

After all, she'd been to Picard's quarters twice already, to see if she couldn't lighten the load of his exile. Unfortunately, it hadn't helped much.

"Well," Barclay said, "I'll see you. And thanks."

The doctor shrugged. "Any time," she replied.

As she watched him go, she shook her head. She felt much the same way the engineer did, but she couldn't show it. As an officer on the *Enterprise,* she couldn't go around undermining its commander—no matter who it was.

On the other hand, she *could* judge him incompetent to run the ship. That was her prerogative as chief medical officer.

But she couldn't do it—wouldn't do it—unless he really was incompetent. And as far as Crusher was concerned, that wasn't a matter of age or appearances.

Probably, she thought, McCoy wasn't as sharp as he used to be. On occasion, he allowed his emotions to get the better of him. And he didn't think twice about diverging from procedure—or even specific orders.

However, that was true of a great many officers. Whether she liked it or not, it wasn't grounds for declaring the admiral unfit.

For all his aberrations, all his idiosyncracies, she couldn't say for certain he didn't know what he was doing. Of course, when all the results were in, she knew her opinion might change.

But by then, she told herself, it might well be too late.

Eragian regarded the three Starfleet officers crumpled on the floor of the corridor, surrounded by a dozen or more guards. One of the intruders was clearly human. The other two, he wasn't so sure about.

After all, one had a mechanism that halfway encircled his head—some kind of prosthetic device which the proconsul had never seen before. And the third one seemed too pallid to be a human.

"And they were trying to free the other prisoner?" Lennex asked. "The one who took his own life just a little while ago?"

Commander Barnak nodded. "That is what we have come to believe. We can think of no other reason for their being here."

"Indeed," muttered Eragian. "And this one," he said, pointing to the being with the yellowish skin. "Have you been able to identify his origin?"

Barnak shook his head. "We have not, Your Eminence. However, he exhibited incredible resistance to our disruptor beams." He knelt beside the being, then turned the being's head to one side, exposing the back of his neck. "And we saw *this* when we examined him."

Eragian's mouth went dry. The guard was pointing to what looked like circuitry, exposed by a beam impact.

He grunted, covering up his surprise. People in his station weren't supposed to be surprised—not by anything.

"How interesting," Lennex replied, seemingly unflustered. "And the one in the facial appliance?"

"We have not yet determined the reason for the device," Barnak told him. "Of course, given its placement, it would seem to enhance one's visual acuity."

"Perhaps," the proconsul conceded. "In any case, we'll find out soon enough, won't we? Bring them all to the nearest cell. I'll want to interrogate them at my leisure."

The base commander inclined his head. "As you wish, Your Eminence."

"And, Barnak . . ." said Eragian.

The Romulan looked at him. "Yes, Proconsul?"

Eragian eyed him. "Don't let this one slip away as the last one did—if you value your life even a little bit."

The base commander swallowed. "I will double the

189

watch," he promised, then gestured to his waiting subordinates.

Immediately, Barnak's men bent to the task of lifting and transporting the prisoners. As he looked on, Eragian crossed his arms over his chest and considered what their presence here meant.

First, it confirmed that his original prisoner was not the mentally unstable buffoon he'd appeared to be. Second, it indicated that the first prisoner hadn't blundered his way here after all—but rather that his mission had been a premeditated and purposeful one.

And third, it told the proconsul that both the prisoner and his mission were important to Starfleet—or they wouldn't have sent a team here in an attempt to retrieve him.

Lennex stood beside him, saying nothing. But he was obviously thinking the same things.

Eragian was more eager than ever to identify the mysterious individual who had destroyed himself trying to escape from the outpost—and to determine why the man had crossed the Neutral Zone in the first place.

Of course, with this new group of prisoners in hand, he was that much closer to finding out.

CHAPTER 16

"Above all," Spock said, "the universe is ordered by logic, in both the realm of normal space that we inhabit and the other dimensions we have observed. Even in the chaos of quantum and subspace mechanics, we can see the elegant symmetry of the universe."

Almost all of his surviving followers were present for the morning lesson. The Vulcan had initially taken that as a good sign.

But before long, he had seen how dispirited they were. The survivors of the failed escape attempt had been welcomed back into the body of students, but it was difficult for them to conceal their emotions.

They felt grief. Despair. And apprehension about their all-too-brief future. And those feelings were clearly shared by the students who had not participated in the attempt.

Unfortunately Spock had no wisdom to offer that

would change their prospects, or allow them to forget what had taken place. He conceded finally that these Romulans were Romulans, and not Vulcans. No amount of education about the Vulcan way would change that— even if they were to live many years instead of the single day left to them.

Yet they were here now, and looking to him for a palliative that would relieve them of the pain they were in. And as their teacher, he would do his best to ease their passage.

"Surak tells us to find order in chaos," he explained, "so that we may better understand the nature of all that is. When asked about the possibility of life after death—a realm most often left to less practical philosophers— Surak said, 'It would be illogical for the universe to create complex, reasoning beings only to dispose of their minds when their bodies no longer functioned.'"

That principle was the basis of the Vulcan practice of preserving the Katra—the sentient soul of the dying—in the Hall of Thought. Unfortunately, none of his students would have their minds saved in such a way.

Few of them had mastered the required mental techniques for the transfer of the Katra to a living being. And even if all of them had the skills, there would be no one to whom they might transfer their Katras.

Still, Spock knew that the universe was logical, and trusted that the natural order was not wasteful. That granted him the ability to accept what would come.

Of course, as he had noted before, his students did not have the advantage of his experiences. He could see them mentally wrestling with the same questions in their minds.

As he pondered this, the Teacher could see his students turn to look past his shoulder at something behind him.

Glancing in the same direction, he saw what they were looking at—a large body of soldiers entering the compound.

The appearance of the soldiers during the morning lesson was unforeseen, but not a surprise to the Vulcan. The failed escape attempt was clearly going to have consequences that affected all of them. He guessed that their fate was simply coming a day earlier than expected.

In some ways, Spock thought, it was best this way. Life was always preferable to death, but he had seen that some of his students preferred death to continued captivity.

The soldiers stopped a good twenty meters short of the Vulcan and his students. But not all of them. Spock saw a single soldier separate himself from the larger group and approach the prisoners alone.

"It's him," said one of the unificationists, hard-pressed not to show her anger.

"Where does he find the gall," asked another, "after what he did to us?"

D'tan muttered a curse. "I should have *known*. He always had a stench about him."

Like his students, the Vulcan recognized the soldier. After all, he had been one of their own, at least on the surface. Underneath, he had been Governor Tharrus's informer.

Aside from the uniform, Skrasis looked no different from when Spock had seen him earlier that morning. His face was expressionless—more so, ironically, than when he posed as the Vulcan's student.

Spock could hear the angry murmurs behind him building to a crescendo. Unchecked, his students might fling themselves on the infiltrator and extract their revenge. Or at least *try* to.

"Do not act," the Teacher ordered without turning

around. Though the murmurs did not cease, he was confident that his charges would not disobey him.

Skrasis had to maneuver through the small crowd of students to speak with the Vulcan. "May I have a word?" he asked. "In private?"

Spock shrugged. "If you wish."

He walked in the direction of the prisoners' quarters. Several of his students trailed them, fearing that Skrasis would inflict some harm on their mentor. D'tan was among them.

But once they were within the entrance to the cell area, the Vulcan waved them away. "It is all right," he assured them. "Skrasis has no intention of harming me."

D'tan started to protest, but was silenced by a look from Spock. Reluctantly he and the others waited there as the Vulcan and the infiltrator proceeded to Spock's room.

Sitting, the Teacher invited Skrasis to do the same. The Romulan sat.

"I . . . I wish to explain," the youth declared.

"No explanation is necessary," said Spock. "I have known of your affiliation with our captors for some time."

Skrasis's face betrayed his surprise. "How is that possible? If the others had known, surely they would have killed me."

"I told no one," the Teacher informed him. "Your death would have served no logical purpose."

Skrasis's brow creased. "I do not understand. You allowed me to continue as your student. Why?"

Spock had thought it was obvious. "You *were* my student. The bond—"

The Romulan interrupted. "Surely, the bond does not apply when the Teacher knows that the student is betraying him."

194

The Vulcan looked at him. "Did you wish to learn what I had to teach?"

Skrasis was silent for a moment. Then he nodded. "Yes, I wished to learn."

"Then my duty was clear," Spock remarked. "And there is another, logical reason that you do not see."

Skrasis considered the Vulcan, his eyes full of pain and confusion. "It seems there is much I do not see."

Spock sighed. "You were the only one of my students I knew would survive."

The infiltrator was stunned by this simple statement. The Vulcan could see the pain on his face.

"But you allowed me to report the escape attempt," Skrasis pointed out.

Spock nodded. "A serious oversight on my part. I assumed the security procedure instituted by Belan would be enough to prevent that. Since you were with me or one of your fellow students at all times, I did not think you would be able to signal your superiors. However, you obviously had sufficient technical means to do so, even while being observed."

A green tinge crept into the Romulan's face, his shame threatening his composure. "A subdermal transmitter. It allowed me to—"

"I do not need to know," the Teacher assured him. "Obviously your equipment was very effective."

"They never would have gotten outside the compound," Skrasis insisted.

"I have no doubt of it," Spock replied.

Silence hung over both of them for a moment. Whatever the infiltrator had to say, it was not coming easily.

"Why did you come to me?" the Vulcan asked. "Your presence here puts you in considerable personal danger."

The young Romulan had regained his control. "I

195

wished to explain my situation to you," he responded. "I wished you to understand that I harbor neither you nor your students any ill will. If it were my decision to make, I would not convict you of any crime at all."

Skrasis didn't bother to lower his voice, though his words were near treason.

"I wanted to thank you for your instruction," he went on, "and to express my regrets about your future. And I wanted you to understand that I take no pleasure in my task. I simply do my duty."

"As do we all," Spock reminded him. "Live long and prosper," he added, raising his hand in the customary salute.

Skrasis didn't return it. He simply nodded, got up, and left the room.

But the other students were still outside, in the vicinity of the entrance. And judging from the sounds that followed, they were not eager to let the infiltrator escape.

The Vulcan had anticipated this. Rising, he went to intervene on Skrasis's behalf. When he got there, his students looked to him, regretting his presence.

"You must let him pass," Spock said, softly but firmly.

Biting their lips, the unificationists stepped aside to let Skrasis go by. The infiltrator continued past them, out into the courtyard and then toward the command center.

Only when he was gone did the soldiers approach the prisoners and set about the task of herding them together. The Vulcan noted that they were at last going to meet their fate—and the uncompromising hand of Romulan justice.

Proconsul Eragian, with Lennex and several officers from the *Vengeance* in tow, negotiated a corridor on his way to the Federation prisoners' cell. He might have opted to interrogate them sooner, of course, but one of the cardinal rules of interrogation was to allow a prisoner time beforehand.

Time to contemplate the nature of his interrogator. Time to imagine what shape the questioning would take. And most important, time to grow fearful.

As a youth, the proconsul had heard a story about a master interrogator known for the subtlety of his work. On one occasion, the man so carefully manipulated the timing and circumstances of his appearance in his alien subject's cell, the alien broke down—and provided all the requisite information—before the interrogator could pose a single question.

Eragian smiled to himself. Certainly, whether or not the story was apocryphal, it was a standard to which one might aspire.

Nor had Lennex objected to it. That implied his approval.

Abruptly, he heard the bleating of his communications device. Stopping, he took it out and activated it.

"This is the proconsul," he snapped. "Speak."

"Your Eminence," said the voice on the other end, "this is Commander Hajak. We've received a message from the homeworld." A pause. "I believe this is the one you were waiting for."

The Tal Shiar shot him a meaningful glance.

Eragian frowned. "Relay it to the terminal in the outpost commander's office. We'll view it there. And, Hajak?"

"Yes, Your Eminence?" came the reply.

"Maintain security protocols," the proconsul advised. "I do not wish any of this message to become common knowledge."

"I understand," the commander of the *Vengeance* assured him. "Hajak out."

It didn't take long for Eragian and Lennex to make their way to the office of the outpost commander, or to close the door so they could be alone. And it took even less time for Eragian to activate the terminal.

Then it was just a matter of accessing the message, which had already been downloaded from the *Vengeance*. Actually, the proconsul mused, it wasn't really a message at all, but a packet of information.

On one side of the monitor screen, there was an image of the prisoner—the first one, who had perished in the explosion of the transport ship. On the other side, there was a block of data. Eragian leaned forward in his chair, to read the small-faced characters.

"Interesting," he commented, "after just a few moments. Very interesting indeed."

His instinct to check the homeworld data banks had been on the mark. There was a file on the human as long as his arm, and then some.

The man's name was Scott. Montgomery Scott. Born—

The proconsul blinked, then leaned closer to the screen. "That date must be incorrect," he said.

"It is correct," the Tal Shiar insisted. "The central data banks do not contain mistakes."

Eragian shook his head. "But, if this is the same Montgomery Scott—and the records show no other—"

Lennex finished the thought for him. "He would have to be one hundred and fifty years old, as the Federation counts time."

For a Vulcanoid, 150 was merely middle age. But for a human . . .

He pored over the data a second time, and a third—

just to make sure his eyes weren't deceiving him. They weren't.

Scott had served on an earlier version of the *Enterprise* under James Kirk, right around the end of the first period of Romulan isolationism.

The proconsul grunted. "Barring a temporal incident, it seems almost impossible that it's the same man. He would have been too elderly to participate in such an escapade. Too frail."

"And yet," said Lennex, "it makes sense in a way, does it not? The Montgomery Scott in the file was an engineer of considerable acumen. And the prisoner would have to have been in command of such expertise.

"Otherwise, he could not have set up a call for help in the form of an engine pulse, or taken charge of the transport that eventually proved his undoing. Perhaps we should *not* rule out a temporal incident."

Eragian scowled. Too bad the human had decided to take his own life, or the Romulan would have gotten to the bottom of this mystery a long time ago. The proconsul fairly licked his lips at the thought of interrogating such a—

Wait, he thought, the color draining from his face. *The Enterprise.*

Excited, Eragian stored the Scott file and called up another—a detailed report on the *Enterprise* of a hundred years earlier. Scrolling quickly, he found the personnel section, which described those crew members for whom biographical information was available.

Using his finger, he went down the list until he came to the name of the vessel's first officer. *There.*

Slowly, a smile spread across Eragian's face as the pieces fell into place one by one.

"How interesting," he muttered.

"Indeed," Lennex agreed. "It seems Montgomery Scott served alongside the reputed leader of the unificationist movement on Romulus—the Vulcan named *Spock.*"

Eragian nodded. "And is it not a strange coincidence that Montgomery Scott should appear in this sector of the Empire just now—when a contingent of the rebels has been captured on Constanthus? A *very* strange coincidence . . ."

"Unless the Vulcan was one of those who were captured," the Tal Shiar suggested. "Which would mean Spock has been in our hands all along."

The proconsul's smile broadened as he pondered the possibilities. . . .

And then instantly faded. After all, it wasn't the forces of the homeworld who had discovered Spock. It was *Tharrus.*

Eragian's teeth ground together. "I wonder if our friend the governor knows what a valuable prize is in his possession? Or is there still time to wrest the Vulcan from him, before he can use his prisoner as leverage?"

"To gain himself even more power than you anticipated," Lennex remarked.

"Yes," said the proconsul. Storing the computer information, he deactivated the monitor and rose from his chair. As he headed for the door, the Tal Shiar trailing in his wake, he realized he would need to obtain additional ships.

His overriding concern was to obtain Spock before Tharrus could make a hero of himself—and that might require some heavy firepower. Or at least the threat of it.

CHAPTER 17

Apparently the place where the unificationists would be judged was located in the command center.

On the way there, Spock watched as his students— D'tan included—formed an informal honor guard around him. The formation was a Romulan tradition that went back to the pre-reformation days on Vulcan.

Nonetheless, the Teacher sensed the gesture was important to his students, so he allowed it. Only a short time earlier, Spock would have been troubled by the use of such a symbol—one that had its roots in the aggressive, passionate behavior Vulcans had left behind thousands of years ago.

Now he was less concerned with making distinctions between what was Vulcan and what was Romulan.

As they entered an enclosed amphitheater, the Teacher winced at the brightness of the sun, its light filtering through a high, narrow window. The seats that rose all around them were filled with Constantharine citizens. Spock placed the number of spectators at a thousand, conservatively.

Directly in front of the unificationists, a triangular wooden structure formed a stage jutting out from the spectators' seats and into the open area. On a raised position at the rear of the structure sat Governor Tharrus, surrounded by two dozen formally garbed Romulans.

The Vulcan recognized these as government and military officials. He noted with interest that the configuration created by Tharrus and his tribunal strongly resembled the honor guard that his students had made—and abandoned inside the arena, so as not to reveal Spock's position as their teacher.

At the bottom of the tribunal, among the soldiers standing guard, the Vulcan could clearly see his former student, Skrasis—though the young Romulan did not meet his teacher's eyes.

Excellent control, Spock thought. He regretted that he would not have a chance to commend him for it.

Once the unificationists were all present in the amphitheater's central pit, Tharrus stood up behind his judicial desk, regarded the tribunal assembled below him, and then turned to the students of Surak.

"We are here to carry out the justice of the Romulan Empire," he said, his voice echoing throughout the arena. And beyond, the Vulcan mused, since the cameras posted at intervals suggested the event was being broadcast over subspace channels.

"In these proceedings," the governor went on, "we address a horrific threat to the Empire we all serve. We will look into the faces that would destroy all we have achieved as a people. And having judged them, we will devise their punishment—in the process, reaffirming the glory and might of the Empire."

The crowd roared its approval. Pausing to let the applause die down, Tharrus considered Surak's followers with a scornful eye.

"Thousands of years ago," he said, "the seeds of the Romulan Empire were grown on the planet Vulcan, among a powerful race of conquerors. However, on the eve of their greatness, before the mightiest on that world could unite it in a common purpose, a plague was visited on Vulcan. A philosophy of weakness overcame the population.

"The strong on Vulcan were faced with a choice—rule over a race of passive and cowardly people, or strike out into the reaches of space and found an Empire, before which the entire galaxy would one day shudder. This became *our* Empire."

Pointing to the unificationists, the governor raised his voice a notch louder. "These traitors who stand before you would destroy that strength. They study the teachings of the very weaklings on whom the Empire turned its back. They seek to spread that philosophy among us, and reunite the Empire with Vulcan under a tyranny of cowardice."

Tharrus lowered both his accusing finger and his voice, forcing the crowd to listen carefully to his next words. "But this traitorous plot ends here, and it ends today. Our operatives have apprehended the traitors you see before you, and collected incontrovertible proof of their guilt. Thanks to these efforts, the Romulan Empire will survive. It will *endure.*"

When the governor paused this time, a tremendous din of approval rang through the crowd, even greater than before.

"We are not here to determine the guilt or innocence of those you see before you," Tharrus pointed out, "for their guilt is certain. We are here to see justice done."

Turning his attention from the crowd to the students of Surak, the governor asked, "Do any of you traitors wish to confess your crime, and pledge your allegiance to the Empire, before your sentence is pronounced? Do any of you choose to denounce your treason and die citizens of the Romulan Empire?"

Tharrus, his council, and the crowd waited silently. But none of the students of Surak spoke.

Spock was pleased. His followers would remain true to the movement even now, despite the reemergence of their Romulan emotions.

While they could not embrace all the principles of logic and the Vulcan way of life, they had seen the waste and illogic of the Romulan Empire. If that were possible, perhaps there was hope for the movement. Perhaps some day, reunification might yet become a reality.

Finally, D'tan stepped forward and broke the silence. "We choose the right of statement," the youth asserted.

A murmur ran through the crowd as Tharrus hurriedly conferred with his advisors. A moment later, the governor spoke.

"The right of statement is reserved for loyal citizens of the Romulan Empire. You have given up your allegiance, and therefore that right."

Another murmur wove its way among the spectators. The Teacher knew why, from personal experience.

The right of statement was one of the oldest and most protected of Romulan privileges, one that had not been abridged for centuries. And contrary to Tharrus's claim, it was not restricted to loyal citizens, or even Romulans.

"However," the governor went on, "I grant each of you the opportunity to speak for five minutes—no more."

The murmur increased in volume. A trial of this nature, even when there was a clear-cut case of treason, routinely took days to complete. In some trials, the statements of the accused had been known to go on for weeks.

Tharrus must have a good reason to end the trial today, Spock mused. Enough to risk the repercussions of abrogating the rebels' rights.

Finally, the sound of the crowd ceased—though the Vulcan wondered if the discontent would end there.

For the twelfth time by his own count, Riker peered out of the cell he shared with Data and Geordi, looking past the translucent energy barrier that confined them. The length of a short corridor away, a pair of Romulan guards walked a perpendicular passageway.

As always the Romulans were watchful but silent, offering the prisoners no clue as to their fate. Still, the human thought, he could guess what their captors had in mind.

After all, the Romulans had earned their reputation as cruel and relentless interrogators. Someone in this place must have been drooling at the prospect of working over a Starfleet officer.

Which made him wonder all the more about Scotty.

Suddenly Riker heard a conversation in the perpendicular corridor. More than two voices, he thought. Probably their guards had run into a couple of their comrades.

The problem was, he couldn't hear what they were saying. He turned to Data, whose head was already tilted in an effort to glean some information from the discussion.

Fortunately the android seemed to have recovered from the Romulans' disruptor barrage, though his circuitry still showed at the nape of his neck, where his artificial skin had been seared away. With Data's amplified sense of hearing, he had a much better chance than any mere humanoid.

The android wasn't given to a wide range of facial expressions, but the first officer had known him long enough to discern a positive reaction from a negative one. This was definitely the latter.

A moment later, the Romulans' voices faded to nothing. Data turned to him, then to Geordi.

"What is it?" asked the engineer. "Bad news?"

The android nodded. "I am afraid so," he responded. "They were referring to Captain Scott. Unfortunately, it was in the past tense."

Riker felt the color drain from his face. "He's dead?"

The possibility had occurred to him when his tricorders hadn't turned up any sign of the man—but he hadn't been willing to accept it. Even now, it didn't seem real.

Data looked as sorry as he could look. "It would seem that way, yes."

"How?" was the only word the first officer could get out.

"Apparently Captain Scott attempted to escape," the android explained. "He managed to slip out of his cell and commandeer a transport ship before anyone noticed he was gone. He might have gotten away entirely, except—"

"Don't tell me," said Riker. "The warbird."

"Yes," Data confirmed. "It gave chase. However, it

seems it was not the warbird that destroyed the transport."

"It blew up on its own?" asked the engineer.

"That is the way the incident was described," the android agreed.

Geordi shook his head. "Can't be. Montgomery Scott wouldn't have done himself in."

"I'm with you," said the first officer. "Not if he could help it, anyway."

"Perhaps his lack of familiarity with the Romulan vessel . . ." Data began.

The engineer looked at him. "It was a *transport*. If anything had gone wrong, he would have known about it in time to fix things. He would have . . ."

Exasperated, he let his voice trail off.

For a while, no one spoke. Hell, what else was there to say?

Then it occurred to Riker that the three of them were still alive. And that if they were going to stay that way, at least for a time, they needed to get their minds off Scotty's death.

"You know," he said, "we've been in worse situations than this." He glared at the corridor outside their cell, now devoid of guards. "Much worse."

"Absolutely," Geordi agreed loudly—though his voice didn't exactly reek of good cheer. "A damned sight worse."

He looked at his companions. "You think they heard me?"

"That is difficult to say," Data declared. "However, I fail to see what difference it makes."

The engineer grunted. "Morale, Data. Just trying to keep up our morale."

"By recounting more dangerous circumstances?" the android asked.

"That's right," Geordi told him, warming to the subject. "Oh, say, like the time Professor Moriarty took over the ship from the holodeck."

"That was bad," Riker agreed.

The engineer smiled. "And then that other time, when Reg Barclay evolved into a supergenius and seized control of the ship from the holodeck?"

"Worse," commented the first officer.

"You're not kidding," Geordi said. 'Or how about when some of us were taken over by those alien prisoners—"

"From the holodeck?" Data suggested, extrapolating on the pattern. Obviously he was unaware that he was being humorous.

The chief engineer chuckled. "Actually," he went on, "they were from the penal colony on Mab-Bu Six, but why split hairs? And don't forget when some of us were captured by Lore's Borg." He winced involuntarily. *"I* certainly won't."

Data looked at his friend thoughtfully. "Geordi, are you aware that I was to blame for the first incident you mentioned—and served as one of your tormentors in two others?"

The engineer returned the android's scrutiny. "What are you saying, Data?"

The android shrugged. "It occurs to me that your life would have been a good deal less troublesome had I not been chosen to serve on the *Enterprise.*"

"That's ridiculous," Riker chimed in. "How about all the times you've *saved* us from one threat or another?"

"That's right," Geordi added. "When Ro and I were turned into virtual ghosts by that transporter accident a few years ago, you were the one we depended on to figure out we were still alive. And you didn't let us down. You and your wide-range anyon beam brought us back from the dead . . . in a manner of speaking, of course."

Data nodded judiciously. "I suppose you are right." He scanned their surroundings. "I wish I could provide a solution to this problem as well."

Riker clapped the android on the shoulder. "Don't worry," he said. "Something will come up. It always does. The important thing is for us to be ready for it."

"Well, lad," said a voice from somewhere in the maze of corridors outside their cell, "in that case, I hope ye're ready right now."

The voice was masked by echoes, but they all recognized its owner at the same time. The first officer quirked an incredulous smile as he turned to his chief engineer.

"Mister Scott . . . ?" he murmured.

"But he's *dead*," blurted Geordi. "We heard the Romulans say they saw him die."

The first officer grunted, finding new respect for Scotty's talents. "Apparently," he told the engineer, "our captors' information wasn't as dependable as we might have believed."

A moment later, as if to put an end to their speculation, Montgomery Scott came bustling into view at the end of the corridor. As he approached them, Riker could see that the man had a disruptor in his hand and a sheen of sweat on his ruddy face.

But the way he was grinning, one would never know he was risking his life in the depths of a Romulan outpost facility. One would *think* he was having the time of his life.

"Captain Scott," said the first officer, grinning just as broadly, "you're a beautiful sight."

"Which is nae more than I've been sayin' all along," Scotty replied. "Of course, I'd rather have convinced yer Counselor Troi of the fact, but there'll be plenty o' time for that later. Now, if ye don't mind, I'm goin' to have to ask ye to stand back. We dinnae have time to figure out the security code on this energy barrier."

As Riker and his companions crowded into the back of their cell and shielded their eyes, the older man took aim at the energy barrier's control panel. A second later, a dark blue beam stabbed the panel, eliciting a spray of sparks. In the second after that, the barrier wavered and then disappeared entirely.

"I don't get it," Geordi said, as he and his companions poured out of the cell. "The Romulans said you'd bought the farm."

"Never trust a Romulan," Scott replied, turning and making his way back down the corridor. "Especially when it comes to agriculture. They're nae very good at it. And as for yer other questions—save 'em. I'll answer them *after* we get where we're goin'."

Good advice, the first officer remarked inwardly. He looked forward to finding out just what Captain Scott had in mind.

CHAPTER 18

Spock watched D'tan come forward hesitantly, but with a determined look on his face. Whatever the youth had to say, it was obviously very important to him.

"I spent my earliest years on Tavorus Four," he began in a shaky voice. "At the time, it was one of the newest colonies in the Empire. I was stationed there with my mother and my father, a Romulan soldier.

"Early on, my father taught me that a Romulan's allegiance to the Empire was greater than his allegiance to any other Romulan—even to a member of his own family. Together we studied all the Empire's victories, and followed new conquests as they were made.

"As I got older, I dreamed of serving in the Romulan military, like my father—contributing to victory after victory and adding to the greater glory of the Empire. But in time I came to see that there was something wrong with the Empire's mission, at least on the planet where I lived.

"Tavorus's inhabitants had been conquered in one of

my father's campaigns. Now, everyone who lived there served the Empire, either by working on one of the farms or in the mines—both of which, my father explained, were needed to feed our growing civilization.

"An entire race of people had been made slaves, forced to watch the fruits of their labors sent off-planet. For years, I had believed the government histories that said the Empire brought glory and prosperity to the worlds it touched. But if this wasn't true on Tavorus, I began to wonder if it was true anywhere.

"At about this time, the Tavorans rebelled. My father was called into service immediately. Though the rebels were defeated quickly, my father was killed in the fighting.

"My mother and I went back to Romulus to live with her family. We barely survived on my father's small military pension. Unfortunately my father's loyal service to the Empire was forgotten by the Romulan government.

"On Romulus I learned about the unification movement, which I joined out of curiosity more than anything else. Among these people I heard the stories of Surak. I discovered a way to live where everyone was free, and didn't have to serve an Empire that cast aside its most loyal servants.

"I learned about a rational way of thinking and living, where people made decisions based on the principles of logic. Where it was as important to be fair as it was to be strong. And I learned about Vulcan and the Federation, where people who were different because of how they looked or thought were citizens like anyone else."

D'tan hesitated for a moment and then concluded. "On Vulcan, I would not be sentenced to death for trying to learn something new."

Spock heard a hush fall over the crowd. It considered

the youth for a long moment. And then the spectators began to speak among themselves, the sounds they made strangely disaffected.

No doubt sensing what was happening, Tharrus immediately called for quiet. He signaled for the guards to take D'tan back to his brethren, and to bring the next prisoner forward to begin his statement.

After a few moments, the crowd became quiet again. But the Vulcan wondered if it was in deference to the governor or out of respect for the next speaker.

Each student, in turn, told his or her own story. Some, like D'tan, had seen the cruelty of the Empire to its conquered worlds firsthand. Others had grown up on the homeworlds and described a life of restrictions—which prevented them from exploring unorthodox ideas, reading certain books, or holding opinions that were not sanctioned by the state.

Not all of the speakers seemed to affect the crowd as much as D'tan had, but none were interrupted. And when they finished, each one was accorded a respectful silence.

In the end, even Spock was moved by their testaments, and found a part of himself railing against the waste their deaths would represent. And only then did he understand why Belan and the others had attempted their escape, even though it was destined to fail.

What was happening to the students of Surak was wrong. It was both that simple and that complex. The part of his mind and his Katra that predated Surak and the reformation—a part he had all but denied—now screamed out at the injustice.

Though a lifetime of training prevented any of these emotions from revealing themselves, the Vulcan felt them as strongly as he had felt anything in his life.

Then it was his turn to speak. Coming forward, he

looked up at the row upon row of Constantharine citizenry and mulled over what wisdom he might impart to them.

Finally he spoke. "My friends," he said, "I ask you to look at us. We, the students of Surak, have done nothing worse than embrace peace and a rational way of life. For this, we are considered enemies of the state.

"Why? Because knowledge—any knowledge—is considered a danger to the Empire. And the most dangerous sort of knowledge is that which diverges from state policy. To possess such knowledge is to be branded a traitor.

"However, I ask you . . . is there anyone here today who has not had a traitorous thought—a thought in conflict with official laws, proclamations, or histories? Yet you are loyal citizens. Should having such a thought make a traitor out of you?

"Indeed, what can be the future of a government whose laws make its people traitors? What happens to that people when the Empire's surveillance and enforcement capabilities catch up with its ideology?"

He paused. "I do not wish to alarm you. After all, it is not as if you must fear this government for long. The day is coming soon when the Empire will collapse of its own weight.

"How can I be sure of this?" He fixed on one thoughtful face in the crowd, then another. "How can I speak with such certainty? Because I have studied Surak's teachings. And he tells us that any system which fears new ideas as this one does is destined to self-destruct.

"New ideas are essential to growth. And growth is essential to the survival of any being or system. Not the sort of growth that the Empire pursues, with conquest after conquest, and world after subjugated world—but the growth of the spirit.

"We who follow Surak have experienced that growth. Perhaps some of you will experience it as well, someday. Perhaps you will see that a system based on cruelty and injustice is simply not—"

"Stop!" cried Tharrus, suddenly on his feet, his voice a surf that seemed to break everywhere at once.

"—logical," the Vulcan finished.

The governor's eyes narrowed with fury. He pointed to the Constantharines.

"You have heard the words of treason from the traitors' own mouths. They do not dispute the charges. They freely admit they are guilty of the worst crime a Romulan can commit—the destruction of our society from within."

Tharrus gave the spectators a moment to consider his words. Then he turned again to the students of Surak.

"After appropriate deliberation, this tribunal finds you guilty of the crimes of which you have been accused. The penalty is public execution."

Pausing dramatically, the governor waited for a response from the crowd—the sort of approval that greeted him earlier in the proceedings.

But this time, silence was his only answer. And in that silence, Spock believed he saw the eventual end of the Romulan Empire.

Scotty poked his head around a corner, aimed, and fired. His borrowed disruptor turned the corridor blue with its gleam as it slammed into yet another Romulan, sending the man sprawling.

He took just a moment to make certain the guard was

unconscious, like the two Scott had dispatched before him. Then, satisfied that they were in no immediate danger, he gestured for his companions to follow him.

"Nice shooting," Riker commented.

"I used to be a wee bit better," the older man told him.

As they threaded their way among the three unconscious Romulans, the *Enterprise* officers all stooped to pick up the guards' hand weapons. Not that it would be necessary, if all went according to plan, Scotty reflected—but then, what plan had ever gone forward without a hitch?

Fortunately, *this* one was very near to reaching fruition. At the end of the corridor, Scotty made a skidding right—and saw the proverbial light at the end of the tunnel.

Except in this case, the tunnel was a mercifully short hallway and the light was actually a door. A sign just over it, laid out clearly in Romulan characters, designated the room beyond as a transporter chamber.

Scotty was gladder than ever that foreign-language studies were part of the captain's exam. At least, in *his* day.

Heading for the panel beside the door, he pressed his palm against it. To his relief, the mechanism wasn't security-coded; it just opened. And a moment later, he was inside, with the others following close behind.

"Up on the platform with ye," he told them, making his way toward the control bank.

"I can do that," said Geordi.

"I'm sure ye can," Scotty returned. "But nae this time."

"So how *did* you escape?" asked Riker.

Scotty fiddled with the instruments, which weren't as familiar to him as he would have liked. "I guess the

Romulans never held a Starfleet engineer in one of their cells. It was nae all that difficult to pry off a bulkhead plate and access the circuitry underneath." He nodded appraisingly as he fiddled some more. "Once I disabled the energy barrier, I made m'self scarce. And nae long after, the Romulans saw a transport ship take off—then fail to answer their hails. When it exploded, they thought I was dead. But I was never on that ship in the first place."

"Then how—" Geordi stopped himself in mid-question. "Autopilot?" he asked.

"Aye," the older man admitted. "I sent the transport out as a decoy—so I could lie low until the warbird was gone. Unfortunately, when the three of ye were captured, that was nae longer an option."

"Nonetheless, a clever ploy," Data ventured.

"Nice of ye to say so," replied Scotty, completing his preparations. Tapping one last padd, he came around the control bank and hopped up onto the platform beside the others.

"Next stop, the *Yorktown,*" he announced.

That's when a squad of Romulans came running into the room, weapons drawn. One of them barked a desperate order and they all aimed their disruptors at the quartet on the transporter platform.

Before they could press the triggers, however, Scotty and his comrades fired their own weapons. Some of the Romulans fell.

But the ones that were still standing unleashed a barrage of dark blue fury. Scotty cringed, bracing himself for the bludgeoning impact.

But it never came.

His friends from the *Enterprise* looked a bit surprised, Scotty noted. But then, they'd probably expected the same punishment he had—and here they were on the bridge of a starship instead.

"Welcome to the *U.S.S. Yorktown*," said the voice of the ship's computer. "Enjoy your starship adventure. And please, take all wrappers and other refuse with you when you leave."

The *Enterprise* officers looked at him. Scotty shrugged.

"Nae matter what I do," he complained, "I canna seem to turn the damned thing off."

Of course, they had more important concerns right now. Life and death concerns, one might say. And before they could do anything about them, they had to figure out who was in charge.

Riker must have been thinking the same thing. "You're the one who got her this far," he told Scotty. "Why don't you take the center seat?"

Scotty nodded. "I'll do that."

As he assumed the captain's chair, he saw the first officer take the helm, while Data sat down beside him at navigation. As if by instinct, Geordi made a beeline for the engineering station.

Scotty turned to him. "Activate the cloak, Mister La Forge."

The engineer looked at him. "You've got a cloak on this ship?"

Scotty shrugged. "How do ye think I *got* here, laddie?"

Shaking his head, Geordi worked the necessary controls.

Next, Scotty fixed his attention on the android. "Chart us a course for Constanthus, Mister Data. And get us there as quick as ye can. With this cloak of ours, there's nae need for us to sneak about."

"Acknowledged," the android replied.

But before Data could act on the order, Riker turned around in his chair and eyed the older man. "Are you sure that's wise?" he asked.

Scotty looked at him. "Am I sure *what's* wise?"

"Heading for Constanthus," the first officer explained.

The older man held out his hands in an appeal to reason. "I came out here to fetch Spock home, lad. And I cannae do that without paying Constanthus a visit—now, can I?"

Riker frowned. "My point is that *you* may have come out here to rescue *Spock*—but *we* came out here to rescue *you*. We didn't have any discussion with Captain Picard about extending the mission further than that."

Scotty frowned back at him. "What are ye sayin', then? That ye'd abandon one of the greatest men who ever lived to his own devices? That ye'd sentence him to certain death?"

"I'm saying nothing of the kind," the younger man rejoined. "It's just that we've already made our share of blunders in trying to get *you* out—because we didn't know there was a plan already in motion. By the same token, I'd hate to do something that would complicate any effort on the part of Captain Picard."

"Then yer captain has a plan to liberate Spock?" Scotty ventured.

"His intention," Data interjected, "was to negotiate for the unficationists' release. He was in the process of doing so when we received your distress call."

Scotty grunted derisively. Sometimes he wondered about these people.

"Negotiate, is it? With the Romulans?" He laughed. "Picard must be daft. I'd sooner negotiate with a mugatu than some cold-blooded, stiff-necked, backstabbing son of a praetor. Besides," he went on, "there's something yer captain does nae know—something which changes all the rules of the game."

"And what's that?" asked Geordi.

Scott eyed him. "They know about Spock—that he's one of the prisoners they've taken on Constanthus, I mean."

"They who?" Riker inquired.

"They *Eragian*," he replied. "I tapped into their computer system before I came to get you out. I dinnae know what tipped them off—but now that they know what kind of fish they've hooked, they're nae going to waste any time takin' advantage of the situation."

The first officer shook his head. The engineer muttered something under his breath. And though the android just sat there, the captain sensed that he was concerned as well.

"So as ye can see," Scotty continued, "we cannae leave this up to yer captain anymore. We've got to do something on our own—or leave Spock to the mercy of the blasted Romulans."

Geordi turned to Riker. "Captain Scott's got a point, sir. If Captain Picard doesn't know they've discovered Spock is among the prisoners . . ."

"But he knew they'd find that out eventually," the first officer argued. It was clear he preferred to play things by the book.

And maybe there was a time for that, Scotty conceded. Unfortunately, this wasn't that time. They had to move quickly—or not at all.

"Our window of opportunity will not remain open for long," Data remarked, echoing the captain's thoughts. "Once Proconsul Eragian realizes the *Yorktown* is gone, he will mobilize his forces to find us."

"Lord," said Scotty. "Is everything a meeting with ye

people? Do ye nae give in to yer instincts once in a while?"

Riker straightened at the remark, as if he'd been slapped in the face with a gauntlet. "All right," he said at last, responding to the challenge. "We'll head for Constanthus—and do everything in our power to get Spock out of there."

"Thataboy," cheered Scott. "Mister Data—that course I requested?"

"Not so fast," the first officer interjected. "First, while we're out here on the frontier, we send a message to Captain Picard—alerting him to our intentions. *Then* we head for Constanthus."

Scotty balked inwardly at the delay, but he had to admit it made good sense. "Aye," he sighed. "Contact your captain, then. But for God sake, lad, make it *quick*. Our friend Spock could be roasting on a spit in the meantime."

CHAPTER 19

Picard was pacing in his quarters like a caged jungle cat when he heard a beep, signifying that someone was standing in the corridor outside his door.

"Come," he advised.

He expected that it might be Beverly again, coming to cheer him up. After all, she'd been up to see him twice already, though there wasn't much she could do other than keep him company.

But this time, when the door slid aside, it wasn't Beverly at all. It was someone just as welcome, though.

"May I come in?" asked Troi. Her classically lovely features showed considerable strain.

"By all means," the captain told her, gesturing toward a chair.

The counselor entered. A moment later, the door slid closed in her wake. She sat down in the place he'd indicated.

"What can I do for you?" asked Picard, taking a chair opposite Troi's.

She smiled. "Actually, I started out with the intention of seeing how you were feeling. How you were dealing with the loss of your command, I mean." She sighed. "Then, about halfway here, I realized *I* needed someone to talk to as well."

The captain chuckled. "Perhaps we can console each other, then."

The counselor's dark eyes were wistful in the extreme. "It's been very difficult with Admiral McCoy in charge of the ship," she confided.

"I can imagine," Picard remarked. "And for you in particular."

With a certain reluctance, she nodded. "Being able to sense the emotions of everyone on the bridge is not a pleasant experience right now. There's resentment. Uncertainty. Distrust. Even anger. And of course, I share all these feelings to one extent or another, which makes it even harder."

The captain sympathized. "Tell me, Deanna, what did you make of the admiral's conversation with Governor Tharrus?"

The counselor shrugged. "As you know, I've never been very good at reading Romulans. Their minds are too strong, too shielded."

Picard leaned forward. "I'm not referring to your empathic talents, Deanna. I want to know what you *observed.*"

Troi thought about it for a moment. "What I observed," she replied finally, "was a Romulan with a bit of power who thoroughly relished the idea of increasing that power—even if it meant putting himself at risk."

The captain grunted. "Then you believe he fell for McCoy's ploy?"

The counselor thought some more. After a while, she shook her head.

"Not necessarily. I got the impression that Tharrus was considering the proposal. But the kind of man I believe him to be might not have accepted it at face value. He might have sought out other ways to turn the offer to his advantage."

Picard absorbed the information. "I see. And have you made Admiral McCoy aware of your reservations?"

Troi sighed. "He's not exactly open to my observations, sir. As little as he values your input, he values mine even less. And I can say *that* with a high degree of certainty."

The captain sat back in his chair. "Then what happens now? We wait for a reply from Governor Tharrus?"

"Apparently," the counselor replied. "But the admiral didn't seem to think it would be long in coming. And for all I know, he's right about that."

Picard could feel his fingers clenching into fists. With a conscious effort, he relaxed them.

"I wish there were something I could do," he said. "I wish I could take back my command and pursue a more rational course of action."

"But you can't," Troi told him. "I know that, sir." She paused to share his frustration and his pain. "We all do."

McCoy opened his eyes with a start. It took him a moment or two to remember where he was and what he was doing there.

This was the bridge of the *Enterprise,* and he was seated in the command center. The reason Captain Picard was nowhere to be seen was because he had banished the man from his own bridge.

Not that he'd wanted to. He'd been forced into doing it by the captain's lack of initiative. Hell, the very last thing he'd expected was to have to assume command of Picard's ship.

The admiral straightened in his chair. Somewhere along the line, he must have dozed off or something. He'd have to watch that. It wouldn't do to let the bridge crew see their commanding officer conk out that way.

Bad enough he looked like some old nag who'd been put out to pasture. He couldn't afford to act that way, too.

"Sir?" said a deep voice. It came from behind his back, and it sure sounded as if it expected something from him.

McCoy turned in his captain's chair and cast a glance at Mister Worf. "What is it?" he asked the tactical officer, barely bothering to conceal his annoyance.

Worf frowned. "I merely alerted you to an incoming message, sir."

"A message?" the admiral repeated. "From whom?"

The Klingon leveled a glance at him that could have sliced duranium. No doubt, McCoy mused, Worf resented his presence there as much as Counselor Troi had. Maybe even more, he thought.

"It's Governor Tharrus, Admiral." His mouth twisted as if he'd caught a whiff of something distasteful. "He wishes to speak with you."

McCoy muffled a curse. "Then what are we waiting for, Lieutenant?" He got to his feet—a little quickly perhaps, because he then had to grab an armrest to steady himself. "Give me a blasted visual and step back. I'll show you how a professional reels in a fish."

He saw the Klingon sigh. "As you wish, sir." Worf pressed the appropriate padds on his control panel.

A fraction of a second later, the image of Governor

Tharrus leapt to the screen. To the admiral's eye, he looked different somehow. More confident, maybe. But that didn't really matter, as long as he took the bait.

Full of his own brand of confidence, McCoy took a step toward the viewscreen. Turning on the Southern charm he'd inherited from his father, he smiled.

"Governor Tharrus," he said. "Time's a wastin', sir. If we're going to work together, we'd better get our show on the road—if y'know what I mean."

The governor gave a thin-lipped smile. "I would have liked to respond sooner," he replied. "However, it was necessary for me to consider certain . . . ramifications of your proposal, Admiral."

"And now that you've had some time to think about it?" McCoy returned. "Is there any other course of action that makes sense?"

Tharrus shrugged. "Actually, there is. Particularly the one wherein I maintain possession of the *Vulcan.*"

McCoy's jaw dropped at the reference. He tried to recover, to find words that would cover his reaction. But there weren't any.

"I see you remember your old friend Spock," said the Romulan. "Once I, too, had the opportunity to think about it, I realized there had to be a reason they would send an aged admiral out here—more than likely the same reason you were pressing so hard for the return of the rebels. And what could that reason be?"

Tharrus's eyes narrowed. Clearly, he felt he had the situation well in control as he answered his own question.

"Because you served with Spock on the *Enterprise.* Because you were comrades. And because he is one of the unificationists I hold in my jail."

McCoy's face drained of color, making him feel even older than he really was. He didn't know what to say.

"This doesn't change anything," he sputtered, trying to salvage something out of this appalling mess. He took another step forward and pointed at the viewscreen. "The proposition that was offered to you is still a good one. It still makes sense."

The Romulan laughed. "It does? Which do you think would enhance my position more? To spare the home-world a minor embarrassment . . . or to show the Empire that I have captured the great Spock?" He shook his head derisively. "Really, Admiral. Do you think you're dealing with a child?"

"Damn you," rasped McCoy. "We're talking about people's lives here. Not just Spock's, but a lot of others'. They shouldn't have to die for speaking their minds."

"Perhaps not where *you* come from," Tharrus told him. "In the Empire, it happens every day. Not that I have any intention of killing your friend, Admiral McCoy. At least, not yet. For the time being, I simply intend to make him . . . a trifle less comfortable."

Again, the governor laughed—a hard, cruel laugh. And before it had finished echoing on the bridge, his image vanished from the viewscreen, replaced by a splash of stars.

"My God," croaked the admiral, his eyes fixing on infinity. "What have I done?"

What indeed, he thought. Glancing about, he saw that everyone was looking at him. Pitying him for his ineptitude—for his failure.

What's more, he couldn't help but agree with them. Without a word, he negotiated a course past the command center and the tactical station and allowed himself to be swallowed up by the turbolift.

Once inside, he slumped against the wall. He was worse

than a broken man. He was a broken man who'd just signed his friend's death sentence.

Picard regarded Troi. "You know," he began, "the last time I felt this way was when the Ferengi disabled the *Stargazer* at Maxia Zeta. I—"

He was interrupted by an intercom summons. "Lieutenant Worf calling Captain Picard. Please respond."

Picard tapped the communicator on the left side of his chest. "This is the captain. What is it, Mister Worf?"

Silence for a moment. "Sir, I believe Admiral McCoy has abdicated his command of the *Enterprise*."

Picard looked at the counselor. She obviously had no more idea what Worf was talking about than did the captain himself.

"Abdicated?" he echoed out loud.

"That is correct, sir," the Klingon confirmed. "Admiral McCoy received a message from Governor Tharrus of Constanthus—a message in which the governor informed him that he had identified the admiral and associated him with Ambassador Spock."

The captain cursed beneath his breath. "Go no further, Mister Worf. I get the picture. But are you certain that Admiral McCoy has abandoned his post?"

"As certain as I can be," the lieutenant responded. "As soon as he realized what he'd done, he turned pale and left the bridge."

Picard nodded. "Thank you, Mister Worf. I'll look into this. Picard out."

Troi looked saddened. "That poor man," she said.

"I agree," the captain commented. "He may have been misguided, but he meant well. Tharrus's response must have crushed him."

"I should speak with him," the counselor decided.

"Computer," said Picard. "Locate Admiral Leonard McCoy."

A melodic female voice provided the answer. "Admiral McCoy is in the Ten-Forward lounge."

The captain exchanged a glance with Troi. "It seems the admiral's psyche is in good hands," he observed. "Your services may be put to better use on the bridge."

The counselor smiled. "As you wish, sir."

Rising, Picard pulled down on the front of his tunic and made his way to the door. He had a long, difficult road ahead of him—that much was certain.

But it felt good to be the captain again.

CHAPTER 20

Tharrus still had one loose end to tie up. But he didn't expect it would be very difficult—not when the key to everything he needed was well within his grasp.

Flanked by Phabaris and Skrasis, he approached the warren of cells to which the rebels had been returned after their trial. The sentinels he'd posted there all straightened and saluted him crisply in the Romulan manner. As well they should, the governor mused.

After all, he would be rising swiftly in the political hierarchy after it became known he'd apprehended Spock —more swiftly than he'd ever imagined. And if they served him well, his people would be rising with him.

Emerging from their compartments, the prisoners eyed Tharrus warily. What did his presence here mean? They would find out soon enough, he mused. Motioning for his guards to stay behind, he brazenly walked into the rebels' midst.

They didn't move. Even though the governor was alone

among them, they knew any attack on him would be met with force by their jailers. So they followed him with their eyes alone, and continued to wonder what he was up to.

Tharrus smiled—a reminder of who was in charge here. "It has come to my attention," he said, "that the legendary Spock is among you."

There were glances exchanged among the prisoners. Subtle glances, to be sure, but not so subtle that they could not help confirm what he already knew.

"Unfortunately," the governor went on, "while I know that *one* of you is the esteemed Vulcan, I do not know *which* one. Half of you are too young to be Spock, but the other half are not. And among the half who *are* old enough, Spock could be almost anyone. Therefore, I will need some assistance to identify him."

With that, he turned to Skrasis. Looking neither right nor left at the stares he was drawing from the rebels, the infiltrator stepped forward.

The rebels whispered curses and exclamations of disgust. Obviously none of them had suspected Skrasis of espionage until he exposed the fact himself. But then these were only political radicals, not trained soldiers.

"Skrasis," said the governor, reluctant to waste any more time here. "Which of these bedraggled specimens is the *real* Spock?"

The infiltrator scanned the ranks of the unificationists. They looked back at him, unruffled. Finally Skrasis turned to Tharrus.

"I cannot say," he told the governor.

At first, Tharrus thought he had heard his agent incorrectly. Then, when he saw the smiles emerging on the faces of the unificationists, he realized he had heard him perfectly.

"You . . . cannot say?" the governor repeated. "And why is that?"

The muscles worked in Skrasis's temples. He seemed to be struggling with a decision he could only have made moments earlier.

"Because it would be a betrayal," he said. "A betrayal of one I have come to admire."

Tharrus looked at him. "Tell me you're joking."

The younger Romulan shook his head. "I am not," he advised.

For the love of Order . . . Skrasis had become one of them!

Somewhere along the line, he had adopted the doctrines of those he was supposed to be infiltrating. And by virtue of that, he was now useless.

"You're making a mistake," the governor told him. "A very *big* mistake."

"That may be," Skrasis agreed. "But it is the path I have chosen."

For a moment, the governor felt an urge to kill. He wanted to tear the man limb from limb, like a ravening beast—to pay him back for his arrogance and stupidity.

Then the moment subsided. Taking a deep breath, Tharrus spat at Skrasis's feet. The infiltrator barely flinched.

Turning to the rebels themselves, the governor realized there was still an option open to him. He took it.

"My agent's abject stupidity is your opportunity. I need to identify the one called Spock, and to do that I require your help. What's more, my request—and for now, it is only a request—does not come without its rewards for those who comply with it."

There was a shuffling of feet. A predictable reaction, Tharrus told himself. No one wanted to think of himself as a traitor, especially among *these* people—though he was certain someone would shoulder that burden if the price were right.

And if it were couched in the right terms.

"Let me amend my offer," Tharrus remarked. "Rather than restrict my gratitude to only those who offer assistance . . . I will reward *everyone*. And why not?" he asked. "Am I not the governor of this planet? Do I not hold the power of life and death?"

Of course, he was lying. After broadcasting the trial, he could hardly have spared the rebels their due. But they didn't have to know that.

He scanned the assemblage for some clue that would tell him what he wanted to know. As yet, there was nothing, no indication at all. He was growing even more impatient than when he'd walked into this place.

"Amnesty," he said, getting to the point. "For everyone present. Except Spock himself, of course. And for him," Tharrus went on, compounding his lie, "protection from the homeworld authorities, who would not have been so reasonable if they had discovered him first."

Still nothing.

The governor's teeth grated. "You understand," he explained, "I will find Spock with or without your help. By cooperating, you will only make things easier on yourself—and on him."

He capped his argument with the most compelling remark he could make to these imbeciles.

"It is the only *logical* option open to you."

For a moment, the prisoners remained still. Tharrus could feel the blood rushing to his face. All right, he thought. If that is the way they wanted it, he would be glad to—

Suddenly, one of the rebels stepped forward. The

governor recognized him as the smooth-brow he had encountered earlier. As before, he showed neither fear nor arrogance as he met Tharrus's gaze.

"I am Spock," the man admitted.

The governor smiled again. At last. Now he could proceed with his plans.

He turned to gesture to his guards—but out of the corner of his eye, Tharrus saw someone else step forward. Like the first one, this was an older man, his dark eyes seemingly devoid of emotion. However, he was taller and thinner than his comrade.

"My colleague's attempt to impersonate me is a courageous one," said the second prisoner. "And clever, as well. However, he is perpetrating a falsehood. *I* am Spock."

The governor looked from one to the other. Which one was telling the truth? Before he could decide, a third individual separated himself from the crowd—a younger man this time, and stockier as well.

"Both of you have demonstrated great loyalty," he told the other two. "I am grateful. But I cannot allow you to make this sacrifice."

"This is highly illogical," the first Spock noted. "It will only delay the inevitable."

"My thoughts exactly," the second one replied. "Desist now and save yourselves. There is no point in all of us being destroyed."

The third one spoke to Tharrus directly. "Forgive them. I am the one you seek. You must believe that."

A fourth figure came forward. "I can no longer stand here and watch my friends defend my anonymity. I am Spock."

"No," said a fifth man. "It is I."

"I am Spock," said two more, emerging from the crowd at the same time.

"No, me."

"Me."

Before the governor knew it, a dozen of the unification-ists had identified themselves as the Vulcan—and if he let this go on, he was sure that others would have joined them. He could feel the anger rising in him worse than before, threatening to choke him.

"Enough!" he roared, his voice echoing back on itself.

Abruptly, every self-styled Spock in the cell fell silent. They all looked at him expectantly, some with their heads slightly tilted to one side. None of them seemed the least bit afraid of what he might do next.

"I had hoped to be merciful," Tharrus snarled. "But you've made that impossible." He glanced at Skrasis. "Stand with these rebels, traitor, if you wish. But rest assured, you will share their fate when the time comes."

Then turning his back on the unificationists, the gover-nor strode out of the warren. "Spock be damned," he muttered.

He could hear the footfalls of his guards as they tried to catch up with him. What blasted power did the Vulcan have that enabled him to bind people to his cause?

Even people like Skrasis, who had started out squarely opposed to it?

No matter. When they faced the moment of their execution, they would crack. They would give up their Vulcan savior. And then Tharrus would get what was coming to him.

Guinan wasn't surprised when she saw the admiral deposit himself at the end of her bar. Truth to tell, she had *expected* to see him there at some point. The only surprise was that it had taken him this long to show up.

McCoy scowled and mumbled something to himself. It was pretty clear he didn't expect anyone to actually hear his complaint.

But of course, someone had. "K'jarju?" she echoed.

The admiral looked up. His eyes narrowed as they focused on her, emphasizing the webwork of wrinkles around them. "K'jarju," he confirmed. "Means *idiot* in—"

"In Tautanese," she interjected. "Yes. I know. It wasn't the terminology I was asking about. Just the application."

McCoy grunted. "I was just getting started. Y'see, I'd just decided I was twelve kinds of an idiot, and I was trying to name them all."

Guinan smiled. "Twelve kinds, eh? That's a lot of self-deprecation for a man in your position."

The admiral harrumphed. "In my position," he repeated, putting a bitter spin on the phrase, "you would think I'd know better. After all those years, all those missions, you would think I'd have a little perspective."

"Perspective on what?" she prodded. "And by the way, what's a k'jarju likely to be drinking these days?"

McCoy shrugged. "I don't suppose you'd have any Saurian brandy?" he ventured half-jokingly.

Guinan tilted her head to one side. "Now, Admiral, you should know we only serve synthehol here, and nothing *but* synthehol. Starfleet regulations and all that."

McCoy sighed. "Yes, I know."

"On the other hand," said Guinan, "we do occasionally *bend* the rules a bit. But only when we have a very *special* visitor."

Reaching beneath the bar, she took out a very old, very

dusty bottle full of a green liquid. Then she produced a clean glass to go with it.

The admiral gazed at the stuff hesitantly. "What is it?" he asked.

"It's green," she replied. "What more do you need to know?"

McCoy chuckled despite himself. "Good point," he told her.

Unstoppering the bottle, he poured himself two fingers' worth. The stuff sparkled in the illumination from the overhead lights.

"Cheers," he said, then threw his head back and downed the contents.

"Better than synthehol?" Guinan inquired.

The admiral made a sound of satisfaction, put his glass down, and smiled. "A damned sight." Then his smile faded. "It's nice to know some things still get better with age—even if I'm not one of them."

"You don't look so old to me," she remarked.

"I'm a hundred and forty-five," he admitted. "If that's not old, I don't know what is."

Guinan placed her elbows on the bar and leaned forward. "At a hundred and forty-five," she responded, "I was just getting started."

McCoy stared at her. "You're kidding me."

"I'm not," she assured him.

"How old *are* you?" he asked.

She pointed a finger at him. "Old enough to know you're no k'jarju."

The admiral's eyes fixed themselves on his empty glass, where just a few lacy threads of the green liqueur were languidly making their way down the insides of the transparent surface.

"You were saying something about perspective," she reminded him.

"So I was," McCoy agreed.

"Care to elaborate?"

His eyes rose again to meet hers. "It's the damnedest thing. Back on the *old Enterprise,* the thing I hated most—the thing that would always make me cringe—was hosting one of those Federation ambassadors from hell. The kind who shows up thinking he knows more than the captain and ends up demonstrating he knows nothing at all."

"And?" Guinan prompted.

"And now," said the admiral, "I've *become* the thing I hated. Now *I'm* the all-fired ambassador."

"I see," said his host.

"And just like all those other stuffed shirts, I've managed to make a mess of things by pulling rank. By insisting the captain do things my way." He winced. "It's a good thing Jim's not around to see this."

"You had a great deal of respect for your captain," she observed. "A great deal of affection."

McCoy nodded. "Damned right I did. He was the finest commanding officer who ever lived—in *any* century."

"I didn't know your captain," Guinan conceded. "But I know *mine.* And if you had asked me, I would've said the same thing about him. The finest one who ever lived, I mean."

"He's no Jim Kirk," the admiral told her. "Jim never would've sat there, waiting for the enemy to make the first move. He would've taken the bull by the horns."

"Maybe Captain Picard would have done the same," she argued, "if the circumstances were different. I've seen him take the bull by the horns, too. But most of the time, he finds another way."

"What way is that?" McCoy inquired.

"One that'll work," she replied.

The admiral looked at her for a moment, as if searching for a chink in her resolve. He didn't seem to find any.

He pushed his glass toward her. "I could use a refill, if you don't mind."

She didn't. A moment later, she pushed the glass back toward him, filled again with some of her private stock.

McCoy tossed it back, then put the empty glass on the bar and wiped his mouth with the back of his hand. He seemed to have lost himself in thought.

"So what you're saying," he remarked at last, "is I should have had a little more confidence in your captain. And his method of dealing with the Romulans as well, I suppose, even though it's not the first time I've run into them."

"Different era," she told him. "Different Romulans. If you want to be effective against them, you've got to change with the times."

The admiral sighed. "That's easier said than done."

"You've done harder things," Guinan assured him. "I know you have. You can do this, too."

He smiled. "So, this captain of yours. He's got it all figured out, has he?"

"Not exactly," she answered. "There were a couple of things he didn't quite understand—even before you made the situation a bit more complicated."

McCoy winced. "Such as?"

Guinan shrugged. "The way the Romulans are moving so many of their ships toward their border with the Stugg. There doesn't seem to be any—"

The admiral interrupted her, his wispy white brows knitting above the bridge of his nose. "The Stugg, you say?"

"The Stugg," she confirmed.

"And the Romulans are deploying their ships to that sector?"

"That's what Lieutenant Worf told me just a little while ago."

McCoy looked surprised for a moment. "Damn," he said at last. "So *that's* what he was trying to talk to me about."

Guinan nodded. "Apparently," she said.

Her guest stroked his chin. "Wait a minute. The Stugg could never get together on anything, much less a military offensive. Why would the Romulans be concentrating so much of their firepower there?"

"That's what Captain Picard was wondering," Guinan explained. "And don't even think of pushing your glass this way again. Two slugs of the green stuff is enough for a man your age. Hell, it's enough for a man of *any* age."

"That's all right," said the admiral. With an effort, he pushed himself back from the bar. "I appreciate the hospitality, Guinan. *All* of it."

"That's what I'm here for," she reminded him. "I'll see you around, Admiral McCoy."

"Leonard," he told her.

"Leonard," she agreed.

With a last gentlemanly nod, he walked away, heading for the exit. But it was clear to her he was still pondering something she'd said.

Guinan went back to her duties, satisfied. When they left Ten-Forward with that look on their faces, she knew she'd done her job.

CHAPTER 21

Picard looked around the observation lounge table. With three of his officers at risk in Romulan space, the table appeared strangely undermanned.

Only Worf, Beverly Crusher, and Counselor Troi looked back at him from their customary places—and even they seemed somewhat diminished by their concern for their colleagues. Admiral McCoy had been alerted that this meeting would be taking place, but he was nowhere to be seen.

The captain frowned. Protocol or no protocol, he would give the admiral another minute and no longer. After all—

Abruptly, the door to the room slid aside and revealed McCoy, who seemed more frail than at any time since his arrival on the *Enterprise*. The admiral's eyes flitted from one of them to the next, almost timidly, as if he were steeling himself for some terrific ordeal.

But no one chastised him. In fact, they could barely look at him. Making his way inside, McCoy quietly took the chair normally reserved for Commander Riker—on Picard's right, halfway along the table's length.

"Sorry I'm late," he muttered to no one in particular. "I had some . . ." He drummed his fingertips on the table's surface. ". . . some *thinking* to do."

Choosing not to address that issue in public, the captain opted instead for the matter at hand. "We have received a subspace message from Commander Riker," he said.

"He's all right?" Troi responded.

"Apparently so," the captain told her. "Geordi and Data as well. And they've found Captain Scott."

"Alive?" asked Worf.

"Alive," Picard confirmed.

"That's wonderful," murmured the admiral.

Doctor Crusher looked relieved as well. "Then Will was just reporting that they're on their way back?"

The captain shook his head. "On the contrary. They are taking the *Yorktown* deeper into Romulan territory."

"But why?" blurted Admiral McCoy.

Abruptly, he realized that all eyes were upon him. Sitting up straight in his chair, he cleared his throat and spoke in a more measured tone.

"They got what they came for," he explained. "What are they up to now?"

Picard sympathized with McCoy's confusion. "It seems Governor Tharrus is not the only one aware of Spock's presence on Constanthus. Proconsul Eragian has learned of it as well—or so Captain Scott appears to believe."

"Then that's why Will and the others have agreed to

head for Constanthus," Troi observed. "They're going to attempt to *free* Ambassador Spock."

"That's correct," Picard confirmed.

Worf's nostrils flared. "Their *orders* were to rescue Captain *Scott.*"

"So they were," the captain agreed. "They have chosen to diverge from them, based on new information."

"But they don't know that Tharrus knows," Dr. Crusher commented. "He'll be guarding Spock a lot more closely now."

"Also true," Picard noted. "Which means our friends are reaching into a bigger hornet's nest than they're prepared for."

"So what do we do?" asked the counselor. The captain recognized it as a rhetorical question, designed to open debate.

"I'll tell you what we don't do," said McCoy. "We don't go traipsing after them. That's the kind of shoot-from-the-hip behavior that got us into trouble before."

Picard turned to him, noting how the man's timidity had suddenly vanished. "Then you think we should rely on their resourcefulness? Count on their succeeding without our help?"

The admiral's lips pressed together. "I don't like the idea," he admitted. "My natural inclination is to light out after them and damn the photon torpedoes. But the way things are panning out, maybe we're better off practicing some . . . hell, some *restraint.*"

"Restraint," Picard echoed.

"Damned right," McCoy told him. "If we go charging in after Scotty and the others, we'll be risking even more lives. As for Spock . . ." He sighed. "Spock will find a way to avoid being used as a political pawn no matter what—even if it means his death."

"I respectfully disagree," insisted Worf.

He leaned forward, the muscles working in his jaw. His eyes were fixed intently on the captain's.

"They are our comrades, sir. We cannot allow them to attempt the ambassador's rescue on their own."

Picard looked to Troi. She acknowledged his scrutiny, but said nothing. No help there, the captain mused. The doctor was silent as well. This was a matter of strategy, not medicine.

Picard bit his lip. It was up to him. As it always was, when one came right down to it. In the end, the captain's decision was the only one that really counted.

"Admiral McCoy makes a valid point," Picard remarked at last. He could see the disappointment in Worf's eyes. "As it stands now, there are only four lives at stake—five, if we include that of Ambassador Spock."

"But, sir—" the Klingon began.

The captain silenced him with a gesture. "Let me finish, Mister Worf. As I was saying, risking a thousand lives to save a mere handful is not only bad arithmetic, it's bad command philosophy."

Doctor Crusher swallowed. No doubt, she believed Picard's words were the seal on her friends' deaths. That is, until he added one more, very significant word to his utterance. . . .

"Usually."

Worf looked at him. "Usually, sir?"

The captain nodded. "Under normal circumstances, I might be inclined to sit tight and wait for Commander Riker to find his way home. Preferably, with Ambassador Spock in tow.

"However," he said, "these circumstances are anything but normal. With Spock's identity exposed, negotiation is no longer an option. Nor is Ambassador Spock the only one capable of being used as a pawn by the Romulans. So, now, are three Starfleet officers—four, if you include Captain Scott—and *that* aspect of the situation is *not* to be taken lightly."

Counselor Troi nodded approvingly. But then, she alone had had an inkling of how Picard would stand on this all along.

"What's more," the captain added, "our long-range sensor reports indicate that patrols are remarkably light in Constanthus's sector—as they seem to be in many portions of the Empire these days. And unlike Commander Riker, we know what to expect vis-à-vis the acceleration of events there. Hence, we have an excellent chance of getting through."

McCoy slumped back into his chair. His expression was one of surprise. No, Picard thought—of outright disbelief.

"You're going after them?" he rasped.

"I am indeed," the captain informed him. "There is a time for patience and a time for action. *This* is a time for action." Turning to Worf, he said, "Make sure the battle bridge is in working order, Lieutenant."

The Klingon suppressed a smile as he rose to carry out his orders. "Aye, sir." The doors slid aside as he approached them.

Picard glanced at Troi. "Prepare the crew for saucer separation, Counselor. We will be taking leave of our civilian population in twenty minutes."

Troi nodded. "Right away, Captain." She, too, got up and started from the room.

Next the captain looked at Doctor Crusher. "You'll be in command of the saucer, Beverly. I want you to wait here until we get back. That is, of course, unless the saucer is endangered. At the merest hint of a military encounter, I want you to retreat."

The doctor frowned at the prospect, but she knew her duty. If anyone was good at making the tough decisions, *she* was.

"Aye, sir," she assured him.

A moment later she was gone as well. That left Picard alone with the admiral, who was still staring at him incredulously.

"Well," said McCoy, his voice little more than a whisper. "I guess you've got something in common with that friend of mine after all."

Picard grunted, apparently cognizant of the reference. "I'll take that as a compliment, Admiral."

McCoy shook his head. "Just when you think you know someone . . ." he murmured.

"They surprise you?" the captain finished for him.

The older man nodded. "They do at that."

Picard allowed himself a smile. "Tell me, Admiral, will you be staying on the saucer section?"

McCoy's expression was still full of surprise, but he harrumphed softly. "Not on your life. Spock would never let me hear the end of it."

As Tharrus emerged from the blockish command center, surrounded by a full dozen of his guards, he glanced at the sky. It was a particularly bloody looking shade of green, thickening to blue at the horizon.

It wouldn't rain after all, he noted with some satisfaction—or at least not until the following day. That was good. Rain would have spoiled the spectacle he had planned.

Taking in the courtyard, he glanced at the stone wall that ringed it—and especially at the gate that sat in the center of it like some big, ornately shelled amphibian. Beyond the gate there were plenty of witnesses—a sampling of Constantharines from every walk of life. His men had seen to that.

Still, they were only a minute portion of the audience that would witness the day's events. Tharrus had gone to the trouble of setting up his cameras at intervals along the wall—cameras that would broadcast over subspace channels to points as far away as Romulus.

But then, what was the point of a spectacle if there was no one to see it? Or to learn from it the determination and efficiency of Constanthus's great Governor Tharrus—and the futility of opposing such a Romulan?

Of course, Tharrus reflected, he'd had a wide variety of choices in terms of how to proceed. There were several methods of execution the Romulans had embraced over the years.

A favorite was the poisoned cup, which generally carried some measure of dignity with it. This was the option granted to those who'd chosen the wrong side in an attempted coup d'état, or military officers who had disgraced themselves. Even in the matter of dying, rank had its privileges.

On occasion, however, even the poisoned cup offered little in the way of dignity. The right blend of toxins could cause a man to spit out the bulk of his stomach lining over the course of several days before he finally and mercifully expired. That fate, however, was reserved for outright traitors to the imperial cause. It was one of the reasons Romulans were so very slow to consider treason.

More expedient was the simple disruptor ray. It was

quick, it was clean, and it left nothing to clean up. It was far from painless, but there were few things in life that didn't have their little drawbacks.

Hanging was a method that hadn't been used very much in the last hundred years. Even the sternest of administrators shunned it—not for its barbarism, but for the fact that so many primitive peoples embraced it. Romulans did not like to be compared to savages.

However, thought Tharrus, as he came to stand in the shadow of the gallows his men had constructed, he would run the risk of being called a savage if it got him what he wanted. After all, hanging had the advantage of being most humiliating to the one being hanged—and a Romulan was more likely to fear humiliation than even the greatest agony.

In short, this was part of his plan. To humiliate Spock and the other prisoners, to terrify them slowly and thoroughly, until one of them finally lost his composure and gave up the Vulcan.

What's more, he was absolutely certain it would work. Otherwise, he wouldn't have invited the entire Empire to bear witness.

Looking off across the courtyard, Tharrus signaled to one of the sentinels on the wall. Nodding to show his understanding, the man pressed a control padd, causing the gates to open wide.

A moment later, the crowds milled in. But they didn't show much enthusiasm after what some of them had heard at the trial.

That would change, the governor thought. Otherwise, they would soon find *themselves* on trial.

Tharrus shook his head from side to side. Romulan character was not what it used to be. When he had risen higher in the ranks of the Empire, he would make it his business to work on that.

But for now, he had more immediate business to attend to. Turning toward the prisoners' quarters, the governor caught the eye of one of its several guards. As before, he gestured. As before, there was a response, and the unificationists were directed into the courtyard.

This time, however, each of them had his or her hands manacled together. A necessity for hanging, he thought.

As the prisoners approached the gallows, Tharrus scrutinized their wan and hollow-cheeked faces. After all, he had cut down on their rations since the escape attempt.

In particular, he watched their eyes. Long ago, as a child, he had realized that what the rest of a man concealed, the eyes often gave away.

One by one, the unificationists sized up the instrument of their doom, squinting in the sunlight to get a better look at it. Nor could they doubt his intentions after seeing their comrades killed during the escape attempt.

No doubt they were wondering what it would be like to feel the noose tighten around their necks. To hear the order given—and to have the trapdoor swing away, leaving them to twitch and die at the ends of their ropes.

Tharrus smiled to himself. Their mouths would be turning drier than dust right about now. Their stomachs would be clenching with fear. And somewhere in the darkest recesses of their tortured minds, they had to be considering what their lives were worth.

And what was preventing them from saving themselves? Nothing but a misguided devotion to an obsessive Vulcan—a relic of another era, an empty symbol of an idea whose time never was and never would be.

The only thing that kept them from salvation was

themselves. Surely, they were beginning to see that, if they hadn't already. If they were Romulans like other Romulans, they were beginning to consider an alternative.

Would it be so terrible to turn Spock in? Would it be so bad to give him up to the governor—not only for one's own sake, but for the sake of all those who couldn't work up the courage to do so? In the end, couldn't one be considered a hero for saving the lives of so many of his comrades?

Who was this Spock, anyway? Was he so important that others should perish on his behalf? And if such foolishness wouldn't save him—wouldn't preserve his ability to spread his gospel—what was the point of it?

Tharrus's smile deepened. He could see these things in the prisoners' eyes. Fear. Anguish. Resentment. Doubt. Emotions they hadn't shown before, not even at the trial. The gallows was shaking their resolve, which formerly seemed unshakable.

He had chosen well. Truly, it was only a matter of time.

Out of the corner of the governor's eye, he saw his handpicked executioners ascend to the platform. Each one took up a position behind a trapdoor and stood with his arms folded across his chest, an imposing figure against the blue-green sky.

Their presence would be further proof of his bloody intentions. It was only a gesture, of course, but a significant one. Any moment now, Tharrus predicted. Any moment, one of the prisoners would fall to his knees and beg for mercy, eager to rid himself of the secret of Spock's identity.

Still, at least for the moment, none of the scarecrow unificationists complied. Without expression, without complaint, the rebels marched up to the foot of the gallows and awaited further instructions.

Tharrus took a few steps closer to them, eyeing them one by one. They didn't shrink from his inspection, nor did they welcome it. They simply accepted it, like pack animals. Like beings too dumb to know what was happening to them.

Even the infiltrator showed no emotion—even Skrasis, who had only joined the unificationists to betray them. It seemed he had become just like them.

The governor shook his head. Once again, it seemed, he had underestimated the Vulcan's power over them.

But he would not be beaten. Not when glory and advancement dangled almost within his reach. And certainly not by these stone-faced pacifists.

Grinding his teeth, Tharrus pointed to the woman closest to him and turned to Phabaris. "Place this one on the platform," he said.

After all, there were several females among the unificationists, and several men much too young to be Spock. And then there was the spy.

All of these were surplus as far as the governor was concerned. Expendable. He could sacrifice them without running the risk of killing Spock.

"Yes, Governor," Phabaris replied. With a gesture, he had one of his subordinates pluck the woman out of the line.

As she ascended the stairs, with Tharrus's guard urging her forward, she cast a look back at the other prisoners. It wasn't enough to give anyone away, unfortunately. But at least, the governor thought, they were beginning to make some progress.

He pointed to another female, this one older than the

first and more frail. "That one as well," he told Phabaris. He selected a young man next—almost a child, it seemed to him. "And him."

Before he was done, he had picked out six of the rebels. Four females, two young men. Along with their executioners, they were all the gallows could handle at one time.

The spy, he decided, he would save for the next batch. That is, if he needed a next batch.

Turning to the first woman he had selected, Tharrus saw her take a deep, quavering breath. *Come,* he urged her with his eyes. *Tell me which one is Spock and I'll spare your life.*

But she didn't say what he wished to hear. *Too bad,* he mused. Looking to the guard behind her, he nodded.

Slowly the man guided the noose over the prisoner's head and tightened it around her neck. She winced once when the coarseness of the rope abraded her delicate skin. But other than that, she remained silent.

The crowd murmured, horrified. The governor's mouth twisted in disgust. A pity, he thought, that the populace showed little more loyalty than the rebels. He resolved again to do something about that when this was all over.

In the meantime, the guard up on the platform had finished his preparations. The woman's nostrils flared as she stared off into the distance. All that was needed was a word from Tharrus and a lever would be pulled—and the trapdoor would fall, leaving the rope as the prisoner's only means of support.

The governor raised his hand. Meaningfully, he turned to the other prisoners, but none of them relented. He sighed and let his hand drop.

"No!" came a cry from behind him.

The executioner hesitated, gazing at something behind

Tharrus. The governor whirled—and saw that a half-dozen Romulans had beamed down into the courtyard, off to one side of the crowd. They were surrounded by the last telltale sparkles of the Romulan transporter effect.

What's more, Tharrus recognized one of the intruders—the one whose voice still echoed in the courtyard. It was no less a dignitary than Proconsul Eragian. And beside him was his Tal Shiar watchdog.

Were they *mad?* wondered the governor. What was the proconsul doing all the way out *here*—so far from the seat of his power?

Certainly, he hadn't come all this way just to lord it over a few captured unificationists. That would hardly have made the journey worthwhile—not to mention the risk to his honored person.

Unless, of course, he knew of the prize in their midst. Unless he knew that Tharrus had captured the greatest rebel of all.

The governor cursed under his breath. That was it, wasn't it? By his ancestors, Eragian knew about *Spock.*

The proconsul strode forward, looking for all the world as if he owned the place. The Tal Shiar and his guards came after him. When Eragian spoke, his voice was honey-sweet, though it carried just a hint of a threat.

"Greetings, Governor Tharrus." The proconsul tilted his head to indicate the gallows. "Have I caught you at a bad time?"

With a gesture, Tharrus signaled to his men to turn off the cameras. Then he glared at Eragian. "Let us not play games, Proconsul. What are you doing here?"

Eragian's expression changed. His eyes took on a steely cast. "Is this not part of the Empire?" he asked. "And am I not proconsul? I go where I please, Governor. And right now, it pleases me to be here."

"For what purpose?" asked the governor.

The proconsul smiled and indicated the rebels with a sweep of his arm. "For the purpose of taking these unificationists into custody."

"They are already in custody," Tharrus reminded him. *"Mine."*

Eragian shrugged. "A jurisdictional technicality. I'll see to it that it's taken care of after I return to the homeworld."

"It's more than a jurisdictional technicality," the governor insisted. "I am the authority on this world. I have a right to these prisoners."

The proconsul's smile faded away, leaving a lean and determined visage in its place. It must have been clear to him then that Tharrus knew what kind of prize he held in his hands—and that he was not eager to let it go.

So they *both* knew the truth. And each of them knew the *other* one knew. The lines were drawn, it seemed.

"You are the authority here because the homeworld made you so. Do not forget that, Governor Tharrus."

"I haven't forgotten a thing," said the governor. "Not who appointed me, certainly. And if memory serves, it was one of your rivals."

"Who no longer enjoys a voice on the Senate floor," Eragian countered. "I don't think you should count on any assistance from him anymore."

Back and forth—not unlike a Senate debate, thought Tharrus. Except in a debate, there were only occasionally true winners and losers. Usually, the matter ended in some kind of compromise.

And here? This day, in this courtyard, would there be such a compromise? He eyed the proconsul. Not likely, he told himself.

The governor frowned. It seemed he had a decision to make.

He could yield to the proconsul's authority and avoid further confrontation. Or he could refuse and leave himself open to all manner of punishment, including a prolonged and uncomfortable death.

Everything hinged on the chance that he could identify Spock and turn him over to the Senate. If he could do that, Eragian would be powerless to carry out his retribution. But if he failed . . .

Tharrus set his teeth. He would never have a chance like this one again. And besides, he would rather die than let Eragian have Spock on a platter.

"Phabaris," he cried out, still intent on Eragian.

The proconsul's smile was restored. "I'm glad you've come to your senses," he commented. "You will not regret it."

"Yes, Governor?" replied Phabaris, from his place by the remaining rebels.

"Take Proconsul Eragian and his escort into protective custody," Tharrus bellowed, his voice ringing from wall to wall. "I'd hate to see them get hurt as we carry out the executions."

Eragian's eyes opened wide. "You wouldn't dare," he snapped.

"Wouldn't I?" asked the governor. "You heard me, Phabaris. The proconsul and his men need not be exposed to the unpredictability of the crowd."

"Yes, Governor," came the reply.

At a sign from Phabaris, every guard in the courtyard drew his weapon and trained it on the proconsul's group. Many of them actually closed in on the intruders, cutting down on the chances of their missing.

But Eragian's men were trained to give their lives for their proconsul. They drew their disruptor pistols at the same time. The Tal Shiar made a point of training his weapon on Tharrus.

Not an unexpected development, the governor mused. But despite their response, the proconsul's escort wouldn't fire on him. Not when any melee at all was likely to end in Eragian's demise.

Of course, the proconsul's vessel could intervene. Its crew could begin transporting Tharrus's men into its prison facilities, a few at a time. Or it could simply retrieve Eragian and his escort.

But the proconsul would have to give the order first. And the governor's guards would make sure to prevent that.

"Well," said Tharrus appraisingly, "it seems we have a difference of opinion here." He looked at Eragian meaningfully. "If I were you, I'd drop my weapon and surrender myself. But then, you may prefer to die in a bath of disruptor energy instead. It's up to you, Proconsul."

Eragian's mouth twisted. He hesitated, obviously reluctant to give up without a fight. But what choice did he have?

None, the governor decided.

CHAPTER 22

Spock had observed the confrontation between Governor Tharrus and Proconsul Eragian with acute interest. After all, the unificationists' collective fate hung in the ever-so-precarious balance.

Clearly Eragian—like Tharrus—had divined the Vulcan's presence here, or he wouldn't have argued for custody of the prisoners with such intensity. But the proconsul was likely to show them no more mercy than the governor intended.

Either way, the rebels seemed destined for execution. And Spock himself would become a tool in the dismemberment of the homeworld unification movement.

Of course, the entire situation had been turned on its ear when both sides drew their disruptors. In the words of the humans he'd served with, all bets were off.

Not that the chances of a successful escape were any more promising than before—even considering the fact that most of their guards had been drawn to the center of the courtyard, or the confusion that seemed likely to follow. The Vulcan estimated the odds of their succeeding at ten percent, and even that was stretching it.

But they weren't likely to get a better opportunity.

Reaching back, the Vulcan targeted the nearest guard and slugged him across the face—manacles and all. As the Romulan crumpled, his disruptor fell out of his hand. Spock picked it up two-handed and fired in the dirt at Eragian's feet—his intent not to injure but to incite.

Reacting just as he'd hoped, the proconsul fired back in the direction from which the disruptor blast had come. The Vulcan was on the move, however, and the counterattack struck only the stone wall that ringed the courtyard.

Discharging his weapon on the run—this time, with an accuracy born of years of Starfleet practice—Spock hit the part of the gallows from which the nooses were suspended. With a sound like water striking a white hot coal, the structure sizzled away into nothingness.

As the executioners scrambled for cover, the rebels found themselves unhampered by either noose or guard. Instinctively they turned to the Vulcan.

"Down!" he cried, his voice strong and clear in its urgency.

They did as they were told. Dropping to their knees, they avoided a disruptor blast from elsewhere in the courtyard.

Because by then, the seed he had planted by firing at the proconsul had taken root. Seeing that Eragian's bodyguards had opened fire, the governor's men had done the same.

Now the two sides were exchanging disruptor blasts with bloodless intensity. And as long as the proconsul's men held their own, the unificationists had at least a ghost of a chance.

Spock turned his weapon on his own manacles. They disintegrated down the middle, freeing his hands. That done, he reset his weapon to Stun.

Then he turned to the main body of rebels and held up the disruptor—in his hands, a symbol of hope and freedom. For a strange, detached moment, even in the blood-pounding haste with which he moved, he considered their faces.

He saw the unflinching trust in their eyes, and the incipient cheers that shaped their mouths, and the rise of color in their hollow cheeks—and he hoped he had not led them astray.

Most of all, Skrasis, whom he had the least reason to protect.

Or was it the *most?*

"To the gate!" he bellowed. "Follow me!"

The gate, of course, represented the way out. It was also where the citizens of Constanthus had gathered to watch the executions—no doubt, at the instigation of the local constabulary.

"Come on!" cried Skrasis. "To the gate!"

By that time, Spock was already crossing the courtyard in long running strides, eyes darting about to see who might be firing a blast at one of his charges. He was so intent on protecting the others, he almost didn't see a dark blue disruptor beam slice through the air in front of him.

But it didn't hit him. So far so good.

And he'd covered almost half the courtyard. Judging

from their cries of exhortation, the other rebels were right behind him.

The Vulcan felt one of his hamstring muscles tighten painfully. He gritted his teeth. After his long confinement, he was fortunate his other muscles hadn't cramped as well. In any case, he could tolerate the discomfort—as long as it ended in their freedom.

With every pelting step, the gate and the crowd of Romulans in front of it was getting closer and closer. And so, of course, were those who guarded the gate. Spock hadn't forgotten about them.

Earlier, he'd noticed that there were two sentinels. As he looked up now, it seemed that he'd counted correctly—if the two disruptor rifles pointed in his direction were any indication.

Up until a few seconds ago the weapons had no doubt been trained on Eragian and his escort. Like everyone else, the watchmen had likely forgotten about the rebels. However, it had become rather difficult to ignore them.

Raising his weapon two-handed, the Vulcan slowed down just a bit, so as not to throw off his aim. Then he released a blast at the sentinel to his right.

The blue beam rammed into the Romulan, sending him sprawling out of sight. Spock nodded approvingly.

Turning his attention to the other watchman, he was about to repeat the maneuver when he saw another beam rise up—and envelop the sentinel in a ball of writhing, wrenching energies. As the Romulan fell from his perch, Spock glanced at the source of the beam.

It was Skrasis, with a disruptor pistol in his hand. Somehow, the Vulcan mused, his student had gotten hold of a weapon. What's more, he had no intention of merely stunning his adversaries.

Spock was about to remark on Skrasis's accuracy when he saw the man's expression begin to change. Too late, he realized why.

He whirled to face the crowd ahead of them, where a single Romulan was separating himself from his companions. A Romulan with a disruptor in his hand, who was obviously no citizen but a guard planted there for security purposes.

A spy—just like Skrasis.

The Vulcan had no time to react—to fall to the ground or otherwise avoid the blast. All he had time for was to steel himself against it.

But before it could come, Spock felt a weight slam into him. It propelled him forward out of danger—so when the blinding flash of the disruptor beam reached out for him, it missed.

Still, it hit something. Or some*one.*

Even as the Vulcan hit the ground, he was turning back to see who had saved him. To his horror, it was Skrasis.

In the background, Spock sensed a great many things. He heard screams of agony and shouts of triumph. He glimpsed running, and strife, and the firing of eerie blue beams.

But all that was secondary right now. His entire universe had narrowed its focus to the man writhing at his feet, his tunic partially burned away to reveal a bloody horror of a wound.

He would not let Skrasis die, he thought, as he knelt beside his student. He would *not.*

"The pain—" groaned the Romulan.

"Is a distraction," Spock whispered to him. "Nothing more." He placed a reassuring hand on the youth's shoulder.

Looking up, the Vulcan saw that the rebels' fortunes had taken a turn for the worse. Frightened by the sudden appearance of the guard in citizen's clothing, the unificationists had retreated back toward the center of the courtyard.

And the guard himself was now walking toward them warily, his disruptor pistol aimed squarely at Spock.

The Vulcan sighed. He had dropped his own weapon in his haste to help his student—and it would not be wise to attempt to recover it under such circumstances. He would almost certainly perish in the attempt.

"We have failed," Skrasis gasped.

"Yes," Spock agreed. Just as Belan had failed.

Back in the center of the courtyard, in the shadow of the gallows, some semblance of order had been restored. The unificationists were being herded into a tightly massed group by the remaining guards.

There was no sign of either Eragian or his men. Either they had been cut down or they'd found the means to escape. Judging from the pitch of Tharrus's voice, the Vulcan guessed it was the latter.

"Save yourself," urged his student.

"That is no longer an option," the Vulcan advised him, glancing at the approaching guard. The man seemed uncertain about what to do with them.

"Then we will . . . we will both *die*," Skrasis grunted.

"I believe you are correct," Spock observed.

CHAPTER 23

Get up," the guard said.

Spock, who was still cradling his injured student, lifted his chin in passive defiance. "I cannot," he responded. "This one is hurt. He needs help."

The guard had obviously been pushed to the limits of his tolerance by the escape attempt. He extended his weapon until its barrel was pointed right at the Vulcan's face.

"I told you to get up," he said, "and get up you will— or I will burn down the two of you right there on the ground."

Spock had no doubt of it. But then, he didn't expect to live very long as it was. More than likely, he would perish with the rest of the prisoners.

The Vulcan clenched his teeth. It had all been for nothing. But at least he would provide an example for his followers as he died.

The guard must have realized what he had in mind, because his mouth twisted with anger. "I warned you . . ." he snapped.

Spock braced himself for the shrieking agony of the weapon's disruptor energies. He could almost feel them thrilling through his body, tearing apart cell after cell, reducing him to primal elements.

But it never happened.

Because suddenly the Romulan guard had disappeared. And that wasn't all. The entire courtyard was gone, replaced by what looked like the transporter room of a Federation starship—and an outdated one at that.

Certainly that was enough of a shock. But when Spock saw who was operating the transporter, he stared in openmouthed amazement, scarcely able to believe his eyes.

And yet, the man behind the transporter console was no figment of the Vulcan's imagination. He was substantial. He was solid.

He was *real*.

"Mister Scott," said Spock, struggling to maintain control of his human emotions. "The last I had heard, you were lost in space." He tilted his head as he tried to make sense of the situation. "But that was seventy-five *years* ago."

"Aye, sir," said Scotty, not one iota less animated than the Vulcan remembered. "Ye've got that right. Unfortunately, there's nae time for an explanation now. I've a few more passengers to take aboard—though that was nae exactly our original intention. And without that broadcast t'work with, I've got to rely on existing transporter locks."

Spock was still puzzled, but not to the point that he

didn't understand what the engineer was talking about. Stepping down from the transporter platform, he gestured for the others to follow. They complied, though it was clear they were uncertain of their surroundings.

"You are safe," Spock told them. "At least, for the moment. This is a Federation vessel."

That seemed to calm them. The Vulcan's ability to mask his own disorientation was a help in that regard. A *big* help.

Seventy-five years, he mused. If anyone could survive that amount of time unchanged, it would be Montgomery Scott. But Spock burned to know how he had done it. What seeming miracle had he pulled out of his bag of tricks this time?

He watched his old comrade work the control panel with the consummate mastery of a Vulcan sand-sculptor. Moments later, the ambassador noticed the shimmer in the air that always preceded the materialization stage of the process.

Sure enough, a moment later, a second wave of prisoners took form. And Skrasis was among them, stretched out on the transporter platform, a bloody splotch in the vicinity of his ribcage bearing testimony to the damage he'd sustained.

Returning to the platform, Spock placed his arms underneath the Romulan's limp form. Straightening, he lifted him and hurried through the doors, which parted at his approach. If there was still time to save Skrasis's life, he would try his best to do so.

Unfortunately he was no surgeon. A scientist, yes. And more recently a diplomat. But never a physician.

The human portion of Spock was filled with annoyance. Of all the times to be *without* Leonard McCoy . . .

* * *

Commander Hajak shifted in the center seat and glanced back over his shoulder. This would not be a pleasant scene, he told himself.

As Eragian emerged onto the bridge of the *Vengeance,* his face was a dark and dangerous green, and his eyes were bulging under disheveled locks. Looking angry enough to strangle the first person who spoke to him, he spat out a string of curses that would have burned the ears of the toughest old centurion.

As a result, Hajak didn't speak to him. He merely stood and turned in the proconsul's direction, ready to respond to the man's wishes with as much alacrity as he could muster.

"My entire escort," Eragian growled, his voice hoarse with all the shouting he'd done for a transport. "And Lennex as well. Dead, at the hand of Tharrus's mongrels. I was lucky to get out of there alive!"

True enough, thought Hajak. His transporter operator had found it nearly impossible to pick out the proconsul, what with bodies and directed-energy beams flying everywhere, and no subspace broadcast to guide them.

It was only when a distraction presented itself at the far end of the courtyard that they'd been able to identify Eragian and extract him.

As for Lennex, the commander felt no personal loss on that count. He had never liked the Tal Shiar. But then, he supposed, the Tal Shiar were not recruited for their congeniality.

The proconsul suddenly pointed a finger at Hajak. "Start transporting Tharrus's men into our cargo hold. Quickly—before they kill the Vulcan!"

The commander frowned. "All of them, Your Eminence?"

"All of them," Eragian rasped. "Do it now!"

"As you wish," replied Hajak. Turning to his second in command, he said, "See to it the proconsul's orders are carried out immediately. I do not want a single guard left standing down there. And bring up Tharrus as well, while you are at it."

The man nodded. "Right away, Commander."

But as he left the bridge, Hajak's sensor officer called out. "Commander, our instruments have picked up a transporter beam. And it did not originate from this vessel—or either of the *others.*"

"Then where *did* it originate?" he snapped, crossing the bridge to join the woman at her station.

She pointed to one of her monitors. "This quarter, sir. I was unable to pinpoint exact coordinates."

Hajak looked at her. "A vessel under cloak?" he muttered. There was no other explanation, he remarked inwardly.

"But who could it be?" railed Eragian. "And what were they doing here, lurking around unbeknownst to me?"

The commander shook his head. What in the name of the homeworld was going *on* here?

"Gods," bellowed the proconsul, crossing the bridge. Grabbing hold of the sensor officer's tunic near her shoulder, he twisted and half-lifted her out of her seat until his face was mere inches from her own. "That could have been Spock they transported!"

Hajak glared at the proconsul. No matter what had happened to him or his watchdog, he couldn't allow his officers to be manhandled in such a manner.

It took Eragian a moment or two to realize why he wasn't getting any response. Finally, he released the woman.

Only then did Hajak peer over her shoulder at her instruments. "Keep a watch, Andarica. See if you can

267

detect another transport. And in the meantime, review your sensor logs. If a transport took place, the ship that effected it must have dropped its cloak for a fraction of a second."

The woman nodded. "Of course, Commander."

As she turned back to her duties, Hajak again confronted the proconsul. "It will take time to locate the transporter device," he explained calmly.

"How long?" Eragian demanded.

"I cannot say," the commander told him. "They may not even attempt another transport, if they have got what they wanted. But even if they do attempt one, they will almost certainly be a moving target. It may take several transports before we can pinpoint them with any accuracy."

"And what if they depart before then?" asked the proconsul.

Hajak shrugged. "Then we will have to rely on our ability to identify and track their ion trail."

He glanced at the forward viewscreen, which showed him only a rounded section of Constanthus. There was no interloper to be seen.

"If it is a more sophisticated vessel," he went on, "that will be difficult. If it is somewhat primitive—at least by our standards—we will have an easier time of it."

Eragian cursed again. "Should we not contact the *others?*"

The commander thought a moment, then shook his head from side to side. "No. We do not want to alert the intruder by allowing him to intercept intership communications. The longer the enemy remains in the dark, the better it will be for us."

The proconsul eyed him. "Make sure this mystery vessel does not get away, Hajak. Because if it does, I will have little to lose by stripping you of your command—and a good deal more."

The commander nodded soberly. "I understand, Your Eminence."

As Geordi sat at the *Yorktown*'s helm, he could feel the perspiration making hot, wet trails along the skin by his hairline. He had finished charting a course back to the Neutral Zone several minutes ago. Now he was just waiting for the go-ahead from the transporter room.

Looking back over his shoulder, Geordi saw that Commander Riker was perspiring, too, in the captain's chair. Maybe the *Yorktown*'s life-support systems were starting to break down. It wouldn't have come as any surprise, he mused. With all the old girl had been through, it was a wonder they hadn't broken down long ago.

Beyond Riker, Data was sitting at the bridge's science station, observing the workings of the *Yorktown*'s cloaking device. Needless to say, the android was *not* sweating—not in any sense of the word.

Riker cast a glance at Data. "How's our cloak?" he asked.

The android turned to face his commanding officer. "Still functioning," he reported. "Though it appears to be flickering each time Captain Scott attempts a transport."

Riker frowned. "That's to be expected. I just hope the Romulans don't notice. It'd be inconvenient to have to—"

His remark was cut short by a now familiar bellow, barely diminished by the vagaries of the ship's intercom system.

"We've got the last of 'em," Scotty cried. "I'm on my way up to the bridge."

In a release of pent-up energy, Riker brought his fist

down on the armrest of his chair. Geordi saw the man's eyes glitter purposefully.

"Engage, Mister La Forge. Get us the hell out of here."

"You've got it," the man in the VISOR replied.

Fortunately he'd piloted all sorts of ships in his day, from the quirky little Mars shuttle to the mammoth and powerful *Enterprise*. And even if he wasn't quite used to the *Yorktown*'s antiquated control panel, he'd already logged a few hours on it.

Deftly he brought the ship about. Then, engaging the impulse engines, he took them out of the planet's gravity well at the speed of light. Any faster, he knew, and he would have been inviting structural damage.

Before long they'd escaped orbit. Geordi alerted the others to the fact.

"Engage warp drive," Riker responded. "I'll take the best speed you can wring out of these old engines."

"Looks to me like warp eight," said the chief engineer.

"Make that eight-point-one-five, laddie."

Geordi turned and saw Captain Scott emerging from the open turbolift. Coming up alongside the captain's chair, the older man eyed Riker.

Out of deference, the first officer began to stand—until Scotty stopped him with a hand on his forearm. "Stay where ye are," he told Riker. "This time, the bridge is yers. After all, ye're the one with all the combat experience."

Clearly Scotty had had some combat experience of his own. But it seemed to Geordi, the man felt he was needed more elsewhere.

"Aye, sir," the first officer returned, sitting back down again. He smiled. "Thank you, sir."

"Ye're welcome," Scotty remarked.

Then without another word, he negotiated a path

around the captain's chair and took up a position at the aft engineering console.

"Eight-point-one-five it is," Geordi conceded. After all, Scotty had had a bit more experience with the *Yorktown* than the rest of them.

Pushing the warp drive just a little harder, the younger man scanned his monitors. The engines seemed to be handling the additional load—just as his colleague had predicted.

"Told ye so," called Scotty, unable to conceal an impish grin.

Geordi cast a look back at him and chuckled. "So you did."

He eased himself back into his seat. With luck, the hardest part was behind them. All they had to do now was keep the *Yorktown* in working order until—

Geordi's thoughts were interrupted by an explosive curse from Captain Scott. "We've got company, lads!"

Checking the tactical monitors on the navigation side of the console, Geordi saw what he was talking about. A moment later, Scotty made it easier for him by placing the image on the forward viewscreen.

"Three Romulan warbirds," the older man said out loud, describing the threat that they could all assess for themselves now. "They must be trackin' us by our ion emissions."

"But there was only one warbird in orbit around Constanthus," Geordi complained. Then he amended his own statement. "That we could *see.*"

It seemed they weren't the only vessels circling Constanthus under cloak. They should have thought of that, the engineer lamented. But it was no good second-guessing themselves—not when every moment was crucial now.

"We're not going to outrun them," Riker concluded.

"Maybe not," Scott agreed. "But they're nae going to take us without a struggle, either." He turned to Geordi. "I trust ye've got some evasive maneuvers up yer sleeve, laddie?"

"A few," Geordi responded.

But even as he worked the helm controls to execute the first of them, he knew it wouldn't make any difference in the long run. He didn't have enough tricks up his sleeve to keep them in one piece all the way to the Neutral Zone.

"Perhaps I may be of assistance."

Geordi looked back over his shoulder to see who'd spoken. From the outset, he knew it couldn't have been Commander Riker or Data. Neither of them had a voice so deep, and yet so devoid of inflection.

When he saw who it was, he almost smiled. "If you've got any ideas," Riker told the Vulcan, "I'm sure we'd all be glad to listen to them."

"In that case," said Spock, advancing to a point midway between the captain's chair and the forward stations, "I recommend that we stop all engines immediately."

Geordi was about to balk at the idea—until he saw the sense in it. Apparently Riker saw it, too.

"All stop," bellowed the first officer.

The *Yorktown* shuddered as it dropped abruptly out of warp, taxing the century-old inertial dampeners to their limit. Hanging onto his console, Geordi resisted the feeling of being thrown forward.

But the maneuver had the desired effect. Unable to anticipate the *Yorktown*'s move, the warbirds were hard-pressed to keep themselves from smashing into her as they shot past at several hundred times the speed of light. As it was, they only missed by a couple of dozen meters.

Geordi could only tell that from his instrument panel.

On the viewscreen, even at top magnification, they were nothing more than elongated streaks of light.

"Target photon torpedoes," Riker commanded. "Let's go for the one in the middle, Captain Scott."

"Targeted," said Scotty.

"Fire!" barked the first officer.

A moment later, twin packets of photon fury erupted in the direction of the Romulan vessels. While Geordi couldn't actually see any more than that, his instruments told him that both of them struck their mark.

And at this all too intimate range, the enemy's shields didn't stand a chance.

"Report!" cried Riker.

"Direct hits on their starboard weapons bank," Data announced. "Damage is isolated, but considerable."

"They'll nae be firing at us with those wee bairns," Scott elaborated with a smile on his face and a twinkle in his eyes.

Spock looked only vaguely satisfied with himself. But then, from what little Geordi knew of him, it was typical for him to make such a contribution and then gloss over the value of it.

"Ahead impulse engines," the Vulcan suggested.

But Riker seemed to know what Spock was thinking. "Full impulse, Mister La Forge. On my mark, accelerate to warp eight-point-three. And come as close as you can to one of the warbirds."

Geordi sensed that Scott wasn't comfortable with that rate of acceration, but the older man kept quiet nonetheless. If they were to have any hope of getting out of this, they'd have to take some fair-sized chances.

The surge to impulse speed wasn't bad, especially for an old ship like this one. In fact, Geordi barely felt it. But going to warp would be a different story entirely. In preparation for it, Spock made his way to the navigation console and sat down beside the engineer.

On the viewscreen, the Romulans were nowhere to be seen. Then, suddenly, they appeared as specks in the distance. And before Geordi knew it, they were filling the parameters of the screen.

"Target photon torpedoes!" the first officer ordered.

"Targeted," Scotty assured him.

They'd better make them count, Geordi thought. After this, they'd only have a couple left.

"Engage warp engines!" Riker roared.

As the engineer activated the faster-than-light drive, the *Yorktown* leaped forward with the abandon of a rogue planet, thrusting him back into his seat with bone-breaking force. Geordi could feel the inexorable tug of too many G-forces pulling the skin of his face tight as a drum.

But not before he directed them to within a whisker of one of the warbirds. Any closer, in fact, and their hulls would have scraped together.

Geordi winced, anticipating a massive impact from the Romulans' torpedoes. But the barrage—a sudden and devastating one—missed the *Yorktown* entirely. In fact, he could only see it as a flare of energy on his monitors.

"Fire!" thundered Riker.

As before, the *Yorktown* sent a pair of photon torpedoes after the warbirds at point-blank range. As before, the torpedoes nailed one of them, caving in its shields in the process.

"Direct hits," Data declared. "We have incapacitated another weapons bank."

The first officer nodded. "Good shooting, Mister Scott."

Without turning, Scotty smiled to himself. "Glad to be of help, sir."

But they weren't out of the woods. Not by a long shot.

Sure, they'd bought themselves a head start with their bold and unpredictable maneuvers. But the warbirds were still faster than the *Yorktown*—and now that they'd been burned twice, they'd be more calculating in their next attack.

Just as Geordi was thinking these things, the situation got worse. *Much* worse.

"Damn," he blurted, staring at his instruments in disbelief.

"What is it?" Riker inquired.

"We're losing warp speed," Geordi told him. "Looks like a problem with the power transfer conduits."

"We can fix it," Captain Scott determined. He was already half out of his seat, no doubt headed for the turbolift.

"No," said Geordi, stopping the older man in his tracks. "It's not just one conduit, Scotty. It's *all* of them. The strain of that last maneuver took too much out of them."

In other words, the *Yorktown* just wasn't built for such stress—not even when it was new. Even Scotty, the twenty-third-century miracle worker, had to accept that.

"Aye," said Scott, taking his seat again. He uttered the word as if it were a curse. "But," he suggested, "we can at least reduce power to nonessential systems. That'll allow us to keep goin' a wee bit longer."

"Agreed," replied Geordi.

"Cloak first," called Riker. "Then weapons."

He didn't sound happy. But like it or not, those *were* nonessential systems right now. Particularly the cloaking function, which consumed a great deal of power and wasn't fooling anyone anyway.

"The cloaking device has been disengaged," Data remarked.

"Cutting power to the phaser banks," Spock called from the bridge's science station.

"And I've got the photon torpedoes," Scott responded.

It wasn't going to help, thought Geordi, peering at his monitors. At least, not enough to make a difference.

"We're still losing speed," he said. "Warp seven. Warp six. Warp five-point-five." He shook his head. "Warp five."

"The Romulans are decreasing the distance between us," Data told them. "Estimate that at the rate we are slowing down, they will be in torpedo range in fifty-four seconds."

"Mister La Forge," the first officer intoned, "give me a rear view. And take the shields off-line—everything except deflectors, fore and aft."

Geordi nodded. "Aye, sir." He did as he was told.

A moment later, the image on the viewscreen changed. Instead of open space, they were looking at the approach of the still distant warbirds.

"We continue to decelerate," Spock announced. "The *Yorktown* is now traveling at warp four-point-four."

"Forty seconds," the android reminded them.

There was a pause, during which Geordi couldn't hear anything but the subtle hum of the failing generator coils and the urgent tapping of control padds. Then he heard another, even more desperate sound—from Commander Riker.

"Cut power to life-support," the first officer said.

Geordi shook his head. That would only save them an

infinitesimal portion of what they were losing. It was like trying to put out a sun with a mouthful of water.

But it might buy them another second or two. And to Riker, that was obviously worth it. Besides, they could live without life-support for a while—and it wouldn't be needed if the Romulans caught up to them.

Geordi made the necessary power-net adjustments. "Eliminating life-support," he advised.

"Warp three-point-eight," the Vulcan reported. "Warp three-point-three. Warp two-point-nine."

"Thirty seconds," Data warned them.

Geordi looked to Scotty. There was nothing more they could do, and both of them knew it. Silently they acknowledged the value of each other's efforts. And each other's courage. And each other's company, at what might well be the end.

"Twenty seconds," said Data. "Fifteen. Ten."

"Brace yourselves," Riker told them.

Geordi held on to the console in front of him. He had no doubt that the Romulans would fire as soon as they were in range.

"This exhibit is now closed," commented the ship's computer, in a strangely strained and polyphonic voice. "Please watch your step on the way out."

"Five," said the android. "Four. Three. Two. "One."

Abruptly, Geordi felt something slam into them from behind, rattling his teeth. His control panel showed that they'd sustained a torpedo hit.

It happened again, except the impact was even greater. And again.

Behind Geordi, the communications panel exploded into flame, sending up twisting ropes of black fumes. He heard someone cry out, but he couldn't make out the words with the deck plates groaning in his ears.

The air filled with smoke. Geordi fought to breathe, to stay conscious, but it was an uphill battle. As the ship jerked again, sparks erupted from the science station, driving Data backward against the rail.

The *Yorktown* was dying, the engineer realized. Really *dying*. And they were going to die along with her.

CHAPTER 24

My *God,* thought McCoy. *We're too late.*

On the battle bridge's small, cramped-looking view-screen, the *Yorktown* staggered under the weight of a dozen fiery photon torpedoes. He could almost feel each impact as the barrage tore its way through what was left of the Federation vessel's shields.

Standing beside Worf at the battle section's abbreviated tactical station, in the lurid light of a red alert, the admiral wanted to do something—anything. But he was out of his element.

Picard leaned forward in his seat. "Report!" he cried.

"The *Yorktown* has sustained significant damage to several sections of her hull," the lieutenant replied. "Sensors show no casualties as yet, but all systems are off-line." He looked up from his instruments. "And another such attack will threaten the vessel's structural integrity."

In other words, the admiral remarked inwardly, there's

nothing but spit and bailing wire keeping her together. He muttered a curse.

After all, his friends were on that ship. Both Spock and Scotty. And also the brave young men who had risked their lives to bring them back.

It occurred to McCoy that they could still beam the *Yorktown*'s people aboard. But only if they dropped their own shields or tried to extend them around the smaller vessel. And right now that just didn't seem practical.

"Ensign Middleton," the captain commanded, "position us between the *Yorktown* and the warbirds."

"Aye, sir," replied the brunette at the conn station.

A moment later, the *Enterprise* swung into the space in front of the wounded starship, offering her some measure of protection. But at the same time, it made the larger vessel an easier target.

Nor did it take the Romulans long to figure that out. In a heartbeat they were twisting and looping into a new configuration—one meant to take advantage of the *Enterprise*'s necessarily defensive posture.

Picard turned to Worf. "Program a standard torpedo spread," he directed. "Fire on my mark."

"Aye, sir," replied the Klingon, his fingers crawling over his control padds like some deadly quick variety of insect.

"Admiral McCoy," said the captain, "I'd find a seat if I were you. We're liable to be jostled a bit."

The admiral didn't have to be told twice. Heeding Picard's warning, he made a beeline for an empty seat at one of the aft stations.

"Sir," said Middleton, "two of the Romulans have already sustained damage to their weapons banks. If we could—"

"Noted," the captain answered. "Mister Worf, belay the standard program. Focus all your attention on the alternative weapons capabilities of those two vessels. And prepare the way with surgical phaser strikes."

"Aye, sir," the Klingon barked again.

McCoy was familiar with the strategy. First, create a weak spot in the enemy's shields with concentrated phaser fire—and then follow up with a swarm of photon torpedoes. If even one got through, it hit paydirt.

The problem was, it took pinpoint accuracy and incredible coordination. If either phase of the maneuver was a little off, they'd fail to penetrate the Romulans' deflectors.

And Picard was calling for two targets, not one. That raised the difficulty factor another notch.

On the viewscreen, meanwhile, the warbirds had completed their preparations. They looked thirsty for blood as they dove headlong for the *Enterprise.*

Picard raised his chin as if in defiance of the odds. No matter what, the admiral thought, he was going to hold his ground.

This wasn't at all the same man McCoy had tongue-lashed for his lack of initiative. This was a seasoned warrior, unhesitating in the heat of battle.

"Fire!" Picard called out.

As the Romulans shot past them, the exchange of fire was fast and furious. It filled the screen with a blinding white light and made the deck jerk beneath their feet, forcing McCoy to grab hold of the control panel behind him.

He hadn't put his old bones through the wringer like this in some time. And now he remembered why. It *hurt,* damn it.

But when it was over they were still in one piece. And judging from Worf's exclamation, they might even have gotten the best of the encounter.

The captain glanced at his tactical officer. "Damage, Lieutenant?"

"Shields are down seventy-five percent," the Klingon told him soberly. "But all systems are still functional."

"Casualties?" Picard inquired.

"None," Worf responded.

They'd been lucky, McCoy mused. At this range, under that kind of firepower, he'd known entire crews to be destroyed.

But then, this was a Galaxy-class ship. If anything could stand up to a bunch of warbirds, it'd be the *Enterprise*.

The captain absorbed the information. "And the Romulans?"

"Direct hits on the two previously damaged vessels," the Klingon declared proudly. "We have all but destroyed their weapons capabilities."

"Excellent," said Picard.

But the third vessel had gone unscathed. That was the tradeoff they'd made by focusing all their firepower on the first two.

"The Romulans are coming back for another pass," Middleton announced.

Picard considered the viewscreen. His eyes narrowed with resolve.

"Let them," he said.

It wasn't as if he had any choice, given the poor condition of the *Yorktown*. Still, the admiral liked the captain's style.

Picard didn't flinch as the warbirds loomed on the screen. "Target the third vessel only," he instructed. "As before, phasers as well as torpedoes—but this time, give it everything we've got. Our objective remains the same."

"Its weapons banks," Worf confirmed. "Targeted and ready, sir."

The admiral clenched his teeth. By emptying their larder, the captain was gambling everything on this next roll of the dice.

And why not? In this kind of confrontation there would be no opportunity for clever maneuvers—at least not on Picard's part. Even though his shields were badly depleted, he couldn't budge from his position, and everyone knew it—the Romulans included.

The question was . . . could the enemy take advantage of it? Hobbled as they were, was their brute force greater than that of the *Enterprise?*

"Fire!" the captain commanded.

Predictably, their adversaries had the same idea. The viewscreen lit up with blast after mind-searing blast, until even its built-in light dampers couldn't disguise the hellish fury of the Romulans' attack.

The ship lurched, the bulkheads shrieking with the strain of impact after impact. McCoy tried to anchor himself as he had before, but this time he wasn't strong enough. Tearing loose of the control panel, the admiral felt himself pitch forward . . .

Until something grabbed him from behind. Looking back, he saw that it was Worf. Reeling the older man in, the Klingon held on for both of them.

At the same time, a geyser of sparks erupted from one of the aft stations, sending its operator reeling in pain. Another crew member tackled her before she could strike her head on the bulkhead—just as a second station burst into flame.

The battle bridge was a screaming, sputtering, ember-shot vision of chaos. And above it all, cutting through it all, Picard stood like a beacon of hope, somehow staying on his feet just forward of his center seat.

He stared at the viewscreen as if daring it to tell him he'd failed. And as it cleared, it seemed to relent before his scrutiny, showing him the Romulan ships in a ragged retreat.

As the ship regained its equilibrium, the captain didn't call for a damage report. He just made his way forward to the Ops console, where he peered at the instruments.

No doubt, the admiral thought, there were systems off-line. With luck, they wouldn't be any of the critical ones.

"Repair crews to decks thirteen through sixteen," Picard bellowed. "Doctor Selar, we've sustained casualties. I'll need trauma teams on decks twelve and fifteen."

"On my way," the Vulcan replied.

The doctor in McCoy felt compelled to go with the trauma teams. But the admiral in him was peering at the tactical board, assessing the rest of their situation.

All in all, it seemed they'd weathered the assault pretty well. The shields were down to nothing, but most everything else was still in working order.

Picard looked to Worf. "What about the Romulans, Lieutenant?"

The Klingon took a moment to check his monitors. "Sensors show we accomplished our objective, sir. The third ship has only a single weapons bank still operational. The rest of its offensive capabilities have been disabled. Also, its shields are down twenty-eight percent."

The captain nodded. "Then we've got a chance—if we can capitalize on it. Lock tractor beams on the *Yorktown,* Mister Worf. Let's see if we can't—"

"Sir!" cried Middleton, who'd suffered a cut to her temple in the confusion. She turned to Picard, eyes wide.

"There are more of them on the way—-bearing two-four-two-mark-four!"

The captain's mouth became a thin, hard line. "Rear view, Ensign."

Middleton worked her controls. A moment later the image on the viewscreen changed. Instead of three Romulan vessels in disarray, it showed three *new* ones, whole and eager for battle.

That made it six against one. Or two, if one included the crippled hulk of the *Yorktown*.

McCoy felt a deep pang of disappointment. They'd almost made it, hadn't they? But with numbers like these, they didn't stand a chance.

Picard felt empty inside. His people, his ship—they had done everything he'd asked of them and more. He'd come so close. But now there didn't seem to be any option but surrender.

At the sound of a snarl, he turned. It was Worf at the battle bridge's tactical console.

"The Romulans are hailing us," the Klingon reported, his expression evidence of his own heartfelt frustration. "The communication is coming from the vessel we just stripped of its weapons function."

The captain swallowed his pride. "On screen, Lieutenant."

In an eyeblink, the image of the newly arrived warbirds gave way to a new one—that of a high-ranking Romulan official. What's more, Picard recognized the face.

"Proconsul Eragian," he observed.

"I see you remember me," said the proconsul. "I am flattered, Captain. Now, if I were you, I would lower what remains of my shields and prepare to be boarded."

The very idea went against Picard's grain. On the other

285

hand, to do otherwise would be to seal the deaths of the battle section's crew—not to mention those on the *Yorktown*. He sighed. There was nothing left but to ask for terms and hope that Eragian would be magnanimous enough to grant them.

Just then, he felt a hand on his arm. Turning, he saw Admiral McCoy standing beside him, his eyes focused on the image of the proconsul.

"Let me try something," the admiral whispered.

The captain looked at him. The last time McCoy had "tried something," he'd made a mess of things. But there was something in the jut of the man's jaw that encouraged optimism this time around.

Besides, thought Picard—what did they have to lose?

"All right," the captain replied sotto voce. "Good luck."

The admiral stepped closer to the screen, purposely eclipsing Eragian's view of the captain. "I don't think we've met," he said. "My name is McCoy. Admiral Leonard McCoy."

The proconsul sized him up. "Is it your function to ask for surrender terms?" he asked.

The admiral smiled at him, as if that were the furthest thing from his mind. "It's my function," he replied, "to suggest an alternative to this combat we've been engaged in."

"I see," commented the Romulan. "How thoughtful of you. And why would I entertain one of your suggestions—when I so clearly enjoy the upper hand at this juncture?"

"Well," said McCoy, "you've heard some of this before—but I think it bears repeating. After all, these unificationists present a problem, you have to admit. And you could solve that problem by letting us slip away with them, quietly. That way, you look like a hero—and there's no need to give any credit to that ol' hound dog Tharrus."

It seemed to Picard that the mention of Tharrus had piqued Eragian's curiosity. Some Romulans were good at keeping their emotions to themselves; apparently this fellow wasn't one of them.

"Y'see," the admiral continued, "we're aware of the little ol' tug-of-war going on between Constanthus and Romulus. I won't waste your time or mine by going into unnecessary detail. Let's just say this could be one of those scenarios where everybody wins.

"The Federation gets to sweep an embarrassment to Vulcan under the rug. You, Proconsul, come out smelling like a rose. And the only loser in all of this would be our friend the governor—though, frankly, I don't like that scalawag any better than the folks on Romulus do."

Eragian seemed to consider the human's approach. But after a while, he grunted disdainfully. "I could turn my weapons on you and accomplish the same thing, could I not? Would that not rid the homeworld of the problem just as easily?"

Picard tried his best not to frown. He had seen that hole in the older man's logic from the beginning. But McCoy didn't seem to be taken aback by the Romulan's response.

"You're absolutely right," the admiral told him, wagging a finger at the screen. "The problem is, that would almost certainly be the start of a shooting war between the Empire and the Federation." He paused. "And unless I miss my guess, the Empire has devoted a significant number of ships to its conflict with the Stugg."

Eragian's face seemed to lose some of its color. "The Stugg?" he repeated, suddenly a good deal less sure of himself.

"I see you've heard of them," McCoy beamed. "Well, that's good, because you must also know that the Stugg are united for the first time in many years. Something about a planetwide tricentennial celebration, I believe. As a result, they'll be out for Romulan blood. Now," he said, making a show of how carefully he was choosing his words, "I'm no military strategist. But I'd imagine that with the Stugg knocking on the door pretty hard, the Empire would be in especially poor shape to defend itself against the Federation. That is, if *somebody* had the bad sense to stir things up."

The proconsul swallowed. *Hard.* "I admire your grasp of our strategic situation," he replied. "I did not think anyone in the Federation knew about the Stugg tricentennial."

The admiral shrugged his bony old shoulders. "Life's full of surprises, isn't it?"

It took Eragian another few seconds to come to terms with his abruptly limited range of options. No doubt he hated the idea of giving up Spock. In his place, Picard would have hated the idea, too.

But in life, one sometimes had to do the things one hated. The Romulan lifted his chin. "What if I were to grant you safe passage as far as the Neutral Zone? That would seem to serve *both* our purposes, would it not?"

McCoy's expression turned into one of gratitude. "That would be downright neighborly of you," he said. "I'd be much obliged." He winked. "And maybe next time we meet, I'll stand you to a Romulan ale for your generosity."

Eragian turned to the commander standing just behind

him. "Instruct half the squadron's commanders to provide an escort for the Federation vessels."

The commander looked as if he would balk at the suggestion, then thought better of it. He inclined his head. "As you wish, Proconsul."

Eragian turned back to the admiral. "It is done."

"Then I guess I'll be on my way," the human responded. "Don't take any wooden nickels, Proconsul. McCoy out."

Picard saw the image on the viewscreen change again. Once more, he was looking at the Romulan formation— except this time, half the warbirds were coming about. As he watched, they diminished with distance.

He didn't think Eragian would understand the reference to "wooden nickels." But then, he would have enough on his mind trying to frame a report to the Praetor.

Stepping forward, the captain clapped the admiral on the shoulder. Gently, of course. After all, the man *was* closing in on one hundred and fifty. And thanks to his efforts today, they all had a chance of reaching that ripe old age.

"Good work," said Picard.

McCoy's eyes seemed to light up at the praise. Nonetheless, he dismissed the idea with a wave of his blue-veined hand. "I was lucky, that's all. I'm a doctor, not a diplomat."

The captain smiled. "You may be a doctor," he observed, "but you are also a great deal more than that."

Then, taking his leave of McCoy, he addressed himself to the business of obtaining a tractor lock on the *Yorktown* and setting a course for the Romulan Neutral Zone.

It would be good to go home again.

CHAPTER 25

It wasn't as if Spock had never seen a badly damaged bridge before. It was just that he had never seen *this* one badly damaged. Truly, the place had seen better days.

The Vulcan inspected the havoc the Romulans had wrought with their photon torpedo salvos—the charred control panels and the disabled stations, and the place where Mister Data had grabbed the rail hard enough to leave an imprint of his fingers.

But Spock also looked past the recently inflicted ruin, at a mingling of lines and tones and textures that was all too familiar to him.

The bridge of the original *Enterprise*. Until his abrupt transport from the surface of Constanthus, he had never expected to see it again.

"Mister Spock?"

The Vulcan turned to his stocky, moustached companion who barely looked a day older than when Spock had seen him last—though that was more than seventy-five standard years ago.

"Yes, Mister Scott?"

"Ye looked distracted," the human informed him, his eyes narrowed slightly with concern. "Ye're all right, are ye nae?"

"I am fine," the Vulcan assured him. "I apologize if I seemed unattentive for a moment. Appearances to the contrary, I was listening to every word you said."

Before he could complete his statement, the turbolift swooshed open and their other companion emerged. Nor had McCoy's advancement in years curbed his willingness to speak his mind.

"I wouldn't believe him if I were you, Scotty." The admiral grunted disapprovingly. "Ancient as he is, the man still hasn't learned any manners. You can't take him *anywhere.*"

Spock considered Leonard McCoy, now as wizened and white-haired as any human he had ever seen. The man was doing his best to keep from smiling—with little success.

Even after all these years, he enjoyed provoking his old colleague. In fact, the Vulcan mused, McCoy probably enjoyed it more now, considering he didn't get the opportunity quite so often anymore.

"I might remind you," Spock replied, "that I am three years your junior, Doctor."

"A subject still eminently open to debate," the admiral grumbled, taking a seat at the burnt-out communications panel.

"What's more," said the Vulcan, "as I already indicated to Captain Scott, I heard every word he uttered." Spock turned to Scotty. "It was then that you intercepted the subspace message concerning my captivity?"

Scotty smiled. "That it was, sir. And having heard it, I could nae sit back and let Starfleet worry about retrievin' ye." He looked around cautiously and leaned forward. "Nae while there was someone around who still knew what he was *doin'*."

"Make that *two* of you who knew what you were doing," McCoy remarked. "I've got a newfound respect for that fellow Picard. He may not be Jim Kirk, but he's all right in my book."

The Vulcan was reminded of how Sarek had spoken of Picard. "And in mine," he agreed. "I see now why my father placed so much . . . trust in him."

Scotty turned to McCoy. "Dinnae sell yourself short, Doctor. I heard the way ye put two and two together regarding the Stugg and the lack of Romulans patrollin' the Neutral Zone. . . ." He shrugged. "If ye had nae thought o' that, we might *all* be guests of the proconsul now. And I, for one, have had my fill of his hospitality."

"It was a most clever ploy," Spock conceded. "At least, Captain Picard seemed to think so. Nor was there anyone else on the *Enterprise* who could have executed it."

The admiral seemed uncomfortable accepting a compliment from his onetime sparring partner. "In other words," he said crustily, "it pays sometimes to be older than the hills."

"There are no other words," the Vulcan answered. "There are only the ones I spoke."

McCoy harrumphed and pointed a forefinger. "Don't be so literal, Spock."

The Vulcan regarded him. "I do not see the value of being otherwise."

Turning to his other colleague, Spock changed the subject. "I am intrigued by your method of survival in a

292

transporter unit, Captain Scott. I found some of the details in a library file, but they were rather sketchy."

"And ye want to hear it from the horse's mouth," Scott replied proudly. "Well, ye've come to the right place. Y'see, we'd gone down, trapped in the Dyson Sphere's gravity well. The crash had disabled everything except auxiliary life-support and communications—and those systems were failing as well. It did nae look promising, I can tell ye that.

"With the help of another survivor, I melded the transporter's diagnostic circuits, locking the pattern buffers into a perpetual diagnostic cycle. Then I had the computer cross-connect the phase inducers to the emitter array."

The Vulcan pictured the maneuvers in his mind. "And by doing so," he realized, "you created a regenerating power source—which could keep the mechanism operating until assistance arrived."

"Exactly," Scott confirmed. "Of course, I did nae expect it to take seventy-five years—but I suppose I should be glad it arrived at all."

Spock nodded. "Fascinating."

It made the human smile. "Ye know," he said, "I've waited a long time to hear ye say that. And it was well worth it."

"Speak for yourself," commented McCoy, tinkering with what was left of the communications controls.

The Vulcan sighed. Some things, it seemed, would never change.

As Picard entered Ten-Forward with Riker at his side, his gaze was drawn to the twenty-third-century vessel keeping pace with them off their starboard beam. Somewhere on that vessel, Spock and his old comrades were enjoying a reunion of sorts.

There was something about those three that distinguished them from other people, he thought. They possessed a stature that seemed to transcend the physical. A . . .

"Camaraderie," he said out loud.

His first officer turned to him. "I beg your pardon, sir?"

The captain indicated the *Yorktown* with a lift of his chin. "Those three, over there. They exemplify the meaning of camaraderie like no one else I've ever seen."

Observing the *Yorktown* for a moment on his way to the bar, Riker grunted. "I see what you mean. But then, they served together for a long time. Almost thirty years, wasn't it?"

Picard thought about it as he slid onto a stool. "Off and on, I suppose. On one mission or another."

His exec commandeered the next stool over. "And still friends. Still willing to risk their lives for one another."

Not so long ago, the being called Q had shifted the captain back and forth in time. In a future that might yet take place, Picard had seen his friends separated and at odds with one another—Riker and Worf in particular. On his return to normalcy, he'd sworn not to let matters take that course.

Now the value of avoiding such a future was brought home to him even more resoundingly. The captain very much wanted his officers to be like Spock, McCoy, and Scotty thirty years hence. He wanted them to be able to look into each other's eyes and know that they were in a place where they could feel at home. He—

"What can I get for you gentlemen?"

Turning, Picard saw Guinan standing expectantly behind the bar. He smiled.

"Listening in?" he asked.

"How could I?" she said, answering his question with another. "You weren't saying anything."

The captain chuckled. "That never stopped you before."

"Duhlian Twist," said the first officer. "Spicy, the way I like it."

"All right." Guinan eyed Picard. "And you?"

"Ale," the captain responded.

But before he'd quite gotten the word out, she had produced a foamy mug full of the very stuff. He had to smile.

"You poured that before I said anything," he pointed out.

"Of course I did," Guinan told him, smiling back. "I can't wait all day for you to make up your mind."

Riker shrugged. "You can't beat the service," he observed.

"I suppose not," Picard agreed. "For that reason alone, it was worth rejoining the saucer section."

A moment later, Guinan brought the first officer his drink as well. The color of rust, it came in a squat, round glass.

"So," said the bartender, "what happened to those charges?"

The captain had to think a moment before he realized what she was talking about. "The ones related to Captain Scott's theft of the *Yorktown*, you mean."

"Uh-huh. He's not going to be court-martialed, is he? Not after he managed to pull Ambassador Spock out of prison?"

"No," Picard told her. "He won't be court-martialed."

Riker grinned. "The captain pulled a few strings at

Starfleet Command. After all, it's not the first time anyone's ever stolen a ship for a good cause."

"True," said Picard. "I understand that in Captain Scott's day, it happened on a fairly regular basis."

Guinan wagged a long, graceful finger at him. "You're pulling my leg now."

"Indeed," the captain admitted. "In any case, I had to promise Starfleet that Scott would return the *Yorktown* and refrain from such thefts in the future. I trust that from now on, he'll restrict himself to the shuttle we loaned him."

Riker looked past Picard to the old Constitution-class vessel. "They've been out there for hours already— probably so glad to see each other, we'll *never* be able to pry them apart."

Guinan had to stifle a snicker. The captain shot her a glance.

"What's so funny?" he asked.

"Nothing," she told him. "Nothing at all."

"An emotional act?" Spock cocked an eyebrow. "I must confess, Doctor, I do not see how—"

"Don't give me that eyebrow," McCoy countered, his eyes fiery and passionate as he leaned on the red-orange rail surrounding the *Yorktown*'s command center. "You knew you didn't have a spacer's chance of stopping the execution—but that didn't keep you from belting your guard into the middle of next week. Or are you saying your Romulan friends fibbed about that in the debriefing?"

The Vulcan didn't move a single facial muscle—yet he managed to convey his disagreement. "If you are suggesting that my decision to attempt physical resistance was not thoroughly considered," he said, "I must apprise you of the contrary."

"The contrary," McCoy repeated. "Uh-huh."

This time Spock continued undeterred. "Remember, Admiral, at that moment the only alternative was to allow myself and my compatriots to be killed. It is hardly an emotional response to act to prevent such a result, even if the odds are against one's chances of success."

McCoy grunted. "In other words, you panicked. You felt the icy grip of fear and you lashed out."

Spock leveled a stare at his colleague. "Really, Doctor."

"There's nothing to be ashamed of," McCoy persisted. "It happens to all of us at one time or another." He wagged a finger at the Vulcan. "The difference is the rest of us *admit* it, dammit."

"I *would* admit it," replied Spock. "I would admit it quite willingly, in fact, if there were even a single shred of truth to the notion. However, as it is, I can only—"

He was cut short by the hiss of air that accompanied the opening of the turbolift doors. The Vulcan turned and saw Skrasis standing there.

"I thought you were to remain in sickbay," the Vulcan observed.

"I was released," the Romulan explained. "And allowed to beam over to the *Yorktown,* to assist you in your assessment of the damages." He paused, no doubt observing the looks on their faces. "Am I interrupting something, Teacher?"

McCoy harrumphed. "Damned right you're interrupting something. But don't let that stop you. Pull up a chair."

Skrasis looked to Spock, to make sure he had no objections. When the Vulcan inclined his head slightly, the younger man took a seat at the science station—the place where Spock himself had sat many years earlier.

He couldn't help but note how pleased the Romulan was merely to be alive. But then, the Vulcan was pleased as well. For a time it had looked as if survival was impossible.

"Ye were sayin', Mister Spock?" Scotty prompted. "As it is, ye can only . . .?"

The Vulcan thought about his experiences with the Constantharines in Tharrus's prison. He recalled Belan's doomed but courageous attempt at escape. He remembered how D'tan and the others had come forward, claiming to be Spock, in defiance of all logic. Finally, he considered Skrasis's refusal to point Spock out, even when his life hung in the balance.

He had tried to teach his students the value of objectivity, in the belief that they could aspire to nothing greater. And all the while, without realizing it, they had been teaching him the value of something just as important.

Spock frowned. "I can only admit," he replied, completing his statement, "that emotion may have played some small part in my actions."

McCoy looked at him incredulously. *"Emotion,* Spock?" He shook his head. "Pinch me," he cackled, "because I'm most certainly dreaming."

Scotty's brow had twisted into a knot over the bridge of his nose. "I think I'd better call security," he said. "Someone's impersonating the ambassador."

Skrasis merely looked from one human to the other. He apparently had no idea what they were talking about. But then, he hadn't served on the original *Enterprise* with them, had he?

Spock eyed his former colleagues. "You may find my

298

statement humorous, gentlemen. However, I should note that it was not *human* emotion that shaped my behavior—but rather, Romulan emotion. You see," he remarked, glancing at Skrasis, "I began my efforts toward reunification thinking I had to teach Romulans to be Vulcans."

"And now?" asked his student, obviously captivated by this turn in the conversation.

"Now," said Spock, "I realize that Vulcans and Romulans have a great deal to teach each other. And any worthwhile reunification effort will have to combine the best qualities of both peoples."

Skrasis smiled, no doubt pleased by his master's conclusion. "I will have to remember that," he responded.

"Well," McCoy interjected, "I'd say we're making some progress here. If the ambassador's sampling Romulan emotion, I don't think human emotion can be too far behind. Pretty soon, we'll have him singing 'Row Your Boat' like Enrico Caruso."

"I do not believe I will *ever* do that," the Vulcan demurred.

"Sure you will," the admiral assured him. "After you've gotten settled, we'll spend some time on Earth. Visit Starfleet headquarters, that sort of thing. Remind you of those human qualities you've been missing the last few years."

"Aye," Scott chimed in. "We'll visit the captain's monument, if ye like."

Spock looked at him askance. "His . . . monument?"

The Scotsman nodded. "They built it on the land where he grew up, right in the middle of a cornfield. Paid for with private funds, too. There's a history of his exploits engraved in the stone beneath his likeness and . . . well . . ." The former chief engineer went ruddy with embarrassment. "There's a bit there about each of us," he went on. "Ye especially, sir."

The Vulcan acknowledged the information with a nod. He was glad that his friend Jim had not gone unremembered by the people of Earth, for whom he had sacrificed so much.

Spock would very much have liked to see this monument. Unfortunately it would not be possible to do so. He said as much.

McCoy balked at the Vulcan's response. "What are you talking about?" His eyes widened suddenly. "Don't tell me you're planning on going back to Romulus?"

"Indeed," Spock replied, "that is precisely what I intend to do. I have already made the necessary arrangements with Captain Picard."

"But it was near impossible to get ye out," Scott declared. "Getting ye back in could be twice as hard."

"No," the Vulcan disagreed. "There is a network I helped establish, which from time to time smuggles Romulan dissenters out of the Empire. I will employ the same network to smuggle myself and my students back to Romulus."

"You can't do this," the admiral insisted. "Not at your age. You're too old to go risking your life in that den of snakes."

"Aye," said Scott. "Ye've done enough, sir. Ye've done *more* than enough. Let someone else lead the unificationists."

But Spock shook his head resolutely from side to side. "If I am truly as old as you claim, gentlemen, there is little time for me to leave the galaxy better than when I entered it. And I cannot imagine a greater legacy than to have played a part in reunification.

"Besides," he went on, "two brave and resourceful men put their lives on the line to preserve the leader of the unification movement. How can I allow such an effort to be wasted?"

McCoy swallowed. His eyes seemed to take on a liquid cast. "You're a damned fool, Spock. *Still.*" He paused. "But I'll be rooting for you just the same."

"As will I," agreed Scott. "And we'll meet again, Mister Spock. Ye can bet the whole blasted Romulan Empire on that."

Inwardly the Vulcan smiled at his friend's optimism. "I would not be so foolish as to accept that wager," he replied simply.

For a moment or two, silence reigned on the bridge. It was Skrasis who finally ended it.

"Our time here is short, Teacher. How may I be of service to you?"

Spock turned to him. "You may help me repair the science station."

After all, like McCoy and Scott, the science station was an old comrade—one he would miss when he returned to Romulus.

EPILOGUE

Picard entered Ten-Forward just in time to see the *Starship Gettysburg* come about in space.

Describing a graceful arc, the vessel moved away from the *Enterprise* under impulse power only. Then, once it was clear of the larger vessel, it switched to its warp drive and sped off like a shot, its nacelles emitting blue streamers of high-energy plasma.

Crossing the lounge, he joined McCoy, Scotty, and Data, who had gathered at an observation port to observe Ambassador Spock's departure. And well they might, he thought. After all, the hopes and dreams of two worlds traveled with the Vulcan.

Data turned to Picard. He looked surprised.

"I believe I have experienced a premonition, sir."

"Indeed," Captain Scott replied. "And what sort o' premonition is that, laddie?"

"I have the distinct impression that we will see Ambassador Spock again," the android informed them.

Scott chuckled and clapped Data on the shoulder. "I would nae be surprised, Commander. Nae one wee bit. After all, the ambassador has a habit of returning from places ye dinnae expect him to return from."

Picard understood the reference. After all, he'd had the advantage of mind-melding with Sarek shortly before the Vulcan's demise—so he was something of an authority on Spock's life and death.

McCoy's blue eyes glinted wistfully with reflected starlight. "You know," he rasped, "if Spock's father could see his son today, he'd be proud. *Damned* proud."

Picard looked at him, wondering half-seriously if the admiral had somehow developed telepathy. "No doubt he would," the captain remarked.

McCoy returned Picard's scrutiny. "I guess I owe you an apology," he told the captain. "You knew what you were doing all along, didn't you? And I was a cranky old fool, who couldn't—"

Picard held up a peremptory hand. "I don't know about that," he countered.

McCoy's wispy white brows lowered a notch. "What?"

"I'm not certain I entirely agree," the younger man maintained. "To my mind, it was the decisive action we took that ultimately made our mission a success. The kind of action that you were advocating all along, Admiral."

McCoy smiled as he saw what the captain was getting at. "Tact and toughness. I suppose you've got to have both options in your arsenal if you're going to command a starship these days."

Picard smiled back. "I suppose you do."

Together they watched the points of light that stood in the direction of the Neutral Zone. The stars seemed to shiver, as if with anticipation of a renewed bond between Romulans and Vulcans.

Of course it might take a lifetime for Spock to bring the two races together again. It might not happen at all.

But, the captain mused, if he and Admiral McCoy could work out their differences, nothing in the universe was absolutely impossible.